Other Titles by Susie Bright

the best
american
erotica
2004

edited by
Susie Bright

A Touchstone Book
Published by Simon & Schuster
New York London Toronto Sydney

TOUCHSTONE
Rockefeller Center
1230 Avenue of the Americas
New York, NY 10020

This book is a work of fiction. Names, characters,
places, and incidents either are products of the
author's imagination or are used fictitiously. Any
resemblance to actual events or locales or persons,
living or dead, is entirely coincidental.

TOUCHSTONE and colophon are registered trademarks
of Simon & Schuster Inc.

For information regarding special discounts for bulk purchases,
please contact Simon & Schuster Special Sales at 1-800-456-6798
or business@simonandschuster.com

Designed by Davina Mock

Manufactured in the United States of America

1   3   5   7   9   10   8   6   4   2

Library of Congress Cataloging-in-Publication Data is available.

ISBN 0-7432-2262-8

Contents

Contents

Contents

Introduction

Sometimes the most interesting part of a story is the part that's not mentioned at all. After a decade's worth of *Best American Erotica* prefaces, where I've laid bare the details of my erotic anthologies, I'm finally ready to tell you about the work you've never seen in print. The rejects—the incomplete, the almost-rans.

They each have their own story that is just as intriguing as any erotic tidbit in this volume.

Each year, I adjust myself to the new erotic zeitgeist. I imagine what would happen if I stuffed all the manuscripts I receive in a time capsule, and buried them for our descendants to unearth in the next century. What would *they* say about the things that turned us on? As much as we enjoy certain fundamentals of sex—the flesh, the suspense—there are minitrends that flow in and out of our erotic history, and they make a distinct impression on me.

Let me give you a graphic example in the not-so-distant past. During the height of AIDS hysteria, I received an uncommon number of stories that dealt with the spilling of blood: vampire tales, blood-brother retellings, and dozens of cutting episodes. I am positive that these blood-sharing tales, whether supernatural or realistic, were a reaction to the sudden fear of HIV transmission—blood became the ultimate symbol of trust, and of abandon.

Sometimes sexual trends are more shallow, the hula hoops of erotic pastimes. We've certainly seen a vibrator phase come and go, and there was a moment when hardly a writer alive could resist some comment on White House affairs.

Readers don't see the sex trends in *BAE* with the same statistical parity as they appear across my desk. I didn't want to publish ten vampire stories in one shot—I refused. I am quite a stickler for variety in the series, and I hate to imagine any reader throwing the book down in exasperation, crying, "Every single one has a dyke with a dildo!" I get complaints from people who don't like this or that, but I contend that we would suffer raw boredom if I followed any particular party line.

When I spot a trend, I try, in my editor's hat, to pick a couple of examples I think are the best literature. But in my unpaid role as a sexual anthropologist, I'm drawn to explore the undercover meaning of a sexual blip on the charts. After all, these various writers who all settle on the same erotic subject don't know each other; they have no idea that scores of others are writing and fantasizing about the same obsession. I wonder if they'd like to be introduced to each other, or whether they'd resent the implication that they aren't entirely unique.

This year's furor was the most sobering of all, in part because I didn't catch it the first time. At the cusp of 2002–2003, I got a giant pile of stories that all focused on men who didn't want to be M-E-N—they wanted to be divested of their masculine assertion and authority. These were men who wanted to be thrown down and ravished, spanked in hot pink rhumba panties, and made to cry like a baby. Not all of them were cross-dressers, not all of them were S/M in nature—but to a fault, they all wanted to be told to shut up and bend over.

Hmm, I thought, is this the reaction to that popular video *Bend Over Boyfriend*? Or is it the general craze of anal sex as equal opportunity for all? Maybe when gay men faced the peril of unprotected anal sex as a high-risk indicator for HIV, straight people just went mad for it. I mused on that notion and went to bed.

In the middle of the night, I went to the bathroom and found myself in a pool of deja-vu, stumbling back to my bed and wondering why all my speculations seemed so second-hand. It was as if I'd considered them all before, in exactly the same way.

When dawn came, I turned on the TV at the foot of my bed, where Secretary of Defense Donald Rumsfeld appeared in an interview about military might and right. I sneezed at the sight of him, and it was apparently the perfect combination of blowing my brains out, because I finally realized why I'd been in this same exact place before.

I had indeed encountered a rash of submissive male fantasies in the past, and it was during the original Desert Storm, when President Bush Senior made the first play against Saddam, his former protégé turned enemy—the first time a half million troops went to the Gulf.

Good grief! These pouty boys who wanted to be taken down and stuffed like flimsy lingerie were apparently the erotic response to a ferocious buildup of wartime tension.

I didn't spot it the first time around—it never occurred to me. It was only with the second invasion that the coincidence seemed too much to bear.

Now that I had a new theory, my psychoanalytic antennae were all atingle. Sexual repression is like a jack-in-the-box that you can never entirely stuff back in its hiding place. Whatever we are *not* supposed to think about in a time of masculine aggression—fear, weakness, vulnerability—is exactly the sort of secret fantasies that are going to flourish. No one likes to be alone in the dark, wondering whether they'll be torn apart or survive, but that's exactly the situation you face in a foxhole. The notion of killing a lot of people to make your point may be a source of pride, ambivalence, and nausea, but it has a sexual effect on everyone's psyche. Our erotic instincts are at the core of our emotions and some of our most human, sensitive feeling. Veterans/survivors have had a lot to say on this issue, and so have their families, our whole community. It's one of the bigger ripples in the pond.

The men who wrote all the "bottoming" stories I read this past year didn't provide me with a snapshot of their life history. I don't know if they're soldiers or vets, draft dodgers or pacifists—submissive hawks or antiwar butt boys. I'm sure most of them didn't give one conscious thought to politics as they wrote their story about being taken from behind. Our sexual fantasies always sneak up on us, and refuse to give their names.

Other trends appeared this year that caught my attention, and I expect I'll see even more of them next year. Sexual relationships between black and white lovers—which in the past have been politically correct to the point of flinching, or colossal Mandingo knee-slappers—are finally coming to a place of honest delivery. I look forward to a great deal more American erotica that deciphers individual perceptions of race and sex.

On the authorship trail, male and female authors are continuing to speak in voices that are not identified with their own gender or personal autobiography. I have never had so many stories in one *BAE* volume where women wrote as men, and vice versa. This is common in mainstream literature, but erotica has traditionally had a touch of memoir to it, as if we could count each one in a census.

Now any prospective census taker will have to dig a little deeper, because the gay street-sex fantasy you just finished reading could very easily have been penned by a fifty-year-old mom who made pickles after she turned in her final draft. I offer her, and the other imaginative writers, my highest regards. I'm thankful to taste for myself that tart piece of the puzzle I was always missing.

Susie Bright
February 2004

the best
american
erotica
2004

Confessions of a
Japanese Salary Man
claire tristram

We Japanese are at home in crowded places. We conceive our children while lying together only yards away from our parents, separated by walls made of paper, in houses where we can reach outside the windows and touch our neighbor's front door. We ride in trains and elevators so full of people that the railroad companies and department stores hire white-gloved attendants whose only role is to push the last of us fully inside so the doors might close. While riding in those railroad cars and elevators, we breathe one another's air and feel one another's sweat, and can even stare into one another's faces and never once really look into each other's eyes. It takes great concentration, but if everyone cooperates it's as if each of us had that elevator or that railway car entirely to ourselves. We can create stillness and solitude even where there is none.

It's clear from the behavior of foreigners that they will never be completely at home in this world, with their gangling limbs and fleshy bodies. In the rush-hour trains they mumble "Excuse me" and "Hello," or may even look us in the face and smile, attempting to forge some sort of temporary intimacy, thus imposing themselves on our solitude. I see them sometimes on my daily ride on the Tokaido line from Fujisawa to Tokyo's Shinagawa station and back, a one-hour trip I've made each day now for twenty-five years. I've always paid them little mind, before *this* time, just after I had entered my fiftieth year, when I found myself involved in an incident that still troubles me today.

That morning I was late and almost missed the 7:40 train from Fujisawa. I was pushed into an already-full car by the station guards before the doors closed and we were on our way. That is when I saw her, a red-headed foreigner of about thirty, who was holding onto a strap, her eyes half-closed, her body swaying slightly with the motion of the train. She was halfway down the car's length from where I stood in the doorway, but I could see her clearly over the heads of those who had managed to find a seat. From her dress I could see that she was what we Japanese call *hen na gaijin*—a term we reserve for those Westerners who have lived so long in this country that they begin to think they belong. Her skin was that whitish blue of a person who burns easily. Her breasts and hips had a fleshy weight to them that you never see in Japanese women.

What annoyed me about her so? Not just the wrongness of her, or the way she stood out so different in color and body from the rest of us. It was the way she presumed to mimic us, trying to fit in by making herself as small as possible rather than spreading herself about the way those of her race usually did. By the time we reached Yokohama station, halfway to Tokyo, I was filled with an overwhelming desire to knock her off balance, to make her uncomfortable enough with an elbow or shoulder that she would get off at the next stop and wait for another train and I would be rid of her.

A wave of people disembarked at Yokohama, followed by

a backwash of those entering the car, who swept me forward to where the foreigner stood. But instead of being in a position to elbow or jostle this woman out of her complacency, I found my right arm pinned behind my back in the crush of passengers, entangled in a group of schoolboys. An old woman dressed in traditional *yukata* and *geta,* her back humped with bone disease, had lodged herself against my left armpit. The foreign woman, directly in front, was pressed into me in an alarmingly intimate way. She was perhaps an inch taller than I, and my groin lodged snugly into the valley below her hips. I had merely wanted to jab her in some rough way that she could never be sure was deliberate or not. Instead I found myself embracing her—that was the only word for it—in this embarrassing and familiar manner, unable to move away for the crowd. The crush had left me with my lips a bare centimeter from the nape of her neck, from those absurd orange hairs, from the blue-white color of her skin.

The train lurched and pushed me deeper into her, until I could feel everything about her body, the dip of her spine, the flesh of her hips, the dampness of her clothes, the slight parting of her legs. To my shame, my body responded with a rush of pleasure. I tried to calm myself. I tried to tell myself I had nothing to feel ashamed of. After all, the train was crowded. This woman could never have accused me. She could never have said, ah, this man is deliberately molesting me. Indeed I could not have touched her with either of my hands if I'd wanted to, since they were held fast by the shifting mass of people that surrounded us as surely as if I had been tied with ropes. I was helpless to change the situation.

Another lurch of the train and, I'm sorry to say, I forgot to be ashamed. Instead a kind of reckless joy overcame me. My flesh pressed more urgently into the foreign woman. Meanwhile the grandmother to my left was digging against my side, the top of her balding head grazing my chest as we rocked and swayed along. My recklessness increased. While I could not touch the foreigner with either hand, I found that with only a little effort I could reach down to squeeze this old woman's bottom—softly, as I did not want to alarm her, or even make her aware that the motion was deliberate. Within moments the old woman's mouth opened, her dry tongue extending as if searching for a drop of water.

How powerful I felt then! I became intensely aware of the schoolboys behind me, and the way they were rubbing my back and hips with their squirmings, my right arm still entangled in their midst. I discovered that I could brush my hand against bicep or thigh or chest, and, how curious! that the bicep or thigh or chest would respond to my gropings not by recoiling, but by coming closer. One of the boy's book bags dug into my shoulder in a way I would have thought painful, if it weren't for this heightened loveliness, this awareness of all that was touching me. I grew bolder, allowing my hand to find its way from thigh to testicle, squeezing it before traveling on to another boy, while my left hand continued to massage the old bag's ass. The recklessness I felt seemed to travel through the car, from body to body. A group of college girls wearing Hello Kitty sweatshirts, just out of reach to my right, began to sway with our forward motion in such a way that their breasts would touch, and then move away again, and they would smile. To my left I saw a salary man like myself who appeared to be masturbating against one of the doors. I began to knead the old bag's ass with a fierce urgency until she was rubbing her pubis over my hip bone, searching for release. My right hand began to encounter open zippers, engorged cocks, and other hands that were busy giving pleasure. One of those hands, perhaps the old woman's, found its way into my trousers, where it began to grope about. But it was what was happening to the front of my body that left me weak and dazed. If only I could have freed my hands to touch this foreign woman! I would reach up under her clothing to grab her great and terrifying breasts. I would roll and pinch her nipples. I would violate her red-haired cunt with my fingers until we were both covered with her juice and sweat. I may have cried out in my frustration, one hot exhalation on the nape of her neck with those hairs the color of copper wires. She arched slightly—I'm sure that she did—and a flash fire passed from her to me and from one body to the next until the entire carload of us, old women and the salary men, schoolboys and college girls, all the arms and hips and legs grinding together in that rail car, all gave it up, and I heard soft gruntings of *Iku! Iku!* from every direction, which is what we Japanese say at the moment of supreme pleasure.

Then it was over. We had arrived at the terminus. The hands withdrew. I stood there, my legs weak, and wondered if like all miracles this one was some sort of illusion. The car quickly emptied. Passengers ran away in confusion and embarrassment. I looked to the foreigner for her assurance that indeed some truths exist. Just one look, not even a nod, was all I needed. But she was already out the door, and soon even her memory faded into that restless, milling crowd.

The Cool Cat

steve almond

Langston had worked late again. It was past ten, which meant he'd missed the sitcoms, would have to settle for a drama. His office was downtown, about a mile from the causeway. He enjoyed unwinding in the emptiness, drifting from lane to lane. Sometimes he would smoke a menthol cigarette, fishing one from the pack stashed under the maps in his glove compartment. Langston believed smoking was wrong—both personally and in a broader sense—but he enjoyed pulling smoke into his lungs and watching himself exhale in the rearview. It made him feel dangerous and a little removed.

Construction of a new overhead tram left the on-ramp backlit by yellow lanterns. Two figures were camped beside the road, fifty yards from the entrance to the causeway. The first stood with one hip pointed at the road, a knapsack riding her shoulders. A thicker figure sat on a duffel bag behind her. He wore what appeared to be a fedora.

Langston was the kind of guy who picked up hitchhikers. At least he liked to think of himself in this way. The truth was, he stopped only if they looked relatively benign, clean, and so forth, and if he saw them soon enough. Even if he saw them soon enough, there were times when, pinned within his own daily concerns, he drifted past, staring straight ahead as if he hadn't seen them at all.

It was hard to tell about these two, but he slowed anyway and in a few moments heard the soft crunch of gravel and a hand scrabbling for the passenger door. The girl dropped down into the seat; Langston was immediately regretful. She was bony and soaked in perfume and too much of her skin showed and it was not nice skin.

"Where's your friend?" he said.

The girl regarded him blankly.

"Your friend," Langston said. "The guy back there? Your boyfriend?"

"Just me," said the girl, touching her chest. She wore no bra, that was clear, just a cantaloupe orange tank top that clung to her fallen breasts. Her miniskirt was of the same improbable color, and her thighs were thin, without muscle. She held a can of Diet Coke in one hand. Crumbles of lipstick stained the straw.

"I'm headed to the Beach. That okay?"

The girl nodded and he threw the car into gear. "You don't mind putting on your seat belt, do you?"

The girl said nothing. Langston considered repeating himself but let it ride. The little backpack, held on her lap, was bright pink, emblazoned with a white kitten in blue overalls. The cat's eyes were diagonal slits. The caption beneath the cat read: *The cool cat rides the city night on motorscooter.* It was the sort of backpack a much younger girl would carry, someone in grade school.

"Nice backpack," Langston said. "Cute."

The girl said, "I'm Kim."

"Kim," Langston said. "Okay. Sure. Dave. Pleased to meet you."

The girl dabbed at the straw with her tongue. Her finger-nails were spotted with glitters of polish; the left pinkie nail, left uncut, curled like a prong. There was something obscene and sinister about its length.

Outside, a homeless encampment slid past the passenger side, black men squatting around a fire, drinking quarts. The yacht club was on the other side; boats dipped their prows against the black water, like thoroughbreds. Beyond the moor-ings, a condo tower rose from a dredged island. Light from the terraces shone down on the bridge, fishermen lined along the bay side.

"Can I smoke? the girl said. She pulled a gold lamé ciga-rette case from her pack.

"Yeah, okay. Actually, I'll join you. But let's open the win-dows, okay?"

She cranked her window and the wind threw her hair around like yarn. Langston lowered his window and the stink of low tide knifed into the car. "God, that was a mistake." He raised his window. But the girl, Kim, didn't seem to notice the smell. She shook the lighter from its carriage and lit up, then took the cigarette from her mouth and offered it to him.

"Oh, actually, no thanks," Langston said. "I don't actually smoke menthols. What brings you to Miami?" he added quickly. "Or maybe you're from here?"

She sighed, as if Langston were somehow stalling, and she were leaking patience. "Baltimore," she said. "I'm from Baltimore."

Wasn't that the city with the new stadium? Or was Baltimore the one that had eliminated their smog problem? There was something hopeful sounding about the place, any-way. Langston glanced at the girl. Her face was drawn, the eyes hooded in makeup. In profile, she could have been nine-teen.

"Cold too much for you up north?"

"I had some problems with a judge."

They were on the straightaway now, past the drawbridge. Langston noted, with some annoyance, the strobe of one of those dinner cruises that trolled the bay, disco music shoving couples around the deck.

"How do you keep yourself busy?" Langston said.

The girl said: "I give head."

Langston thought to seek a clarification, but realized he would only embarrass himself.

"Good head," she said. "I suck cock well. If you want, I'll suck your cock."

Langston tried to laugh, but the sound was more a cough.

"Suck cock," she said, now with what seemed to him a slow belligerence. "That's my specialty. That's what I am good at." She tapped her fingertip on his thigh.

Langston came up tailing a Toyota and tapped the brakes. One hand gripped the wheel. With the other, he took hold of the girl's wrist. "I'm afraid I'm engaged."

With a deft motion, she twisted her wrist out of his. "I'm not the jealous type."

"She is," Langston said. "Nothing personal."

"All I want is to make both of us feel good. You like to feel good, Dan?"

"Dave," Langston said. He knew she was teasing him, but felt helpless to defend himself, suspended between fear and some twisted notion of chivalry.

"You do have a cock, right?" Her hand moved quickly, grabbing for his crotch. Langston was so shocked that he lost hold of the steering wheel for a moment. The car swerved. "Damn!" he said.

Kim laughed softly. "Relax. You're fine." Her hand clung to the inside of his thigh. He could feel the jab of her prong.

Langston had imagined scenes of this sort; more so when he was younger, but even in the past few years. In college, a friend of his, Mike Tunney, had taken him to an oriental massage parlor. The story was that the masseuse would jack you off if you paid extra. All you had to do was say, "Front too," and slip her twenty bucks. But Langston had chickened out in the end and snuck out the back.

And then a couple of years ago, after an office party, a guy from the office named Simpkins, a real joker, had roped him into cruising Biscayne Boulevard. They pulled over and Simpkins spoke to a tall, black woman whose lipstick was woefully smeared.

"What'll twenty bucks get me?" Simpkins said.

"A bus ticket to Tampa," the whore said. Langston felt a secret relief.

He enjoyed pornography, the video parlors especially, with their latched booths and TVs that ate quarters and moaned, and the dark close air that hung around him like a salted veil. He enjoyed the knowledge that a world of epic sexual achievement and ease existed, where trained men and women did these things, and that they could be visited, if one dared, then retreated from, demurely.

But this was a different matter, an assumption that he was a part of this world, that he cruised the lavish width of night with just such encounters in mind. The idea—and the actions performed in the service of this idea—struck him now as a grotesque intrusion. An attempt to make him something he wasn't. "Get your hands off me!" he cried. He grabbed the girl's hand and held it firmly, then squeezed until he could feel the bones of their fingers slide against one another.

"Okay," Kim said. "Okay." She tried to play it cool, but her pale hands were trembling. Langston found his eye drawn, again, to the backpack on her lap. There was the bright kitten, the cool cat, its slitted eyes and strange mantra. Her possession of this backpack struck him as more perverse than anything else about her—more than her brazen offers and mottled skin.

The girl snuffed out her cigarette and her head fell against the window, where her breath clung. They were gliding past Star Island now, pillared homes where celebrities nibbled at each other in the cleanliness of marble foyers.

"Look," Langston said. "I'm sure you're very good at what you do. I'm just not in the market."

"I been tested, you know. I got a report." Kim made a show of rummaging through the knapsack. "Fuck."

"Why don't you take a few bucks anyway." Langston reached into his pocket and drew out a five and laid it on her knee. "Just for the principle of the thing." He had no idea what he meant by this.

She slipped the bill into her top.

Langston clenched his jaw and gazed at the lane dividers between his knuckles. The tires roared dully on the pavement. They reached the red light at the base of the final bridge, and Langston eased the car into neutral, his hand resting on the stick shift. He felt a yank. She held his hand now with an unexpected power.

"Just so you know," Kim said, leaning close enough to nose his palm. "This is how I do it." She lowered her mouth onto his index finger. Langston felt the warm-wet pull of suction, her tongue widening, his middle joint thocking against the grooved roof of her mouth. He thought of an expression he had overheard his father use, at a cocktail party long ago. "That girl," he told a grinning associate, "could suck the rust off a drainpipe."

That seemed the right spirit, the one that should apply to his current circumstance, but her suckling sounded foolish and he couldn't help thinking of her mouth as a trap; moist bacteria, germs. He tried to withdraw his finger, but met the sharp rake of her teeth. A brief and comic struggle ensued, Langston's finger seesawing until, with one devious jab, he slid his finger against her uvula. Kim gagged and coughed and Coke spilled on her lap. Langston began at once to apologize, feeling put upon and foolish.

"I should kick your sorry ass," Kim said. A brown stain was spreading on her skirt. "You motherfucking dickless asshole."

"I wanted my finger back."

"My boyfriend is going to kick your ass." The girl began to weep, then abruptly stopped and assumed a stony silence. She looked out the window. They were on the Beach now, gliding down Fifth. Shops glowed on either side.

"Where do I stop?"

"Here," the girl said. "Anywhere."

Langston pulled over and the girl, Kim, opened the door. But she didn't get out. Instead, she leaned toward Langston and he could smell menthol on her breath and something darker, more rotten. She spit in his face. "Okay," she said. "Okay?" Only then did she remove herself from the car, swinging her knapsack, the small white kitten in blue overalls twirling wildly while Langston kept his face still, very still, trying to avoid any movement which would make her any more a part of him.

The Pitcher

sharon wachsler

I was the catcher, she was the pitcher, the way God intended.

"Oh, God," I gasped later, when she plunged three fingers into me. "Oh, God."

"Oh God!" I jumped when she threw a windmill pitch so hard it knocked me onto my ass. "What in God's name do you think you're doing?" I stomped to the pitcher's rubber.

God was to have a big role in our relationship.

"Oh, Gaaawd," she drawled, mimicking me in a too-girly tone. Her Southern accent stopped me short, panting. "Don't be such a pussy," she said, looking at mine.

"Listen, the only reason I'm on this goddamn team is because slow pitch is full. And *you* keep losing players." I pointed at her pussy, just for good measure.

"I'm just supposed to be a warm body," I added. "So don't call me a goddamn pussy." I kicked dirt on her shoe, then turned toward home.

"Well, your body better get a little warmer behind that plate," she sneered. "Pussy."

Pussy was to have a big role in our relationship, the way God intended.

I tried to yank off my face mask to throw at her, but the strap got caught on my ear.

I was a New York Jew, soft and round and loud. She was an Alabama Baptist, sharp and pointy like a stick. Usually I don't like skinny. Skinny can feel brittle, insubstantial. But she had a way of making skinny overwhelming, scary. I liked that.

I didn't know how to play softball. The team stuck me as catcher because I couldn't field or throw or bat. Also, the equipment fit me. I guess their last catcher was also short.

The equipment was heavy and dusty and smelled like boy sweat: astringent and raw. All the joints creaked, stiff with salt and mud. There was a spot of blood on the mask.

With the thick padding on my chest, my knees, my ankles, I felt invincible. The metal on the mask was cool and hard. I felt like a man. A man with a cunt. I didn't want to play softball so much as I wanted to squat behind the plate, my hand in my shorts, masturbating for her, the pitcher, while a succession of women stood in front of me, swinging a big piece of wood while a white leather sphere was thrown at them.

I couldn't believe this game was legal.

"Get a room!" the short stop yelled when I told the pitcher to "fucking fuck off and just throw the fucking ball like a normal fucking person. We aren't all Dot fucking Richardson."

We played the game. I don't remember most of it. I remember the perspiration crawling all over my scalp, pooling beneath my breasts, under the elastic on the backs of my calves and thighs. My thighs ached and spasmed from the extended crouch. I could have asked someone to switch positions with me, but I'm not really a switch.

I looked at her through the metal grid on my face. She threw the ball into my glove. It stung where it landed. My hand was red, tingling. The mitt smelled like leather and soap and dirt. Not the dust on the field, but soil: dark, rich, almost like oil. That's how she smelled, too, I found out later—like rotting earth and tough hide.

After the game the pitcher grabbed my braid. "So, what does your warm body look like under that chest protector?"

"You'll never know." I turned to walk away. My cunt jumped at her hand sliding down to the back of my neck. She didn't need to know *that*, though. She already knew that. I needed her to know that.

She swung in front of me. Her shirt was stained. A smear of dirt spread across her upper arm and her neck. Her breasts looked small and hard, the nipples scraping against her tank top. I wanted to bite them, to feel them give, to taste blood. She put her hand at the base of my throat. Under the chest protector I was on fire. My hidden body was molten, burning the armor onto me.

"Even with that mattress on you, I have a pretty good idea," she smirked. I grabbed her wrist to fling it off. She snatched my hand out of the air, brought it silently to my side.

"This equipment belongs to the league, you know," she spoke softly into my neck. "I'm responsible for making sure it's all returned."

"I know where it goes." I heard the tremor in my voice and cleared my throat. "I know where the storage closet is."

That's when I saw her smile. That's when I knew. God knows, I knew.

We walked to the brick school building, into the gym. She pulled out a key and let us into the locked cage that held basketballs, soccer nets, hockey sticks, and big blue mats with yellow foam sticking out. They were piled in haphazard lumps.

"Be a responsible citizen," she intoned, "turn in your equipment."

I tried to pretend she wasn't there. I played it like I was unself-conscious. I bent to unhook the elastic bands across the backs of my thighs and knees. It was only after the third clasp that I realized I was sucking air with each release. The pitcher was gasping in time with me. She was catching what I pitched.

My skin felt strange and new in the cold air; goose bumps rose and I shivered. The heat of my body came off in the fabric of the shin guards as I peeled them back from my legs. The guards stuck out horizontally, still attached at the ankle. I knelt to unhook the ties around my ankles, staring at her legs in front of me, light hair on clay-colored skin, veins riding over muscle.

I didn't want to take the chest protector off. I felt so hot underneath, molded into its shape, as if I'd been wearing it since I was born. The pitcher reached both her arms around me, releasing the ties on the back of the chest protector. I saw the grime on her neck and a red splotch where she'd been scratching. When she pulled the quilted pad away from me I actually expected to look down and see my naked body, my breasts hanging like white plums. She threw the chest guard onto the pile of blue mats. Numbly I reached up to take off the mask.

"No." She grabbed my hand. "Leave it on."

She laid her palm against my chest, then pushed. I fell onto the mats. She turned, closed the metal gate, its white paint peeling around the lock, twisted the key. "Now we're locked in."

I knew that we weren't. I knew that the key was on the chain that hung from her belt loop. I knew someone could walk in and find us. I knew I should probably leave. While I was deciding to leave she slid her hand up my thigh, her gritty fingers on my new skin.

The pitcher's other hand was still on my catcher's mask, her fingers entwined in the bars across my face. She lay down on me, her arm pinned across my throat and chest.

The pitcher slid her hand up my thigh and under my cutoffs, slipping a finger under the elastic of my panties. I inhaled sharply, waiting for her to touch me. But she didn't. She just ran that finger under the elastic, from side to side. I was wriggling, trying to force her finger closer, higher. But, pinned under her sharp body, her arm like a bat across my throat, I couldn't move. The mats were swallowing me; I felt engulfed in the deep blue indentation. The pitcher kept her finger moving but wouldn't touch my pussy. She wouldn't send me home.

"You're not a very good catcher," she commented offhandedly.

"I . . . I never—" I stammered.

"I hope you're a better fuck," she added.

"Fuck you," I struggled to get up but she grabbed the crotch of my shorts and yanked me back down, knocking the wind out of me. My ass thumped against the top mat. She had ripped the right leg of my shorts almost to the zipper. I glared at her through the mask.

When I'd caught my breath I realized she'd moved her hand so that it lay on my mound. She was that kind of pitcher—smooth and sly. She let her skinny hand whisper across the ends of my pubic hair, not touching my skin. The vibrations tingled down to my skin.

I moaned, lifting my hips, trying to make her touch me, but she just kept sliding her hand away. She was not the kind to let a runner steal a base.

"Hold still," she hissed, then yanked my mask so hard that my cheek was pressed against the mats. She brought her face right up to the metal grid, looking me in the eye. "Hold still and be quiet. You don't want some janitor wandering in here to find out who's moaning, do you?" she asked.

"No," I whispered, embarrassed.

"No," she repeated, turning my head from side to side, gripping tight to the mask. "No, no, no," she incanted.

"No, no, no," I agreed, softly, dizziness descending as she rocked my head on the mats.

In a hypnotic rhythm I continued shaking my head, mumbling "No, no, no, no," and felt her middle finger and forefinger slide to either side of my engorged clit. Deliberately she rubbed up and down, capturing my clit between her fingers. I rocked my head faster, gasping, slurring, "No, no, no, no." I couldn't see her face. I saw the ceiling and the mats and the cage and this wiry hand over my face, all blurred in the constant motion of my skull and the thrill of her fingers riding my slippery clit.

"Shut up!" she hissed suddenly. "I hear something. Someone's coming." She didn't mean me. The pitcher held absolutely still. So did I. It hurt to breathe.

I could feel the pulse in my throat pounding against her arm, in my swollen clit against her fingers. The stillness made me ache that much more to have her inside me. I must have groaned because she jerked my head and spat "Shut up."

In the rank locker-room air, her fingers huge and crimson in front of my eyes, her other hand still inside my shorts, I wanted to beg her to fuck me. I was afraid of someone coming in, seeing me like that. I didn't know what to do.

The pitcher pushed three fingers inside me, hard. I gasped. It hurt. I wanted to tell her, *No, too many*. I wanted to tell her *More*, to take her whole fist. She started skimming in and out, slowly at first, then faster. "Be quiet, don't move," she kept muttering through gritted teeth.

I gripped the blue mats hard. Later I found bits of foam under my fingernails. She pumped in and out, bumping against my clit with the heel of her palm, pressing into me. My legs went numb from her bony weight across them.

Every time I gyrated against her hand, into those skilled pitcher's hands, into that hypnotic stroking and probing, she'd pull out and yank my pubic hair, growling "Quiet." While I gasped in surprise she'd plunge back in. I was so grateful and scared.

I could feel my orgasm building. It felt rich and full, the

striated meat of her hand, her slick fingers, my numb legs, my head tilting crazily. She saw it coming, yanked the mask up onto my forehead and pressed her hand over my exposed mouth. I broke open like a glass of water, spilling in every direction. I was calling to God, but she couldn't hear because her hand was muffling me. My cunt contracted around her fingers, the waves of heat washing over me, her hand pressed hard against my face. I think I must have bitten her, sunk my teeth right into her palm, but neither of us said a word. When I saw her at practice the following week she had a bandage on her hand. Said she'd cut herself slicing a bagel. No one believed that.

When I was done the pitcher pulled her hand out from under my shorts. "Shut your eyes," she said, "and suck." I sucked her fingers—my own bitter juices, her sweat, the oily leather of her glove, and a tangy metallic edge that made me want to taste her mouth.

She stood up, then pulled me onto wobbly legs. "Here, don't forget to leave this." Gently the pitcher peeled the mask from my damp forehead. She laid the mask on top of the other gear. She opened the cage door, which squeaked as it swung wide. She locked it and we went out into the bright sun. I couldn't believe it was still daylight.

"See y'all next week," she called as she headed toward a silver mountain bike chained behind the batters' bench. I just stood there with the sun on my hair, watching her turn her key in the Kryptonite lock.

I walked toward the subway, smelling my rank, sexed-up smell. I was already hungry to see the pitcher again, to watch her throw, to taste the bite her hands left on me. My pussy ached as I walked, reminding me of her, the way God intended.

Two Guys, a Girl, and a Porno Movie

rachel kramer bussel

I met Danny the same way I meet most of the guys I date: at a bar. Danny was this much older guy, 37 to my 22, and although he had a wife and kids and house in the suburbs, he fashioned himself a hip "down with the kids" kind of guy. And the truth is, despite his big, burly exterior, workman's hands, and old-world Italian sensibility, he got along pretty well with our younger, artsy crowd. He spent so much time in my neighborhood that he knew more about it than I did—what parties were going on, the hot new restaurants, where to meet all the cute waitress chicks. He was on top of it all.

So one night I was at this divey local bar, where I was hanging out getting trashed with some friends of mine. I got introduced to Danny briefly at the beginning of the night; one of my friends had invited him, but I didn't pay too much attention. I was so engrossed in my own gossipy conversation, and Danny just didn't seem like someone I'd have much in common with, so I pretty much ignored him. He was busy talking to someone and I was busy pounding down Heinekens like I'd never get any more after tonight. After I'd drunk about five beers, Danny decided he wanted to talk to me. Me! Why, I don't know, but he sat down and we started shooting the shit.

Well, at first it didn't go that well. He proceeded to tell me that I'm a "typical woman" because I'm a Democrat and voted for Hillary, then went through a litany of other "typical" beliefs, most of which I held. This got me pretty fired up, but somehow, instead of wanting to knock him over the head with my beer bottle, I found it endearing. I liked arguing with him, and enjoyed his comebacks more than I could ever have imagined. His way of thinking, his attitude, his strong accent, his macho manliness were all different from the liberal types I usually hang around with. And as much as I love to read or hear someone saying something I agree with, I have even more fun debating with someone, especially if they're up for it. It wasn't his views I liked so much as the fact that he had them and felt strongly about them. Lots of people just drift through life without being able to take a stand, and I'm just the opposite, so when I meet someone who also has strong opinions, it's a treat. So we sat there arguing passionately for three hours, during which we lost our friends, who had to go home and go to sleep (what wimps!). I found that even though I still disagreed with him toward the end of our conversation, he wasn't the big stupid guy I'd thought he was at first.

So I let him give me a ride home, and we made a detour to get something to eat. Against my better judgment, I found myself suddenly flirting with him, letting the alcoholic swirl overtake me as I leaned against him while we waited for our food. At that moment, I wanted to attack him right there in the restaurant, to run my hands up his chest and claw my way back down, but I settled for the next best thing by touching his knee under the table while I gobbled my sandwich. I didn't care that he was married or that we were utterly incompatible or that after tonight I might never want to see him again; none of those things mattered when my whole body was on fire waiting for him to touch me.

In the car, I made out with him in that sloppy, drunken way I tend to do, like I don't have a care in the world and it doesn't matter if I'm making a mistake because tomorrow it'll be like this night never existed. It'll go down in my memory as just another blaze of drunken, hedonistic glory, something I can feel proud of for being so brazen, but not something I'd do on a regular basis. So I just let myself go and enjoyed the moment. He bit my tongue as soon as I stuck it in his mouth, and the unexpectedness of that action, and the way it felt kind of good even though it hurt, sent me over the edge. I guided his hand under my skirt, and he stroked my cunt through the layers of my tights and panties as I squirmed against him in the car. If we'd been on a deserted street, I might've even fucked him, but I had the presence of mind to know that there was only so far we could go in his car.

I should've called it a night and chalked it up to a fun but silly escapade, but I made the mistake of giving him my phone number. It seemed like a fun game we were playing, and maybe I didn't even need to be drunk to continue enjoying it. When he called a few days later, I agreed to meet up with him, even though I had some misgivings. I knew that if I wanted him to, he'd be in my bed in a heartbeat, but I didn't want that. I wanted to continue flirting with him, to continue with the teasing we'd enjoyed the other night. I told him we could meet at my place, then go to a bar around the corner.

He calls from his cell phone to tell me he's downstairs, and I buzz him in. As soon as he walks through the door, we start messing around. It feels good, I'm a little nervous, not sure how he'll take my ultimate refusal of his sexual services. I'm also nervous about my own desire, that I have to force myself to say no to him, instead of that just coming naturally because I know he's married. Maybe because it's been so long since I've fucked a guy, any guy, since I've been so busy lately chasing after cute girls, that this forbidden thrill seems tempting. And knowing that I'm tempting him in return makes it even hotter.

We stand in the doorway of my bedroom with my long skirt hiked up to my waist, him pressing against me. I wiggle my ass against his cock for a while, pressed between him and the door, his erection hard and eager. Then I drag him out to the living room, unsure I'll be able to resist my own command to not let him any closer than that. We splay ourselves out on the couch, where he resumes his tongue-biting from the other day as I rub my cunt against his denim-covered dick. We make out for a few minutes as his hands fumble to undo my bra and get at my tits.

Then, all of a sudden, he says he needs to use the phone. "Who are you calling?" I ask.

"My cousin. He's waiting for me in the car."

I just stare at him. "That's so rude, to leave your cousin there waiting for you. What, you were gonna let him sit and wait for you while we fooled around?" I can't believe that he would do that. I make him call his cousin's cell phone and tell him to come upstairs.

When his cousin, Steve, enters the apartment and introduces himself, I notice that he has the same build and style as Danny. He walks in and checks out the meager surroundings, fixating on one of my porn videos. Its big shiny cover, filled with pictures of girls bending over and showing off their gorgeous asses, usually attracts attention. "Let's watch this," he says.

Figuring I'll go with the mood, and since it's one of my favorites, I put in the tape. I settle onto the couch with Danny, and Steve dims the lights before making himself comfortable in a chair. As soon as the video starts, they're engrossed, their tongues practically hanging out and their dicks getting hard as they watch cute girls flirting and spreading their ass cheeks. With each juicy movement onscreen, they lean closer, as if they can enter the video if they just get in the right position in front of the TV.

Though I'm lying on top of Danny and can feel him playing with his dick underneath me, like the two of them, I'm engrossed in the movie. I've seen it before and enjoyed it, but it's even more naughty to be watching it in the dark with two big horny cousins who seem like they're about to come on my TV screen. Since they're letting themselves go, I figure I will too. I suck in my breath and plunge my hand into my panties as one girl's latex-covered fingers delve into another's eager ass. As the girl getting fucked onscreen starts moaning louder and louder, all of our hands move faster against our own bodies.

Danny starts to lift my skirt, and I let him, straddling him as we lie across the couch, and he spanks me. He doesn't know that this is a particular turn-on for me; it's probably something he does with all his girls, but I don't care. It's just what I need to get even more excited. His hands are big and strong; they deliver hard, powerful smacks without even trying. My pussy is getting wetter and wetter with each one. His cousin's eyes roam from the sex on the screen to the spanking right next to him. After a little more spanking, while I can only marvel at the heat generated by his spanks and the way they send tormenting shivers through my cunt, Danny returns to his own needs. I lie on the couch, gasping. I move over, away from Danny, pull my skirt down, and watch the movie, wanting to touch myself but holding off for a little while.

Danny and Steve already are, their pale white dicks hanging out of their jeans, hands squeezing and swaying them all around as they exclaim over the movie. "That girl is so fucking hot, I'd marry her." "Look at that ass! Oh man, how delicious." Danny tries to touch me and I push him away. "Why not?" he whines. "Those girls are getting fucked up the ass and doing all kinds of crazy things, and I can't even touch you?"

"No," I reply in my haughtiest voice, and push his hands firmly away.

Even though I'm lying here with two of the straightest guys I've ever met, there's something decidedly queer about our arrangement. They are so horny, so overcome by their cocks that they'll share them with each other to get to me, or to relieve their arousal. They don't seem to see anything strange about seeing each other jerk off, about being so close to each other. Meanwhile, I'm getting off on the onscreen antics, which now feature one girl lying down on a carpet getting fucked into oblivion by her boyfriend. That scene switches to other girls testing out a buttplug on a virgin user. The girls' asses all seem so round and firm, and I envy the way they eagerly offer their butts to be fucked and filled; no girl has ever done that for me.

I look at Danny and Steve and smile. I love the power being a girl seems to give me in this situation. If I wanted to, I could get both of them to fuck me right now, their dicks mere inches away from each other as they slide up my slick pussy and into my ass, me smushed in between them. I'm sure the fact that this is very queer doesn't even occur to them; they're like guys in a circle jerk, so intent on coming that they don't notice the homosexual undertones. I like playing with them, teasing them, making them want me and then pulling away. As obnoxious as that makes me sound, it's true.

I almost let things get really wild, just for the hell of it, to see exactly what they can do, but I realize that I don't have to fuck them to enjoy this. I lie back on the couch, avidly watching the movie, as Danny hovers below me, pulling down my panties and staring adoringly at my pussy. Steve joins him on the floor and they both eagerly stare at my nicely shaved cunt, abandoning the video. I let Danny take a few licks, enough to bring me almost to the point of coming, then I let my secret domme side out and kick his chest to push him away. He doesn't mind, though; at this point, any contact with my body is a treat for him. Steve looks so eager that I let him lick me too, and his tongue is big and rough—in a few seconds, it has me wiggling around and dripping my juices down his chin. He moved away and Danny, horny again, rubs his dick against me, begging me to let him enter me, but I refuse.

If he were someone else, someone I trusted or knew just a bit better, I'd be sprawled across the bed, screaming for him to fuck me as hard as he can, but for some reason I'm holding back. I enjoy teasing Danny, making him beg just to touch me for a minute, fondling his dick but not letting him come. Having them so close, I wish I could ask them to perform some very naughty tricks for me, but I know they wouldn't go for it, even if I promised to fuck them all night.

Instead, I lean back, close my eyes, and imagine Danny licking Steve's asshole, Steve pushing back against his tongue and moaning eagerly, his own dick throbbing and hard. I picture Steve, with his big, powerful tongue, sucking Danny's dick, his tongue moving up and down and making Danny spasm in seconds. My mouth opens and my breathing quickens as I picture this scenario. I work my fingertips against my clit, pushing and pulling and kneading it to give me the pressure I need. I squint my eyes open and notice Danny and Steve next to each other on the floor, dicks in their hands, eyes on the screen, once again involved in their fantasy world. *They have their fantasies, and I have mine,* I think, as I feel a stream of hot liquid shoot out of me. I keep at my clit, waiting for more, this time opening my eyes to see one of the stars of the film screaming in ecstasy as one girl fucks her with a big pink vibrator, while another works her well-lubricated fingers up her ass. Danny and Steve grunt, lost in their passion as first Steve, then Danny, come, shooting their victory onto the TV, their come dripping down the hard screen and obscuring the movie. We never make it to the bar, but that's okay. We've had more than enough fun for one night.

The Disabled Loo
from *Tommy's Tale*
alan cumming

The biggest difference between a disabled loo and a—no, I will not say normal—a nondisabled loo is that the former is so *spacious*. Of course there are all those handrails, but the most startling thing is there are just *acres* of room. I am writing this as though you have never been in a disabled loo. I hope this is not the case—they are a wicked luxury that everyone should know of. But even if you haven't, I hope you can understand that the assignation that Sasha and I were about to have, whilst losing some of its cramped, bang-your-head, sweaty, oops-excuse-me, no-you-go-first quality, was going to be an altogether much more languorous, better-lit, sumptuous and yes, *spacious* experience because of the type of toilet facility mentioned above.

I actually had to guide Sasha to it. She was all for just popping into the ladies and taking our chances, so I could tell that I was the veteran from the word go and therefore immediately took control. I locked the door and turned to look at her. For a moment there was silence. I loved this time. The lull before the storm. Just those few seconds when you could look way, way down inside someone and know you were going to have them.

"You are a dirty bitch," I said without moving.

She smiled, not quite sure what to do. I smiled back and walked over to her, pushed her up against the wall and kissed her. She had beautiful lips and her mouth tasted fresh and dewy. Our tongues explored each other's mouths and my hand went down to her crotch, feeling her heat.

"Do you want some coke?" I asked. Her eyes lit up. I knew the answer. "Do you want to take it a different way from usual?"

Sasha, it turns out, is another in that long line of girls who, contrary to popular opinion, love a bit of bum action. The coke was administered with my finger and then to make sure it had got where it was going I gave her an oral check. She was leaning face-front against the wall, her arse stuck out like a pervy Betty Boop, her little suede skirt flung to the far corner of the loo. I was on my knees behind her, one hand clasped around the ankle of her little black boot, the other around my cock. Then we tried some coke on her pussy, and that was a great success too. If you've ever partaken of the same, you'll know the wondrous qualities that cocaine has on the mucous membranes of the vagina. My wishes came true and then some. When I came up to kiss her mouth my face was *dripping*. I was having such a good time.

There was only a little bit of the coke left, so we put it on my cock so that Sasha could get some. Now I had the tingling everywhere. We were both sweating and various body parts were fairly numb so that meant we were a little more vociferous than we might have been. At one point she was on the floor, her head was against the door and I was kneeling astride her, my hands grabbing on to the door handle for support while I fucked her face.

Good clean fun.

Really.

And then we were cleaning up afterwards. Have you heard of a pearl necklace? Well, this was more a pearl veil. After I came she spread it all over her face with her fingers. I had her juice all over my face and down my chest and on the crotch of my black jeans—if was drying now into one big, nice milky-white stain. Fabulous.

"Let's just stay here and chat for a while," I said. My teeth were grinding and I could feel the red splotches exploding across my face. I looked in the mirror—another nice disabled loo touch, your own hand basin ensuite—and I looked like an advertisement for not taking drugs. My eyes were saucers, I was pale, with only the aforementioned blotches breaking my otherwise alabaster complexion. My mouth was a constant whirr of grinding, and I was covered in a mixture of sweat, cum, and vaginal juice. I felt great.

"I think you are fucking sexy," I said to Sasha.

"Well, you know, Tommy, the feeling is really mutual," she replied kindly, a damp paper towel at her temple. "You look like you're all cookies and cream but you are a very dirty little boy, I'm glad to say." She laughed and pulled another towel from the dispenser. "Do you have a girlfriend?"

"No," I snorted. "No, not for a while." I immediately thought back to India. I'd fallen BIG for a woman after three days and then she turned out to be not the person she told me she was, and I was left disillusioned, hurt, and broke. That was India. I could feel a black mood coming on. Coke could do that if I let it. India could too.

"Actually, at the moment the nearest I have is a boyfriend," I said.

"Oh, really?" She was unfazed. "Is he that big guy you came in with who's now chatting up that bald bloke?"

"What, Bobby? Don't be daft. No, he's my flatmate, my best friend, well, my equal best friend. No, my sort-of boyfriend's called Charlie, and he has a little boy called Finn."

"Ooh, sounds complicated." She had finished washing up now and turned toward me curiously, her little cheeks still red from our sex. She sat on the edge of the sink and looked at me. There was silence for a moment. One of *those* silences. "It sounds like you're a little confused, Tommy."

I laughed. One of those laughs I mentioned earlier where you're in the middle of laughing and you hear yourself and you think, Who is that desperate person?

"Well, yes, I am confused, but not in the way you think," I said, knowing that being obtuse was a stupid idea because she was only going to ask me to explain and if I really did I would . . . what, what would I do? . . . I would, you know, I might . . . cry.

Yes, get this. In the disabled loo of the Almeida Theater, Islington, London, England, U.K., our little Tommy might burst into tears in front of a girl who he has only clapped eyes on less than an hour ago, a girl whose every orifice he has had his tongue down, a girl whose pussy juice is still wet on the neck of his T-shirt, whose sweet-smelling bum hole he can still conjure in a nanosecond; our Tommy could cry in front of this stranger, isn't that weird? And for why? Because she had said he sounded confused and she, this stranger who had just gagged on his penis (and it wasn't the Charlie type of polite gag), she was the first person who had said that to Tommy in many years, and even though he knew the kind of confusion she thought he was suffering from was far different from what was really going on—these tears would not be about whether he preferred boys to girls—the fact that she had cared enough to listen this far and mention the word *confusion,* and the look of genuine care and concern on her little moist face, and the fact that he had just gone to a place with her that made them so close at this moment, all this made Tommy start to cry. Yes, no, he really did. Big, blubby tears and heaving sobs formed years ago way, way down in the very pit of his stomach.

Tommy lost it. Tommy lost it so bad he couldn't even bear to talk of himself in the first person right now. The girl tried to help him, she cuddled him and kissed his forehead, but Tommy was inconsolable. He was shuddering. He was emitting noises that shocked even him, so it was no surprise, but no less depressing, when the girl made her excuses about having to get back to work and started to leave.

But before she had gone, when she had managed to lever his eyes toward hers by lifting hard on his chin, she had said, "What is it? Can you tell me what it is?"

"I want to have a baby," whispered Tommy, and started to wail again, because he felt so ridiculous. He felt like the girl who after one bout of sex starts talking about marriage and children and then of course the boy thinks, Fuck me, panics, and leaves, just as Sasha (the boy in this instance) was now leaving and I was left alone looking in the mirror (a bad idea if you want to stop crying, believe me) and wondering what the fuck was I going to do.

What.

The fuck.

Was I going.

To do.

Sex in Space: The Video
david r. enoch

I **sat in** front of the computer, my erection ebbing. I had just watched the digital video once again, beginning to end. It was finished—I was satisfied the movie was as good as I could make it. Hard to believe I still got aroused watching that last scene, after everything.

I closed the video editor, opened my e-mail, and typed out a message.

> To whom it may concern:
> I work for NASA. You might be interested to know about a secret project on the International Space Station. Check it out at *www.sex-in-space.com*. This is not a joke.
> Signed, Commander Robert Deece

After thinking for a moment, I changed the first sentence to read, "I used to work for NASA." Then I typed in the addresses for ABC, NBC, CBS, and CNN. I blind-copied Suzanne. It was 3:00 in the afternoon. That should give the networks enough time to download a clip for the evening news.

I toggled back to my to-do list and checked off "e-mail media." The next item read "print labels, burn DVDs." The orders for my video disk were sure to start pouring in tonight. I loaded label paper into the printer and opened the file containing my cover design.

A color photo appeared on the computer screen, underneath the words "Sex in Space." The photo showed a close-up of a woman's hand, holding an erect penis. Mine. I had just ejaculated. There was no gravity pulling on my ejaculate, so a true "pearl necklace" dangled upward—six beads of semen, all connected on a string of seminal fluid. Suzanne is floating naked in the background, fascinated, her long chestnut hair fanned out around her head.

I figure a lot of people will see that photo on my website and want to spend $49.95 to see what happens next. In the video, Suzanne laughs in delight. "It is beautiful," she says. She floats over me and then down, slowly taking the necklace into her mouth, like a weightless piece of spaghetti. Then she kisses the head of my dick.

Tomorrow, she'll just want to cut it off.

I never dreamed I would be the first man to have sex in space. *No. Way.* There were a hundred reasons it couldn't happen— the main one being there were no female astronauts I had even a remote interest in. And if you had told me I would return from Utilization Stay 12 to become a porn star, I would have assumed the masochists in flight-sim had left you on the whirl-and-hurl overnight.

But then Dr. Suzanne Ritschards flew from Switzerland to Johnson Space Center for final training. She and John Weisendorf and I were finishing lunch, after having spent the morning doing a space-walk-sim in the weightless tank. We were just getting to know each other, and Weasel asked how Swiss elections worked.

"Oh, the politics are very different. Especially the Swiss woman from the American woman."

"Really?" I asked. "How so?"

She winked. "Well, when we want some dick in the president's office, we just vote for him."

Weasel and I laughed. I liked a girl with a blue sense of humor, especially a cute one with an accent. Weasel answered with his own joke. "Hey, do you know what they wrote under Monica Lewinsky's high school yearbook photo?"

"I can't imagine," said Suzanne.

"Most likely to suck-seed."

Suzanne and I laughed again. It was a pleasure to watch her; she leaned forward, open with her delight, letting forth a cascade of giggles and flashing her white teeth.

Pleased with himself, Weasel pushed back his chair and stood up, holding his cafeteria tray. Our separate afternoon briefings were about to begin.

"You know," I said, before Weasel walked off, "that's just what we need, Weeze. An OMGRAMS."

He arched an eyebrow, waiting for the punch line.

"On-Board Micro-Gravity Monica Simulator."

"Hoo-boy," said Weasel. He turned and headed toward the tray depot. I grinned at Suzanne. She didn't smile back. At first, I thought I had offended her.

Then she leaned toward me, put her hand on my arm, and lowered her voice.

"Maybe you don't need a simulator."

I blinked. Had I heard right? She looked at me for a moment, and then laughed. "Poor Deece." She patted my arm. "We need to find for you a nice, sexy Martian."

Another joke. I relaxed and smiled back. "Good idea. Do you know any?"

"Oh yes." She leaned toward me again and whispered, "They run about everywhere in Switzerland. They like chocolate."

"Mmm," I nodded. "I'll have to bring some Toblerone to the Station, for bait."

She giggled again. "That should work." She took her hand off my arm. I looked at my watch.

"Oops," I said. "Getting late." We rose, dropped off our trays, and walked together down the corridor. I stopped in front of the astrometrics lab.

"See you later, Deece," she said. She touched my hand lightly as she continued down the hall, toward biophysics.

"See you, Suzanne." She looked back just before turning the corner. We both waved.

Damn cute. I shook my head and walked into my meeting, a few minutes late.

The three of us were scheduled for lift-off in mid-November. The weeks before launch were always stressful, so Major McLeod, who oversaw training, invited the entire flight support staff to a Halloween party at his ranch. Suzanne hadn't heard of Halloween—the Swiss celebrated All Saints' Eve. When Weasel and I explained we had to wear costumes, she clapped her hands in delight.

"Really, everyone must wear an outfit? It will be fun! What will you wear?"

"Mmm, I don't know," I said. "Maybe a flight suit and my shit-kicker boots. I'll be a space cowboy."

"You already wear that every night to bed," said Weasel.

"Hey, it beats your nightgown."

Suzanne interrupted us. "We should dress alike," she announced. "We should dress all the same, the three of us."

I looked at Weasel. He shrugged. "As what?" I asked.

We all thought for a moment. Then Suzanne clapped her hands again. "Martians!"

"Oh, God," Weasel and I said in tandem.

"Yes, it's perfect," she laughed.

I held my nose and said, "Take me to your leader."

Two days later, Suzanne reported she had bought costumes for all of us, and held out three bottles. When we saw what they were, Weasel and I both shook our heads no. Hair dye. Suzanne put on a pouting look.

"You promised," she said.

"No we didn't," said Weasel. Suzanne looked at me, and I held up my hands.

"But we *have* to dress the same, the shuttle crew. You Americans don't know how to have any fun."

"Suzanne," I appealed, "we don't know how to use that stuff."

"So I will do it for you."

That gave us pause. Eventually, Suzanne made Weasel and me both promise to come out to her duplex before the party, where we would all get ready together and she could help dye our hair.

I drove to her apartment that Friday, arriving before Weasel did. Suzanne answered the door with bright blue hair. I refused all over again, but Weasel showed up and Suzanne convinced him it would be fun and easy to wash out. He sat on a stool and leaned his head back into her kitchen sink. I drank a beer while I watched her wet down his crew cut and tint it canary yellow. He looked in the mirror afterward and bitched and moaned, but it was obvious he had enjoyed the attention. And it did look funny. I let Suzanne pull me to the sink and dye my hair a vivid shade of red. We all walked out to my car wearing silver paint on our faces and hands, and green coveralls.

Major McLeod answered the door wearing a large cardboard box spiked with cardboard tubes and a tag saying, "Hi, my name is Sputnik." Suzanne said *"Prevyet,"* hello in Russian, and kissed him on the cheek. Weasel bowed and said, "Greetings, Earthling." I made some beeping noises.

The guys from propulsion and telemetry started hitting on Suzanne pretty hard, which kind of annoyed me. She seemed to enjoy the attention, though, line-dancing with a few of them. Around midnight, McLeod started talking exclusively in Russian and handing out shots of vodka. Weasel, who doesn't drink, caught a ride home. Suzanne and I stayed until things started to wind down, and then we said good night to Mackie.

I helped Suzanne into my car and we drove through the warm night, talking easily. In her driveway, I shut off the car, turned toward her, and pinched my nose. "Flying Saucer X-23 returning to port. Mmm-Beep."

Suzanne laughed. The silver paint had rubbed off of her lips.

"Merci, Monsieur Beep. I enjoyed being your Martian friend tonight."

"Me, too," I smiled. We sat for a minute, holding our distance. Finally, I opened my car door. "Let me walk you in."

I walked around the car and opened the door. She reached for my hand as she got out, and didn't let go as we moved up the walk. I turned to say good night, but she took my other hand and leaned into me. We kissed. For a while. Then we stopped, but didn't move from the stoop.

"We're launching in three weeks," I said.

"Yes. The timing is not so good." She traced her finger up and down my arm, her head against my chest. I waited, smelling her perfume.

"You know," she said after a minute, "we are not really NASA astronauts tonight."

"Mm? What are we?"

"We are new Martian friends just beginning to know each other."

"Ahh. And what do new Martian friends do?"

She looked up at me. "They wash each other's hair."

"Oh, really."

"Yes, really." She turned and unlocked the front door. *"Viens.* Come with me, Monsieur Beep." She took my hand and I followed her into the apartment. She led me past the kitchen, through her bedroom, and into the bathroom.

"I take it we're not using the kitchen sink."

"No. I don't think we both could fit." She reached into the shower stall and turned on the water. Then she started to take off her coveralls. She smiled and stripped off her shirt, as though we had been nude together hundreds of times. There was nothing to do but follow her lead. In a moment, we were both naked. We stepped together and kissed again, caressing slowly.

She was slender, soft, nicely proportioned. I was hard immediately. Glancing at the mirror, I grinned at how silly we looked in our makeup. "Okay, Martian friend," I said, "time to wash your hair." We stepped into the shower. I guided her under the spray and massaged her scalp. The blue dye rinsed out, flowing down her shoulders and breasts. The tint collected at her crotch. "You're blue everywhere," I laughed, and rubbed the back of my fingers softly against her pubic hair. The dye streamed down her legs and swirled into the drain.

"And you are turning red," she said, pulling me full under the shower. I watched the blue water on the floor turn maroon. Reaching for the bar of soap, she began to wash my chest and stomach.

"Ooo," I said. "Aaah. Beep-beep-beep."

Suzanne laughed. Then she pretended to look angry. "What is this?" she said. "I see you have deceived me. Martians do not have these."

"Mmm," I moaned. "How sad for the Martians."

"No, sad for you. Your masquerade must be punished." She stroked me softly.

"Show me mercy, o Martian Queen." It was getting harder to make jokes. "I was seduced by your alien beauty."

"Martians do not know mercy," she said, and kissed my shoulder. "Now, you must do my bidding."

"Anything, Your Royal Blueness. I mean, Highness."

She continued to massage me for another minute, creating a mass of red lather. Then she let go of me and stepped away. Blue dye continued to drip from her hair, streaking her body. Holding my gaze, she leaned back against the shower wall.

"I am tired of being blue," she said. She tapped her vagina and raised her arms above her head.

She whispered through the steam. "Turn me purple, Earthling."

I awoke to see Suzanne watching my face. Her hair, still wet when we had finally gone to bed, was wildly tousled. She looked lovely.

"Do you want to make love again?" she whispered. I nodded. She climbed on top of me and began to rock slowly. She looked for a long time into my eyes.

"Is this just sex for you?"

I shook my head gently. "No."

I was surprised to feel like I meant it.

Afterward, we lay on top of the sheets, holding hands, and decided what we had to do next.

Our relationship had to stay completely secret, at least for now. NASA had put all of us—me, her, Weasel, the two cosmonauts already on the Space Station—through extensive personality testing on paper, to make sure we could spend four months on the Space Station together without killing each other. If mission control learned we were romantically involved, there was a real possibility one or both of us wouldn't fly.

"Bobby?" she said.

"Mmm?"

"We have to pretend on *Alpha*, too. The whole time."

"I know. Four months."

She was silent.

"It's going to be hard," I added.

"Is it?" She rolled toward me and grabbed my penis.

"Ha-ha." I caught her hand. "Is that my Martian punishment? Locked up in orbit with you and nowhere to be alone?"

"I warned you the timing was no good."

"Some warning."

She kissed my neck and said we would just have to get our fill before we left. We made love nearly every night after that, including the night before launch.

Our flight was flawless. Suzanne and Weasel and I joined Sergei and Yuri on board *Alpha* just before Thanksgiving. After acclimating for a day, we all quickly got to work. Our schedules were busy, which was fine. It kept me distracted. Suzanne and I barely touched during our first three weeks in space.

But then the "Canadian Hand," our remote dextrous manipulator, froze. After several space walks, we still couldn't fix it. Without the Hand, two of us had to go extravehicular every Tuesday, crawling out to the exterior of Leonardo module to switch out the panels we used to measure near-Earth radiation and micro-meteoroid levels. And another one of us had to act as the walk-choreographer from inside. This messed up the schedule pretty good. Normally, NASA had all of us take sleep and presleep at the same time. But the two spacewalkers invariably came back so cold and exhausted that they'd skip presleep and go straight to bed. And the choreographer would have to take his mandatory daily hour on the treadmill during presleep.

The way it ended up after the second "Tuesday EVA," Weasel and Yuri sacked out early, Sergei strapped himself to the treadmill to beam his heart rate and respiration levels back to Houston, and Suzanne and I were off-duty for forty-five minutes.

It didn't occur to me to take advantage. But then Suzanne said to Sergei, "Looking good, Gei. I'm going to catch a sunrise from the cupola." She drifted feet first out of Habitation toward Kibo module. I was entering some data on my laptop. Just before she disappeared, she cocked her head slightly and winked at me.

"*Ya vizhou vas zavtra,*" said Sergei, continuing to jog. "See you tomorrow." It was an old joke; we had sixteen "tomorrows" every day, counting by sunrises.

I closed the laptop. "I guess I'll grab a look too," I said as nonchalantly as I could. I somersaulted to face Sergei. Two spring-loaded tethers were attached to a harness around his torso, pulling him down onto the rolling track. "You need anything, Gei? Water?" Sergei touched the bottle strapped to his belt. I nodded and pushed my way out, through Zarya module and the Unity connector toward Kibo. The Kibo cupola had the biggest illuminators on the Station, four thirty-inch windows looking over the solar arrays and down at Earth.

Suzanne was waiting for me, eyes bright, surprised at our luck. "Welcome to the backseat of my Chevy," I said, pushing myself over to her.

"I can't believe we're alone." She grabbed me in a big hug. We kissed quickly. It felt so good to hold her close.

"Man, have I missed you," I said.

She took my face in her hands and kissed me again, a

dozen times on the lips, making up for the last three weeks. I laughed. Then she kissed me once more, slow and deep.

"We probably shouldn't start something we can't finish," I said.

"Who says we can't finish?" She brushed her hand against my crotch.

"Don't tease me."

"Nah-nah." She pushed away, unzipped her jumpsuit, and lifted up her T-shirt. Her breasts jiggled slightly; she often didn't wear a bra back home, and she clearly didn't need one in space. I grabbed her shoulders and pulled her close again. Then I lifted her up and sucked her nipples. She moaned. Her scent made me slightly dizzy. I floated even with her again, and our eyes locked.

"Do we dare?" I whispered.

She paused for a moment. *Alpha* was quiet during presleep—no voice traffic, no music. The drone of the air-scrubbers muffled the sound of Sergei tromping on the treadmill. I realized I was holding my breath. Then, Suzanne reached for the zipper at my chest, and pulled it down.

"Turn me purple, Earthling," she whispered back. "But do it quick."

We discovered three things, our first time.

One, cinch your clothes under a restraining strap. My shorts seemed determined to wrap themselves around my head, and her jumpsuit nearly floated out of Kibo altogether.

Two, move slowly. We kept disconnecting inadvertently, until we realized that hurrying was just working against us. McLeod's docking-sim advice proved unexpectedly useful: Greater control comes with short, smooth, low-power thrusts.

And three, position was everything. Standard missionary was clumsy; doggy-style was incredible. After a few miscues, I got behind Suzanne and held her hips. With little effort, I could move both of us any way I wanted, change my angle, my depth. I could even rotate her from side to side, with me as the axis. Floating in front of me, she could open and close her legs, and reach back to cradle my balls or caress herself.

The sensation was otherwordly. As long as I held on to her hips, we stayed engaged, but we had complete freedom of movement. We drifted through the room together, shifting easily from spooning to barely touching. We explored each other for the first time, all over again.

We bumped into a wall, and Suzanne grabbed a handrail near the illuminator. She tucked her feet under another rail, and held herself still while I stayed connected behind her. I spiraled so that we formed an X; it looked and felt so bizarre, we both started to laugh. Our clothes drifted by as we giggled and moaned and hushed each other.

"We need to finish soon," she whispered.

"That won't be a problem." I rotated to parallel again. I let go of her hips and latched onto the same handrails she was holding. She pushed back into me, and I sped up. We both came over the Pacific Ocean at 16,000 mph, and it felt like it.

We were tingling afterward, whispering and giggling, putting our clothes back on. We could still hear Sergei, running on the track. I heard him cough in the distance and I glanced toward the passageway back to Hab-mod. With a start, I saw a black lens pointing back at me.

I looked down and then right at the other two lenses, knowing they were there. The three digital video cameras were all wall-mounted, aimed at the center of the room, intended to capture x-, y-, and z-axis views of our micro-grav experiments.

"Oops," I said.

Suzanne froze. "What?"

I pointed to the digi-vid next to the hatch.

"Oh my God. Are they on?"

"Shouldn't be." I pushed over and checked the switches on the central control panel. Each button had wording in both Russian and English.

"Off," I said.

"What about the other panels?"

I thought for a minute. "Well, Sergei is right next to the masters, but there's no reason he'd turn them on. Houston could maybe do a remote activate, but they wouldn't unless we reported a glitch." I realized we were okay, and smiled. "Maybe McLeod is watching us right now, trying to figure out what experiment we're working on." I waved. "Hey, Mackie!"

"That's not funny."

"Don't worry, Beep." I hadn't called her that in weeks. "No one was watching."

"You really scared me." She hugged me tight. I kissed her on the forehead. We both felt relieved. In more ways than one.

Then she squeezed my butt. "So," she said. "What are you doing next Tuesday?"

Unfortunately, I was going outside with Sergei. Mackie had scheduled the two of us to alternate spacewalks with Yuri and Weasel. As usual, our tethers and gloves made for slow going. It took us almost seven hours to switch out all the radiation panels and return through the airlock. My feet were freezing, and I always felt drunk after coming off pure oxygen. By presleep, I was bushed. I went into my sleep-chamber right after dinner, with Sergei right behind me.

An hour later, I was still awake. I couldn't get comfortable in my sleep-sac, the electrode net kept tugging at my hair, and someone was pounding away on the treadmill. I realized I hadn't taken my melatonin supplement with dinner, which helped fight micro-grav-induced insomnia. I finally disconnected the medilog cap, unzipped my sac, and pushed my way back into Hab-mod.

Yuri watched me float into the room, which smelled of his sweat. He was on the treadmill, jogging steadily. "No sleeping?" he asked.

"Nah. Forgot to take my sleep pill with dinner."

"Tonight you are only using pill from last week."

"Yeah, I know. I guess I should have taken two pills last week."

"It is damn EVA. Now you are too tired to sleep."

"I think you're right." I rubbed my eyes. "I need something to drink."

"*Da.* You need good Russian vodka."

"You got some?"

"Already gone." We both laughed.

"You're heating up this place pretty good," I said, and pushed over to the main controls. I thumbed down the thermostat a notch. Out of habit, I looked at the master switches for the digi-vids in Kibo. Ever since our secret rendevous, I always checked to make sure the switches were off. They were.

For the hell of it, I turned on the monitor bank. Each of the six monitors could display the view from any of twelve different cameras mounted inside and outside the Station. The monitors were all blank, as they should have been. Under the first monitor, I flipped the switch marked "Kibo-v1." A fuzzy image came on and the auto-focus went into gear.

The image resolved and I gasped. It was Suzanne, nude, holding onto a handrail. The screen didn't show her lower half, and it didn't show me, but I knew we were both there. I didn't understand. How could the monitor be showing an image from last week? How could we have been recorded? How was it playing back now?

In a panic, I flipped the switch for Kibo-v2 under the second monitor. The screen became brighter, and the auto-focus for the second camera went into gear. As it did, the odd thought occurred to me that the auto-focus only initiated when you first turn on the camera. Something didn't make sense. Then the second view pulled into focus.

She was with Weasel.

She was with Weasel and he was naked and they were naked together and it wasn't a recording and she reached for him and they pulled together and she took his penis in her mouth and she sucked on him and he closed his eyes—

"What are you doing, flying home for vodka?"

I snapped back into the sweaty room. My hear was racing, and I felt like I had run out of air. I finally managed a croak. "Uh?"

"You are flying us home for vodka?"

It was Yuri. I turned. He was behind me, facing the other way on the treadmill. He hadn't seen anything. The dimensions of the room seemed to warp. Was I dreaming?

I turned back. The monitors were still on. Suzanne was still there, still sucking Weasel. The images on the two screens moved in sync. This was no dream. I began to feel sick.

"No," I said. "Aaah. Just. Making sure everything is off." I flipped the monitor master switch and the screens went blank. Yuri kept running, his feet like a metronome. My nausea began to rise.

How could it be? When had it started? I took four long, deep breaths, like Mackie had taught during flight-sim training. It didn't work. I looked back down at the switches. The monitors were off, but the two digi-vid cameras were still on. Looking at Suzanne. With Weasel. Watching her do with him what was only for us.

I closed my eyes and gritted my teeth, working to force back the acid tang curdling in my throat. The taste of betrayal. Fool. *Fool!*

Then the nausea disappeared with a flash of cold, white anger. *You fucking bitch,* I thought. *Everything is off all right. Except for this.*

I reached over and snapped on Kibo-v3. And then I hit Record.

The idea of revenge came whole. I'd record her with Weasel. Make it public. Put it on the Internet. Even better, I'd sell it. They'd be unwilling porn stars, and I'd get paid for it. NASA would fire us all, but tough shit. They deserved it, and so did I. What a chump.

It turned into a project. Project Revenge. It had two steps. First, they couldn't know I knew. I did a good job on that part. I was already hiding everything from Weasel and the two Russians anyway, so I just added her to the list. We stayed there for eleven more weeks, and I acted like we were all still friends. No one had a clue. I even kept on fucking Suzanne. Every other Tuesday.

Step two was, it had to be good video. It was twisted, my perfectionist streak, but I wanted good composition, good lighting. People might not pay to see crappy amateur shots. When I got home, I spent a lot of time with the video editor, choosing footage.

The DVD starts out showing all five of us doing "normal" micro-grav things—grabbing floating liquid balls with our mouths, posing next to each other with one of us upside-down. Gives the viewer some context, establishes the setting. Then I cut to Weasel and Suzanne, alone, floating into Kibo one at a time. They both get undressed, except he leaves on his socks. They tuck their clothes under a retention strap. They kiss for a minute, and stroke each other. "So wet," he says. She moans in reply. It's obvious they have no idea they're on tape.

As soon as Weasel gets hard, they fuck, front-to-front. He holds her ass and she puts him inside and they interlace their legs to keep from floating apart. They drift through the module, wiggling like a weird sea-worm. They bump into a bulkhead and float partly out of view, then back on-screen. Weasel says "Oh cunt, oh cunt, oh cunt," like he always does, and comes. Suzanne keeps wiggling for a minute. Their breathing slows down, they unwind and push apart. Weasel pulls two sheets of paper toweling out of the dispenser and hands one to Suzanne. They wipe themselves off. Then they get back into their clothes, push off the wall, and float out of the room.

On Earth, it would be almost boring. Five minutes of insipid humping. But this was sex in outer space. Weightless astronauts stripping off NASA jumpsuits, fucking while floating, and the happy couple didn't even know they were being recorded. My plan was to ruin their lives, and make some money to boot.

The problem was, I couldn't get any variation. They kept doing the same goddamn thing. On my EVA Tuesdays, just before presleep, I programmed a two-hour record for all three Kibo digi-vids. The next morning, I transferred the captures onto my laptop and waited until I was alone to see what I had caught. It was like they only knew one thing to do. She gives him some quick oral sex. They wrap around each other in the sea-worm position. He grunts, sometimes she does too. They disconnect. Wipe themselves off with paper towels. Get dressed and leave. Same scene, every fucking time.

I couldn't sell a porn tape showing the same exact thing a dozen ways.

And it was infuriating to watch. Over half the time, she didn't come. He was selfish, sometimes almost violent. He was built well, but so what? Why did she do it with him? Her sex with me was clearly better. Clearly.

Or was it?

I decided to find out. After one of Weasel's EVAs, I turned

on the digi-vids before I met her in Kibo. I admit I had an advantage, knowing the cameras were on. But my scenes were vastly superior. I got some great close-ups by maneuvering us near the cameras. I talked dirty better. I used my mouth, my hands, tried different positions. I was tender. You could see she was more into it with me. Her final spasm lasted for half a minute. It really was great footage. Once I saw it, I couldn't *not* use it.

After that, I turned the cameras on every Tuesday. When it was my turn, I secretly planned our sex, scripting out movements in my head. I even brought props. One time, I told her I wanted to have sex by candlelight. I dimmed the lights to half and pulled out two pen-sized flashlights. We did a floating 69 while the pen-lights twirled slowly around the room. The cameras caught it perfectly.

My best footage of all was the docking sequence. I saved it for the last scene on the DVD. Like I said, I still get hard watching it, even now.

Suzanne and I are floating free, in the middle of the room. I'm holding on to her hips, and her feet are hooked around my waist. She's leaning away from me, her arms above her head, like our first time in the shower. I'm pushing in and out with a slow rhythm. Her eyes are closed and her face is flushed.

"Pull your knees up," I say. "Higher." She does, with her hands. I arch away from her, my hands still holding her hips. Then I spin her counterclockwise, slowly.

"Oh my god," she says. I turn her all the way around, and stop. In and out. I turn her the other way, slowly. In and out. She starts to come, the flesh on her buttocks and breasts quivering. Then I spin her again, a good, firm spin, and let go.

"Oh my god," she keeps saying. I hold still, arching backward. Slowly, she spins off me, floats away. "Come back," she says. "Bobby, come back. I want you in me."

On the DVD, she drifts out of the picture, leaving me alone on the screen, my penis poking out. Then I fade to black and show the whole thing again—but in reverse. I got the idea while I was editing, during a rewind.

I used a different angle, my feet toward the camera. The scene starts out looking like I'm alone in the module. Then Suzanne appears from screen-left, floating toward me slow-mo. She's holding her knees, spinning. I don't touch her. My cock lifts up and she docks perfectly onto my erection.

On the sound track, I dubbed the voice traffic between me and McLeod when the shuttle arrived at the Station. "We have connect," I say, just as Suzanne spins on to me. "Docking complete."

"Docking complete. Good job, Deece," said Mackie. "Very pretty."

"She flies great," I say. I take Suzanne by the hips and spin her the other way.

"Welcome to *Alpha*," says Mackie.

"Home sweet home."

It's great porn, if I say so myself. It shows the world how much better I was than Weasel. And it shows that Suzanne is a fucking slut.

That night, the telephone rang. I let my computer answer. At first, I thought the caller had hung up.

Then I heard something, a choking sound. It was her. She was crying so hard she couldn't speak.

Finally, she caught her breath. "Bobby. Pick up the telephone. Please, answer."

I didn't move.

"Bobby, please." She wept. "Don't do this. Take the video off. Please. I will have nowhere to go."

I listened to her sob. The telephone icon flashed on my computer screen. I watched it blink.

Then she screamed, really in anguish. "BASTARD! I HATE YOU! FUCKING BASTARD!" She was frothing, hysterical. I heard her slam the phone against the wall, and the connection broke. After a moment, the telephone icon stopped blinking and disappeared.

I smiled thinly and reached for my mouse. "That was really very genuine," I said to the empty room. "And I *am* a fucking bastard. A *fucking* bastard." I clicked on the computer directory and opened the audio files.

There was still time to add her message to the end of the sound track.

Dicks, Digits, Dildos
dawn o'hara

Penises. **Vibrators,** dildos, tongues, even pens in my hungry youth. Fingers—mine, men's, rubber-gloved doctors', and one fumbling young girl's before boys occurred to me. Spermicides, sponges, diaphragms, condoms, lubricants. Seven-day yeast infection treatments—they didn't used to have the quick and tidy fixes they do now. Acidophilus tablets, vinegar douches, progesterone creams. Chocolate syrup. Tampons I could never tolerate—they just never felt as good as on those horseback-riding ads. Two miscarriages. Thermometers when we were still trying for kids. A quack regime of herbal vagi-packs during my holistic phase. Four-hundred ninety-two periods. Sixty-seven speculums. Forty-three pap smears. One cryosurgery. One hysterosalpingogram, as difficult to tolerate as it is to pronounce. Two biopsies. Eleven ultrasound wands. And this particular cock, my husband's, 4,682 times. I'm sure I've left some things out. At my age I have a hard time keeping track of what's trespassed between my legs.

Shouldn't all this have earned me some loyalty? After seeing it through so much—the ups and downs of a lifetime, so to speak—my vagina picks a hell of a time to betray me. It's our thirty-first wedding anniversary. And we've never had an anniversary without nooky. But I'm dry as a dead insect stuck in the lampshade. Parking lot closed for business, neon sign flashing, parking arm down, tires will be slashed if you enter the wrong way.

There I am, spread-legged while my husband hunts around in his softening state like a worm lost at the edge of a leaf. Not that he was rock-hard to begin with. Instantaneous erections only happen in the mornings, now.

Never mind the lubricant. I feel fragile, that I will rip and tear if he succeeds in his coaxing entry—like my grand-mother's transparent skin, bruised by a whispered touch. Even my husband's soft cock feels angry against my desert tenderness.

You'd think there would be nothing left to shame me. This man has seen my flesh jiggle in every possible sexual position over the course of thirty years. I'm twenty pounds heavier than on our wedding day, when I foolishly starved myself into a dress I couldn't fit into two days later. Once, in the emer-gency room, he stood behind the doctor as the speculum was tightened. "The cervix," the doctor announced with a flourish of his gloved hand, as if he had created its hidden wink. "Wow," was all my husband said.

I have been inadequate in producing the requisite children. Deficient in jeans size, cooking skills, apologies, and in-law relations. I got over all that and concentrated on blow jobs and yoga stretches instead. You think my husband minded unmatched towel sets and shopping without coupons?

But feeling sexually inadequate after all these years, when the lack of children gave us space for sexuality that so many couples don't have? When is my body going to cut me a break?

Fourteen years ago, reaching for the box of tissues to wipe up (he, always solicitous, tucks a tissue between my legs before he tends to himself), our hearts still pounding, my husband looked at the clock. "It takes us half an hour now. Used to be twelve minutes." Oh, we laughed at that one. But there's nothing funny about not being able to do *it* at all.

My vagina is a handpuppet with nothing to say. I am the mouth of a rolled-up sock, crusty and used, discovered with mothballs under the bed. No O'Keeffe flower, but a cracked lobster claw. The *Star Trek* alert sirens go off all around us: *Frigid vagina alert! Menopause approaching at warp speed!* I beam myself out of the room, after first meditating on dinner choices and considering the *feng shui* ramifications of our bed placement and wall color. Intense concentration has earned me many orgasms in the past, but I don't want to think about what's happening down there, my husband the spelunker rooting around for the opening of a collapsed cave. Think I'll get him one of those head lamps for Christmas. At the moment I wish ole Columbus would give up, abandon the exploration as a lost cause, so I can return to my flower bulbs.

He knows I've vacated the continent. I've got the same look as the one I wear when I'm naked on the scale. As on the first day of my period, when I don't want him to watch me dress, feeling like I've tripled in body size. Not a hostile look, like when he crawls into bed with cigar farts or enters halfway through a five-hankie TV movie and snorts at the obvious stupidity of the characters. It's the "Stay Off My Planet" look.

"Never mind," he says, rolling off me. "I have an idea. Something new."

After one-third of a century together, what else can be tried? Creative positions have gotten trickier with the need for glucosamine supplements. I could tell you what we've done on every piece of furniture in the house, but lately we stick to the basic bedroom standbys.

He fumbles around in the special dresser drawer, his thwarted pecker dangling below his belly flab. I admire his ease. Orgasms never elude him. Unexpectedly flaccid states don't disturb him. His confidence remains firmly rooted in his slightly above-average cock size (he's measured), and nothing seems to shake it. Not weight gain, hair loss, or below-average height. Even when he wore a dress a couple of times, his penis was *present* in his attitude. He never tires of my watching him, no matter which end of a diet he's on.

But now he turns away from me. His bum never changes no matter how the rest of him morphs over the years. "I got us a present," he says.

This current dilemma hasn't blindsided us out of the blue. My body's been working its way up to emergency drought levels for months, but I've ignored the signals and haven't practiced water rationing. I have procrastinated the doctor's visit, dreading the prognosis and resultant pills—but it now appears that *he's* been taking some preventative measures.

"I thought we said no presents this year." After three decades together, we buy for ourselves when the mood suits us. No more dropping months-long hints that the other one never gets.

"No, *you* said no presents this year."

There is a great deal of rustling going on. He's dropped down to the floor, so I can't see him over the side of the bed. I even hear him giggle. A fifty-four-year-old man, giggling! I giggle in response. We're a pair that way, like pizza and acid reflux.

He stands and faces me. "Tah-dah!"

He has strapped a miniature dildo to his leg. A little Bacchus sprouting from Zeus's thigh. It is lifelike in shape and color, as if his cock has reproduced, a tiny silicone replica of the real thing.

He climbs onto the bed next to me. "Come on. There's more holes here than just one."

"You're gonna fuck my ear?" Fifties kids, we still love the thrill of foul language. Not during sex, but as a part of our banter. "Wanna fuck?" we say. Or, with his Midwestern lack of verbs, "I need fucked."

"No. Your nostril. Now open wide."

I flare my nostrils, one of the few small muscle movements I can manage. He can wiggle his nose like a rabbit, but when I try it, my whole face contorts.

He wags Bacchus in my face. I swat him away, laughing.

I know what his intentions are. And he's incorrect. This isn't something new. Although I rarely let a chance go by to point out that he's wrong, since it's maddeningly infrequent, I keep my mouth shut. But we *have* tried anal sex before. Years ago. Before the twelve-minute era came to an end. We tried it only once, just for kicks during my Dickens phase, when I learned that at that time anal sex was the preferred method of "birth control." The literary experiment didn't work out, and we never attempted the back-door method again. I never saw the need while my other hole was cooperating.

He lies beside me, his hand on my chest. My breasts have always fit perfectly into his palms. "I got a really small one, just for you," he says. "I remember that the last time it hurt."

So, he *does* remember.

"Come on." He nudges me to roll over. I sigh and roll my eyes, but comply. He rubs oil between his hands and massages my back. He sits back on his haunches, and Bacchus tickles my left buttock.

"Watch the armpits!" You'd think after spending more than half a life with me he'd have memorized the ticklish spots, which encompass most of my body, and tread a fine line with my erogenous zones.

"Yeah, dummy," Bacchus pipes up in a high-pitched nasal tone. Inanimate objects in our house have developed voices over the years, usually in falsetto, facilitating our highly evolved and effective means of dysfunctional communication. It is best during arguments to have a third party to blame, especially when the object has no vocal cords and cannot defend itself. We attribute the long-term success of our marriage to this system, though the African violet resents taking the heat for eating the last cookie, or for certain foul odors permeating the room.

"Sorry."

He skims his hands up and down my spine, across my tush. I begin to relax. I'm warm and expansive. I am an O'Keeffe blossom under the New Mexico sun, splashed on the bed in purple and pink hues.

He spreads me, and I let him. I know that my ripe and rippled derriére will never make a magazine photo spread, but I also know that these cheeks look good to him. He slips inside, a centimeter at a time. It's not difficult at all this time, like the last time we tried it in the prehistoric age of our careless youth. Maybe it's because of Bacchus's minute size, or the lubricant, or our ability to work together, or that my lifelong lover has learned patience and self-denial. Whatever the reasons, I moan. I let him enjoy pleasuring me while he receives no physical gratification in return, only the sensation of giving. His real cock dangles and knocks against my lower back as he moves, right above my birthmark. His leg hair prickles my bum.

He can't tell what my vadge is up to, but I'm well aware of the state of his cock. It rapidly returns to its instant fossilized state of youth. He stabs my birthmark now with each gentle thrust inside me. My vagina stretches, yawns, and blinks, discovering that her coveted spot in the hierarchy has been usurped. Worse, the instigator is not even a member of the immediate household, but a Lilliputian godhead. Jealous, she puts up a fuss, causing a commotion between my legs. She even resorts to calling in the reserves, and my clitoris joins the clamor.

"I think Bacchus needs some air," I say over my shoulder.

My husband—this lifelong friend and lover who knows me better than anyone and yet doesn't know me at all—rolls off and lies beside me. He gazes at me, not expecting anything, though his Big and Little Dippers demand otherwise. He plays with my hair. For years he looked forward to its turning gray, saying with a wink that he wanted to sleep with an older woman. I know that in his rich inner life I've often been the siren schoolmarm seducing his helpless virginity, so I've never wrestled with hair dyes, despite the random streaks through the still-shiny black.

Then I'm on top of him, our puzzle pieces connect, and my body swallows him in one easy gulp.

Bacchus taps my rump, as if to say, *Hey, did you forget about me?* But he doesn't say a word.

Recent Reports on Progress Toward Fusion

bill noble

Hannie Arenson was born one minute after midnight on April 27, 1969, in Mackinaw City, Michigan. So was Steve Arenson. Y'see, from the belly button up, Hannie and Steve are two separate guys; from the belly button down, they're just one.

Hannie's blond, with a big Scandinavian jaw holding up an easy smile. Steve's darker, with a clown's sadness behind his eyes. Hannie's generous. Steve's judgmental. Hannie makes appreciative love, then goes to sleep all wrapped up in you. Steve dangles you at the edge of coming till you beg.

How do I know all this? Hey, who should know better? I'm Meg Kapinski. They're my husbands.

I met them in May on their twenty-sixth birthday. My friend Myra knew them from college, and invited me to their party. They blew out their candles by leaning around opposite sides of the cake and emitting a huge simultaneous puff. I can't truthfully tell you whether it was Hannie's sunny face that got me, or Steve's elusiveness, or imagining one-and-a-half guys making love to me—one straight-home cock and all those hands. You know us ex-Catholic girls. Kinky.

It took me a week to figure out they were virgins, and that just made me hotter. We were in this noisy seafood bar in Ann Arbor, drinking beer and scarfing oysters. I took two of their hands and with a sudsy leer asked them how they handled good-night kisses. Hannie laughed, but Steve looked away.

Hannie said, "Meg . . ."

I said, "I'm sorry," talking to the tears in Steve's eyes. A klutz. I was a complete klutz. I leaned across the table and kissed him without thinking. He resisted at first, then opened his mouth and kissed back like a tiger. Hannie's eyes were like golf balls. So I kissed him too.

I drove them home—Michigan still hadn't figured out how to give driver's licenses to two guys with one set of legs—and stayed and talked. Between the beer and being an outspoken broad, I wasn't about to let them get away with anything. I brought a chair over to the couch and scooched up close.

I smiled my brightest all-American Kapinski smile. "So, would you guys like to work on kisses three and four?"

Hannie closed his eyes and leaned toward me, a grin fighting with the pucker he was trying to hold. As I kissed him, I looked sidewise into Steve's guarded, hungry eyes and felt a slick of wetness between my legs.

It was a great kiss. Hannie and I got our hands into it, faces, fingers through hair. I let my mouth relax, let Hannie come to me.

When we finished, I turned to Steve, smiling. "Not tonight," he said, not looking me in the eye. "Just not tonight."

I picked up his hands and buried my face in his palm. I gave each of his fingertips a wet kiss with lots of tongue. Hannie put a hand on my shoulder and started to breathe hard. Without any warning, their bodies stiffened. Steve gasped and went red. Hannie let out a long, pent-up breath he might have been holding for twenty-six years. The two of them had just come for me. I stared at the blotch on their pants. Nobody knew what to say.

Three dates later, we were at their sunny, bay-windowed flat again. We'd backed off after that first explosion: the last thing I wanted was for my Godzilla libido to hurt these guys. But now, lace curtains blowing, Norway maples June green all along the street, I was ready to roll again.

"Esalen massage. Really, guys."

"Massage?" They both said it together.

"You know," I deadpanned. "Rub-a-dub? Like California."

Hannie glanced doubtfully at Steve. "That okay with you?"

Steve put on a studied nonchalance, but he was running his eyes-somewhere-else routine. "I'm game. If you are."

"What do we do?" Hannie looked about twelve years old.

"Just take off your clothes and lay down on the bed." I waited, an ache in my belly.

Steve made the first move, undoing the top button on his shirt. It didn't help my ache any to notice that they already had a pretty good erection loading their jeans. Steve, despite being Republican, dropped his shirt on the floor. Hannie, the Democrat, laid his neatly over the back of the bedroom chair. I was having a hard time breathing, so I knelt down real quick and undid their belt. I snaked their pants down and confirmed Meg's First Conjecture: They didn't wear underwear. Meg's Second Conjecture was that they weren't circumcised. Confirmed. The Third? Go ahead, guess. But I was right on that one, too.

This was the only time in the years I've known my guys that I remember their coordination failing. As their gorgeous thingymabob hoisted, they tried to hide it by turning toward the bed—each in opposite directions. All they succeeded in doing was fwapping it across my cheeks, twice, once in each direction. You've never seen a blush until you've seen bare-assed Norwegian Siamese twins go red right down to their toe tips. They finally lurched around and fell face down on the mattress.

"Guys," I said.

They twitched, but didn't really move.

"Guys, turn over." I saw frantic eye signals, then finally, laboriously, they turned over. Each one tried to pretend their grossly inflamed dingus belonged to the other guy.

"Watch," I said. They did.

I undid my top button. Then the next one. Grossly inflamed became more grossly inflamed. I took my blouse off and lofted it across the room. I took off my bra and lofted it, too. I hefted my breasts and slurped a nipple, smirking through well-batted lashes. I was directly wired to that Macarena cock. I dropped my skirt. My darlings' dick hung a long streamer of silver, anchored yummily in the fine hairs on their belly. I wriggled out of my panties, then wafted them past their noses. I tugged a chair to the foot of the bed, and sprawled in it, legs flung wide. I raised my middle finger and lowered it toward my puss. I slipped the finger in, then took it out and licked it. My guys licked their lips. I was the god-damn Pavlov of the boudoir! I drew the wet up around my clit and circled.

One thing I'd extracted from our long evenings of talk was the mind-boggling news that they'd never "touched them-selves." Hah! Meg the Kinky Sex Maven was about to change that.

I petted myself close to coming, and then I danced. I strad-dled them on the bed, pulling open my puss. I almost—but not quite—grazed their lips with my boobs. Mama, I was mer-ciless. After nearly an hour of tease, I sat back in the chair and propped my legs wide apart on the corners of the bed.

"Touch yourself." I breathed the words in my best Marlene

Dietrich baritone. Steve's hand crept down. He was almost cross-eyed, staring at their cock. Hannie flung a panicky glance at him.

"Touch yourself. C'mon. Both of you."

They each put reluctant fingers on the shaft of their penis and gave a shudder of pleasure.

"Stroke," I said, holding their eyes.

Hannie took the initiative. He wrapped his hand around it and began to stroke. Steve joined in. I was beginning to shake.

"Slower," I said as I diddled myself again. "Real slow."

"Slower."

Hannie's mouth was locked open, gulping air, *heh, heh, heh.* Steve's face darkened toward purple. He was looking at me, but I'm not sure anything was getting recorded in his brain.

"Jeezus," I called, riding my wave. "Slower!" I kept my eyes locked on theirs.

The muscles in their thighs were vibrating. I was trying to stay with them. They both shouted at the same time—I shouted, too, but I have no idea what—and a second later this fountain spurted out of them. They snapped nearly upright; a big glop of semen caught Steve across the neck.

I struggled to stay upright on the chair, deep in those two pairs of eyes. *Holy shit, this ain't kink anymore. You're in love, girl.*

"All right," I said, not nearly as in charge as I was acting. "It's time for the massage." And I gave them one. Really. Just a massage.

Weeks later, we were in the lap of August, sitting under jack pines above the clearest little backwoods lake on the Upper Peninsula.

We were making love. And talking about marriage. And swimming. They'd been picking raspberries for me and they were licking raspberry juice off my nipples. This is why I've got two breasts. I may be the first woman in the history of the world to really understand that about boobs.

"You can only marry one of us, you know," Steve said, looking out at the lake.

"No way," Hannie and I said together, and then we grinned.

But Steve's voice had an edge. For the first time in their lives Hannie and Steve were rivals.

If another Ice Age came, I felt like I'd personally push back the glaciers with animal heat. "I want both of you," I said.

I pushed them over and smooshed raspberries all over their warm, big intellect. Then I sucked it all the way down my throat. They both hollered when I did that. I grinned at the looks on their faces and then popped them out of my mouth for a minute. "I can do anything I want."

All the while I sucked there were hands wrapped in my hair, hands over my shoulders, fingers tracing the lines of my back. *Anything I want. Anything.* I came before they did, and then I came again when they exploded.

One of their doctors explained it to me with an unprofessional leer: Two brains pumped hormones through one set of equipment. Five or six times hardly seemed to wear them out. In fact, it was usually me who begged for mercy. But the same doctor also told me that their lower body was the rarest thing in joined twins: a chimera. They came from two different eggs, but their cells had mingled. Their immune systems had learned each other's chemistry: They were two separate bodies, mingled as one. They made two sets of sperm in one set of balls, Republican and Democrat, and launched all that stuff into Catholic me every time they came. And came. And came.

When we ran out of raspberries we went swimming. They leapt up with their weird, top-heavy grace and sprinted toward the cliff, catapulted into the air. Hannie grabbed a pine bough and pendulumed them upward. Steve caught a higher bough to swing even higher. They sailed out over the lake, twined in a Tarzan duet. I dove in after them.

When I surfaced, they were nowhere in sight. Two heads tickled up between my legs. Two mouths blew bubbles, one up my butt crack, the other tingling my clit. They burst to the surface. We clung together, laughing, half-choking on lake water, and then laughing all the more because of it. All those hands were holding me up.

By early October we'd gotten to the hard parts. One particular afternoon, I was trying to hammer home the subtler arts of munching my puss. Problem was, the guy who wasn't employed never had any idea what to do with himself. Hannie was lying face down, listlessly stroking my belly and breasts, clearly uncomfortable. Steve was doing Olympic-level tongue-fu. But all those hands I'd loved so much were just distracting. We were on our way to a first in our relationship: I wasn't going to come.

I rolled them over and impaled myself. I kissed my taste off Steve's mouth and then tried to kiss Hannie. He wasn't having any. I fucked them, hard and steady, staring into Hannie's eyes, willing him to open up. I swooped and jiggered, broke my rhythm, went slow, went fast, milked them with my puss. "Hannie, where you at?" I said.

"Meg," Steve cut in, "I thought you and I were the ones making love." His lips were set in a line.

I sucked his tongue into my mouth and then bit it till he winced. Then I did the same to Hannie. I pushed their heads together, ear to ear, and bent hard over them, kissing one and then the other. I wanted to come so bad, but it was as elusive as ever. If I kissed one of them for long enough they'd respond, but when I switched back to the other, the first one'd go all distant again. I closed my eyes. I humped cock. Sweat ran down me and dripped onto their chests. I tried to pull them closer to each other, but it wasn't working.

I stopped moving.

I wanted a circle of love, and I was living in a fucking isosceles triangle. I pulled them out of me and stood up.

"Guys! This isn't working. I feel like I'm sneaking around having two separate affairs."

"Meg, I think we're all in this together." Steve was trying to joke, looking out the window at the yellow maples, but I knew they both understood what I meant.

I grabbed my blouse, but my shaking fingers buttoned the damn thing one button out of whack. A button rattled to the floor as I tried to undo it. Tears spilled. "I only ever get to make love to one of you. The other one's always acting like they want to watch TV."

Hannie turned to his brother. "She's right, you know."

"Fuck if she is."

"Steve, we always—"

"Shove it!"

"Steve—"

"Damn it. I don't want to hear this shit!"

I was crying full out now. "I'm leaving, Steve. It just makes me feel lonely."

Hannie tried to touch my cheek, but Steve wasn't letting him lean forward far enough. His hand fell back in their lap.

"And get your goddamn hand out of my crotch!" Steve spat at Hannie.

Hannie winced and blinked away tears. Shaking, he reached up to touch Steve's cheek. Steve struck Hannie's hand away. His shoulders were bunched, his face all twisted up. I stopped trying to get dressed. Hannie gave me a long, steady look. All of a sudden he wasn't holding anything back, tears, truth, anything. He turned to Steve and cradled his brother's face. Their legs shifted unconsciously on the bed to support them. Steve glared, but didn't move.

"Steve."

Silence.

"Steve, we . . . we *are* in this together, y'know." Hannie put a soft kiss on Steve's forehead. Steve flinched, but didn't bolt. "Steve," he said, in the softest voice I'd ever heard. He lifted his brother's face up and kissed him on the mouth. To my amazement, Steve's face relaxed. He looked into Hannie's eyes, searching. Thinking hard.

Steve turned. "Meg. Hold us."

I hesitated.

"Just hold us. Please."

I came and sat on the edge of the bed with my puffy face and my draggled hair and one boob hanging out of my half-buttoned blouse. I put my hands on their shoulders. I was shaking. Shit, one way or another, I always ended up shaking. Hannie's face was a big, open question. Steve was headed someplace, and Hannie was ready to go.

"Whatever we feel, we both feel." Steve reached down and touched their cock with the greatest tenderness. He wasn't holding anything back now, either. A first.

"Whatever we love, we both love. That's just the way it is."

Hannie nodded, just the briefest movement. Steve's fingers began to stroke.

"Feel that?"

Hannie nodded again, a solemn big-eyed boy.

"So do I. Feel Meg holding us?"

The ghost of a smile passed over Hannie's lips.

"When I talk about Meg, you feel what our body does?" Steve squeezed their cock and it bloomed.

Hannie's eyes blinked tight, then opened. This time the smile was unmistakable.

I couldn't tell who started the kiss. I felt a sudden flood, not just in my puss, but everywhere. I never knew men could be so tender.

Steve pulled Hannie's face closer, kissed him deep. Hannie

took over stroking. We had some lube beside the bed, so I grabbed it and poured it all over their cock and Hannie's hands.

Hannie stroked the shaft and Steve made a little tent with his fingertips for their cockhead. I watched the muscles in their one precious pair of hips bunch and release. They made tiny sounds into each other's throats while I held them. I don't know how long it went on. You can't believe what four hands can do. To a cock, to faces, to bodies, to two men who discover love.

I was afraid they'd break. They held their chests so close— I didn't see how it was possible, the way their body was made. But it wasn't frantic. I watched a patient dance.

I watched the little eye in the tip of their cock open. I felt their come move through their entire body, I swear. Pulse after pulse. I just held them, watching their lips just touching.

When it was time, they turned and brought me into the center of it.

"Hey," I said in a little voice.

"Hey," Steve said, in a voice just as small. Hannie smiled his little-boy smile, but didn't say a word.

Our lips and noses and tongues tangled, breath passing soul to soul to soul. Our arms wove a circle to hold it all. One of my nipples was crushed against Steve's curly chest, the other rubbed Hannie's smooth one.

"Get hard for me, husbands." As I said it, they swelled. Their cock made little scratchy sounds rising through our pubic hair.

I raised my butt. Hannie and Steve held my eyes and edged their mouths together. Their tongues danced, following the dance of my puss on their cockhead.

They darted their tongues and I jabbed their pink head in and out of me. Steve slipped his tongue behind Hannie's upper lip and I slickered their cock over my clit. That squeezed an involuntary "Yuuuuf!" out of me. The two guys cracked up, and that made me lose it. We started roaring with laughter.

We howled so hard I couldn't hold my butt up; my puss fell all the way down on Hannie and Steve's pole. There isn't a word for the sound we made sliding together, but there oughta be.

We stopped laughing.

Hannie took our hands and leaned back—and then the three of us were swayed back at arm's length, hands locked, our two bellies fused: Three separate, loving people, joined into one.

We curled our hips up, and we could see the column of our cock entering. If we strained, we could make out the rim of the head slipping out, but then our belly muscles would relax and it'd glide back in. It didn't matter who had an innie or an outie. It didn't matter if we came. Well, maybe a little bit.

The distance Hannie and Steve always held was gone. The little smart-ass separation I'd always kept from men was gone, too. I pressed that sweet cock in and rocked and felt it bend and unbend inside us. Our pupils widened in unison. A salty tear ran right down into my wide-open mouth and I started to climb the hill of a gargantuan come. They climbed too, the three of us did. When we burst over the top, indistinguishably one, a whole new country opened up beneath us. October sun rushed in and filled the room. Leaves danced down our street for joy.

They're for My Husband

john yohe

Jim walked with his wife into the lingerie store, heart beating fast, holding on to her hand tightly. His first time in a lingerie store. Finally after so many years of walking by them and looking in, he would see what one was like.

He immediately caught the eye of a young blond salesgirl. She gave him an approving look, recognizing that he was an attractive, well-dressed man. The fact that he was with his wife seemed to make the salesgirl even more interested, a trait in women which he never understood.

If only she knew, though, how he felt, and what was really going on. He was terrified. After many nights of sharing his fantasies with his wife, after the progression from confessing how much he liked seeing women in sexy underwear, to his wife forcing him to confess that *he* liked the idea of being dressed in women's underwear—after all that his wife had decided it was time to take that next step.

He loved his wife, Katherine. A sharp, successful business-woman, he considered himself lucky to have her, as a lover and a friend who understood him even better than he understood himself. They both enjoyed their "naughty" sex life. Katherine seemed fascinated with how powerless he became when she would taunt him during sex, or when she would take off her clothes and have him watch her in her lingerie. She also became fascinated with seeing him masturbate, or "jack off," as she called it. She liked to hold his balls and talk to him while he did it, make him tell her about panties, and stockings, and pantyhose (she'd been so surprised at that!).

Yes, lucky. But now, this new step. It was fine when it was a fantasy in the privacy of their bedroom. Her daring awed him. She had promised they would go today and buy him panties. The terrifying part being she would not pretend they were for her. She had vowed that she would tell the saleswoman exactly who they were for. He'd thought she was joking, but walking into the mall he'd seen the way she'd set her jaw: She was serious.

They walked deeper into the store. Panties, teddies, nighties, and other frilly things everywhere. Heaven. Everything soft looking, with wonderful colors. They came to a table of panties laid out in rows according to color: red, white, purple, gray, tan, black (his favorite). They were all one design, his favorite again, with the back part covering the whole butt. Thongs were nice on some women, but he loved the idea of a woman's ass encased in soft material.

Katherine picked up a pair of purple panties and held them up to his face. "What do you think of these?"

He looked around nervously, scared everyone was watching. Katherine was dressed in her sexiest black dress, tight in all the right voluptuous places, with dark pantyhose with a trace of glitter that drew attention to her muscular legs. To him, she exuded the signals for sex, and so he couldn't help thinking everyone else could see how obvious they were being. But no, no one was watching. Except, here came another saleswoman in a green dress, low-cut, which went well with her red hair done up in a bun. She smiled at them. "Can I help you two with anything?"

He tried to say no, but Katherine spoke first. "We're looking for panties. Sexy ones."

"Of course. Do you like the cut of these? They would go well with your body type."

"They're not for me."

"Oh?"

Jim was sweating. Please don't say it.

"They're for my husband."

He wanted to close his eyes and run out of the store, but something made him try to keep calm. The saleswoman, whose name was Gloria, raised one eyebrow and looked at him. "Oh?" Then she looked at Katherine and winked. "I understand. His first time?"

"Yes, though I hope to make this a regular part of his wardrobe."

What? She hadn't said anything about that to him. But he said nothing, aware now of how hard his cock was.

"Are these his favorite style?"

"Yes, on me at least. And I think I like the idea of his ass covered in soft material."

"We could do French-cut panty."

"Hmm . . . maybe. Let's try these first." She put the purple panties down and picked up a pair of black ones. "Let's try him in black."

Gloria smiled. "Ah, sexy and mysterious. I was going to suggest pink."

Katherine laughed. A laugh he'd never heard from her before. Cruel. "Yes, that would be funny. I think, though, that Jim would like black. He's jacked off into my black panties often enough."

"Excellent. Would you like to come to the dressing room to have him try them on?"

"That would be great!"

What? He tried to say something. "But Katherine, I thought . . . I thought we were going home . . ."

"Oh, come on, Jim, get a spine."

She'd never talked to him that way before. He followed the two women to the back of the store, watching his wife's hips wiggle the way they did. Magnificent. And those legs. Had she really just insulted him?

At the door to the dressing room, Gloria paused. "Can I suggest something? He might look good in some thigh-high stockings. I mean, if we're going for the sexy mysterious look."

"Oh, that's a good idea. It's good we didn't go with pink, then."

"We do have pink stockings."

"Oh, really? But I'm already in the mood for black, I guess."

They were ignoring him. Gloria pulled out a cardboard package from the hosiery section. "These are the kind with the black seams up the back, which I like. Makes men go crazy for me."

"Oh, that would be wonderful. Don't you think so, Jim?" She turned to him with a very serious look on her face.

He gulped. "Um, I guess . . ."

They went into the dressing room. It felt warm and comforting somehow, with the mystique of having had so many women who had changed into sexy underwear there. Gloria drew back the curtain of a stall and told him to go in. Told him. He hurried in, scared somehow that she would be upset with him if he didn't. She gave him the panties and stockings, told him to get dressed, and pulled the curtain shut.

He looked at himself in the mirror. He knew that this was the point to refuse if he was going to. That if he didn't, things between him and Katherine would change forever, that his life would change forever. He wasn't sure if it would be for the good or bad, but he started unbuttoning his shirt.

As he undressed he listened to the two women talk. Katherine was telling Gloria about his fetish, and how he liked to jack off for her. And Gloria seemed to know everything about him anyway, asking questions like, "And he likes to have you squeeze his balls, doesn't he?" or "I bet he likes to lick your ass, right?"

He wasn't sure he liked the idea of his wife sharing their secrets with this strange woman, but Katherine seemed to like her, and he did trust Katherine's judgment. At least, the old Katherine. This new Katherine, with the evil laugh, he wasn't sure about.

Naked, he looked at himself. His cock had sagged down a bit with fear. He hoped it wouldn't shrivel. Katherine hated when it shriveled. He put on the panties quickly, anticipating the feel.

They were tight. He was sure Katherine had planned that, as she'd said as much in their fantasies, that she wanted to see his cock and balls pulled tight. The panties were nylon, with a flowery see-through design in the front, giving a glimpse of his cock, which to his relief was getting hard again.

The stockings. He felt them with his hand. He loved the feel of nylon. When Katherine wore her stockings or pantyhose, he would spend what felt like hours caressing her smooth, shiny legs. He felt this pair. How soft and flimsy! He put them to his face and rubbed. Heaven!

He slid them on. God, how erotic to slowly slide the stockings on his legs. He never knew how sexy a woman must feel putting them on before a night out. Like masturbation; pleasurable in itself.

When they were on he looked at himself in the mirror again. He didn't know what to feel, knowing he looked ridiculous, yet also feeling he looked sexy. Or maybe it was the feeling of *doing* it, of wearing women's underwear. But no, the look too. He turned around to see his ass.

"What are you doing in there, Jim?" asked Katherine.

Both the women giggled. Gloria said, "Come on out, Jim, and let us see you."

He'd been hoping they wouldn't make him do that, that they'd call off the game. But it wasn't a game, was it? He walked out, hands over his crotch.

Both women immediately looked down to his panties and legs, and he got a glimpse of how a woman must feel when men look at her. Like a piece of meat.

Katherine crossed her arms and frowned. "Jim, take your hands away from your cock. I know you're insecure and need to touch your penis, but I want to see it."

He took them away but felt odd, holding them at his side. Gloria noticed and smirked. "Why don't you put them behind your head and pose for us?"

They laughed, and when he did it they laughed even harder. But he liked how they were both looking at his cock.

Katherine led him over to another mirror. She whispered, "I love seeing you in panties." Then louder: "This may be a new look for you. And the stockings! Gloria, what a wonderful idea. Jim, turn around so I can see them in the mirror."

He turned and looked back at himself, loving the black lines running up his calves and thighs.

"Now bend over. I want to see the material stretched tight over your sweet ass." Katherine had never talked that way. He remembered saying things like that to her when they'd first gotten married. Is that where she got it from?

He bent over. Gloria came up in front of him, so his face was in front of her breasts. He could see the outlines of her lace bra through the green silk blouse. She looked down at him, "Hmm, nice ass." She spoke to Katherine. "Is he taking it in the ass yet?"

What!?

"No, I hadn't really thought about it. I mean, he doesn't fuck me enough already. If he started taking it in the ass, I'd *never* get fucked properly."

"Was it that good anyway?"

"No."

Katherine! He prided himself on making her come!

"Well, you can always take a lover. Or two. I don't think Jim is in a position to mind. Or rather, to protest."

"Hmm, do you think so? I've thought about it."

He couldn't believe it. Of course he knew women had fantasies, but she'd never shared this idea with him. But he didn't say anything, just stood there bent over as they talked.

Gloria spoke. "Do you mind if I grab his balls? I really can't resist when a man's in panties."

"No, go ahead. I understand. Jim, stand up for her."

Gloria got close and reached down with her right hand. He felt her fingers close firmly around him as she turned her face to Katherine. "The good part of having a panty-whipped husband is you don't have to worry about him cheating on you with some young thing."

"Really, why is that?"

"Well, the young thing might think he's a suave handsome man, but when she sees him in panties, she'll know that, one, he's marked: property. And two, he's a panty-pussy. It takes a mature woman to tolerate a man like that. Did you see that salesgirl out there checking Jim out?"

"The little blond slut? Yes."

God, he'd tried not to be obvious. It's not like he encouraged her to look at him.

"I'll go get her. Wait here."

He knew what was coming, knew Gloria was right. Knew somehow that any chance of a discreet night with a younger woman was gone.

Gloria came in with the blond girl. The girl looked at Jim and gasped, horrified. "Ew, that's disgusting! Pervert!" She averted her face in disgust and stomped out. He took one last look at her young legs. Gone.

Katherine smiled at him. "Thank you, Gloria. I feel much better. Well, I guess I'll take them. The stockings too, of course."

"Just one pair of panties?"

"I think I'll buy some more black. But I'll take some purple ones. And pink. Jim, you don't like pink, do you? Too girlish?"

He tried to plead with her. "Please don't make me wear pink."

Katherine turned to Gloria. "Yes, a couple pairs of pink, too. And some pantyhose for me. I don't think Jim's going to be needing access to my pussy anytime soon."

"Excellent. Let's go pick some out while Jim gets dressed." They started to leave.

"Wait!" Jim called.

They turned and looked expectantly at him.

"Can I come?"

There was a pause.

"Do you need to?" asked Katherine.

"Well, yes."

"Then go ahead."

"Don't get any on the floor," added Gloria.

They turned away and he called out again. "Can I . . . can I do it with you watching?"

Katherine sighed. "Can't you wait till we get home?"

"I . . . I want to come for Gloria."

"Oh, all right. Go ahead, jack it."

Katherine put her hands on her hips and Gloria crossed her arms, an amused smile on her lips. Jim reached into the— no, *his* panties, and started to pull.

After a minute of frantic jerking, the women turned to each other and started talking.

"He *does* have decent-size balls. Too bad about the cock."

"I know. He's got a good, sensitive personality, though."

"Well, sometimes a woman needs a good fucking, and to hell with sensitivity. Do you still like to give blow jobs?"

"No."

"Well, maybe Jim will do the honors for you."

That last put him over the edge. "Oh, god, I'm coming."

They turned to watch Jim, and Gloria said out of the side of her mouth, "See?"

"Jim! Catch it in your hand like I showed you."

He jacked with his right while his cum shot into his cupped left hand. When he was done, the women turned to go. Gloria said, "Don't put that anywhere in the store."

Katherine said, "And I'm not going to walk out with it still in your hand. Get rid of it."

They left. He stared down at himself. The panties, the stockings, the handful of cum. There seemed to be only one thing to do. He raised his hand to his lips . . .

The Conductor

a. w. hill

T he railroad yards are still at this time of night, the
invisible pivot between one day and the next. Still, but not
quiet. Railroad yards are never really quiet. They creak like
the bedsprings in an old cathouse; they moan softly when the
river wind detours through the open door of a cattle car. The
atoms of memory in these old diesel juggernauts still groan
with the stress of laboring through the Cumberland Gap. And
there are memories in the plush upholstery of the fine old passenger cars, as well, of the groans and sighs of another sort of
exertion.

I have come here to enjoy a recollection for one last time,
before age and infirmity deny me the ability to recall. For
seven years, from 1957 through the spring of 1964, I was a
conductor on a private and highly exclusive leg of the
Chesapeake & Ohio run from Newport News, Virginia, to
Louisville, Kentucky. The train, known to all as *The Fast Flying
Virginian*, left Newport News with two engines and seven
passenger cars and arrived in Louisville with one and four. I'll
tell you what happened to the rest of the train, for it's a story

that can now be savored as myth. As far as I know, none of those whose reputations might be damaged by the telling of it are still among the living. None but me, and I have neither reputation nor virtue to lose. If witnesses to debauchery were named as accomplices, I might be held to account at the gates of heaven, but that would be only if God is a moralist, and if I once believed he was, I no longer do. Whatever occurs on earth between man and woman, he permits by way of divine abstention.

The Chesapeake & Ohio was born as a coal line, and the *Virginian* ran the old track laid by hand and hammer through the voluptuous Shenandoah Valley and the strip-mined wilderness of the Appalachians. In my time, Number 96 carried not coal, but those made rich by its extraction. Just west of Charlottesville, however, at a point equidistant from Richmond, Virginia, and Washington, D.C., the train continued to make, as if by habit, what used to be the last water stop before the steep ascent into the mountains. Even in 1957, this was an anachronism: the engines no longer ran on steam. But there was, at Mount Pisgah, a solitary depot at which I and my crew of six black porters waited patiently, playing pinochle. And there was, more often than not, a phalanx of black limousines lined up behind the depot, camouflaged by night, big V-8s purring, their passengers eager to get on board and begin what they invariably called, in a Southern lilt, "the festivities." Some of the limos had driven all the way down from the Capitol, others from cities nearer by; some appeared as if delivered out of the mist that draped the perpetually damp and fertile valley. In the later years of the *Virginian*'s run, when regular passengers had come to know me and I them, my crew and I were sometimes joined for a hand or two by those who had tired of the mute company of their drivers and the pliant leather of the backseats. They were hard men in soft suits, and their varnished accents inevitably dipped toward the vales and hollows of their birth when they felt themselves to be in the company of "working men" like myself and the porters. They observed decorum only when accompanied by either their "distinguished guests" from Washington or their feather-hatted mistresses, some of whom had come all the way from Hollywood and whose familiar features were lent only the flimsiest disguise by the black mesh which covered their faces. I have played pinochle with senators and ambassadors, torch singers and movie stars. During those years, more celebrities passed through the Pisgah depot than had likely passed through the lobby of the Plaza Hotel in the same span of time.

At Mount Pisgah, Engine Number 1 decoupled from the lead car and rolled through a switcher onto a side track. There, it waited for Number 2 to bring it the three first-class Pullman cars: two sleepers and a club car. Number 1 then rejoined the four remaining coach cars and continued on to Louisville with all its regularly ticketed passengers. In all those years, none of those passengers—save for one curious young man—ever questioned the unscheduled stop or the loss of half the train. A blind eye is bred into all good Southerners. Oh, there was talk, plenty of that. Gossip is the libretto of Dixie's opera. But no scandal, no exposé. In that day, the lions of the print press understood that powerful people have powerful appetites, and probably understood also that discretion might one day earn *them* a pass to the "festivities." Given what they'd heard, it must have seemed a small price to pay, for whatever itch desire inflamed could be scratched aboard my train. As for the young man I mentioned, he was a sailor on leave from the base at Newport News.

He left the train to get a breath of mountain air and wandered across to the side track, where he stood and gawked as three showgirls in silk dressing gowns were escorted aboard by no less than an admiral in full-dress whites. The officer paused on the grated steps for a moment and stared down the recruit, ready to swear him to silence upon pain of court-martial, but then had the good sense to beckon the sailor on board and treat him to the ride of his life, a far better guarantee of his confidence.

And so, as the *Virginian* dieseled on west to Kentucky, my Number 96—now dubbed *The Sportsman II*—headed north along the Great Valley, with the Appalachians on its left and the Blue Ridge on its right, and Front Royal, Virginia, our final destination. They tell me that it's one of the most beautiful stretches of rail ever laid, but I honestly couldn't say. We traveled between the hours of midnight and 5 A.M., so the great, heaving mountains were never more than a looming presence, flanking us as we cleaved our way through a blackness only fleetingly pierced by the light of a clifftop cabin. The limousines followed up the old state highway, which ran, for parts of the journey, parallel to the track. Occasionally, I'd step between the club car and the sleeper for a cigarette and spot a pair of high-beams—then another, and another—breaking around a bend in the road some quarter-mile distant, tailing us like a procession of slow barges moving up the canal (though, somehow, the limos always arrived at Front Royal before we did). I was once joined out on the platform by an ash-blond woman in an ermine stole who'd just consumed the semen of seven men as lustily as a New Englander swallows Masapeake oysters. She was smoking a cigarillo and said, while exhaling a plume of blue smoke, "Too bad we can't lose them. I'd ride this train forever."

It will by now be apparent that *The Sportsman II* was a pleasure train with a highly exclusive clientele, though by no means was it merely a rolling bordello. None of the women who boarded her over those years was ever paid, as such, for her company. They came, just as the men did, to experience that freedom from all prohibition that only transit can provide. Nor were the women ever treated poorly (had that occurred, it would have been my sworn duty to stop the train and put the offending party off to make his way through the wilderness). No, our patrons had the good breeding to know that if you wish for a woman to behave like a pagan, it's best to treat her like a goddess. If anything, the women of *The Sportsman II* were more lascivious than the men. God knows, they had greater endurance. I've come to believe in the years since that my train provided them with something closer to the "natural state" of things, and this notion was most piquantly affirmed by a well-known society hostess who'd come aboard in the company of her Cuban houseboy.

"You know what?" she asked me. She was seated on the toilet in the gentlemen's room (which, for reasons unstated, she preferred to the ladies') and had asked me to "stand guard" just outside the cracked door. "In a perfect world . . . a world with no 'bad girls' or 'good girls' . . . no husbands or wives . . . I'd screw everybody." I said nothing, but I must have shifted my weight or chuckled unconsciously. "I would," she insisted. "Even you, sweetie. Why not? It truly is what I do best."

The club car, which was the center of the festivities, was a fully restored classic Pullman from the 1910s, down to the red plush booths and polished brass. Each and every accoutrement aboard *The Sportsman II* had been hand-selected by the Proprietor for its quality, and this was equally true of the libation dispensed at the bar. We served only Kentucky Bourbon whiskey and its derivatives, at least twenty varieties from private old family distilleries, none aged less than ten years. There was seltzer and branch water for those who favored it, and our highball glasses were of cut crystal mined from caverns deep beneath the Kentucky bluegrass. One of the club car's time-honored erotic sacraments involved the application of a smoky-sweet liqueur distilled from thirty-year-old mash, a favorite *digestif* reputed to have aphrodisia-cal effects. A lady, after being caressed to the brink of fever by the men present and freed from constraint by good bourbon and the primal rhythm of the rails, would disrobe down to her shoes and her hat (for reasons of ritual, a lady's hat was sel-dom removed and the fine mesh veil rarely left her face). She'd plant her pumps in the soft carpet in front of the bar and then lean in, resting her bare arms and a rouged cheek langor-ously on its lacquered oak surface, so that the span from her shoulderblades to her tailbone described a forty-five-degree angle. The bow-tied bartender, acting as celebrant of this car-nal mass, warmed a snifter of the liqueur over a Bunsen burner until it reached the temperature of a warm bath, then gently pushed aside the woman's hair to expose the nape of her fine neck. The woman, as you may have guessed, was to serve as both altar and rail. Meanwhile, the communicant—the first of three gentlemen selected by lot—had knelt behind her on the ceremonial velvet cushion, his nose at the height of her anus, his waiting tongue extended just short of the plump teardrops of her buttocks, within tantalizing reach of her upended cunt. It was against the rules for any but the desig-nated third man to make contact with her flesh. The penalty for violating this rule was excommunication from the festivi-ties.

Before dispensing the liqueur, the bartender urged the woman to extend her coccyx and lift her ass until she was able to feel the heat of the gentleman's tongue a scant half-inch from her sex. This exercise not only made the rapture more dizzying for both supplicant and goddess, but contracted her back muscles to form a gently banked channel which neatly contained the liquid amber as it flowed down her spine from nape to tailbone and dripped bountifully into the communi-cant's mouth. As he rose from the cushion and left her, the sec-ond man approached and the ritual was repeated. By the time

the second man had drunk his fill, there were urgent murmur-
ings among the onlookers. Breasts had been freed from lacy
bodices to be fondled; groins were feverishly pressed against
willing backsides. I often found myself perspiring beneath my
cap and experiencing a sort of sexual vertigo (the Proprietor
required strict celibacy of the *Sportsman*'s crew). The third
man came forward and was stripped to the waist by a pair of
"ladies-in-waiting," who then pressed him to his knees and
administered three lashes each with a cat o' nine tails. Now
the viscous firewater, color of blond tobacco, flowed for the
third time down the sacral spine, only this time it was allowed
to run down the cleft of her ass and onto the tender lips of her
vagina, where its astringency begged for the healing balm of
saliva. The experienced ladies could stand nearly a full
minute of the exquisitely fiery torment before they cried out
for the tongue; the novices screamed out and pleaded
instantly for relief. But whether novitiate or abbess, each
ended up with a man's nose pressed into her rump and came
with the profane fury of a maenad.

There were many such entertainments performed in the
club car of the *Sportsman II* as she climbed snow-dusted
foothills under jeweled skies. Some were boisterous and
giddy, others almost reverential in tone. Common to all of
them was a single element: a rarefied appreciation of the
juices squeezed from sexual congress, most especially of that
admixture of the male and female essences which results
when the pot is stirred (rumor has long held that each bottle
of the Proprietor's special sour mash liqueur contained a
thimble full of it). Not a drop was ever wasted; no stains
were ever found on the combed wool carpets or in the plush
velvet booths. All of it was, in some fashion, consumed. I
cannot tell you how or when the festivities were originated,
or why all who boarded my train—yes, even the first-
timers—seemed to know them as familiar, as if recalling

some long-dormant memory of tantric excess in Eden. It is said by the old hands that the Proprietor learned much in his track-laying days from a Chinaman by the name of Li Po, a railroad worker whose strength and stamina were said to have exceeded that of men twice his size and whose sexual wisdom was legendary.

I won't attempt to catalog all that I saw during those years; that would risk reducing a kaleidoscope to a mere peephole. For purely selfish reasons, I don't wish to diminish the memories. But if you can imagine it, wish it, desire it, it occurred, if not in the club car then certainly in the sanctum of the private sleeping compartments, where crisp linen sheets were cast in the hue of virgin snowdrift by blue night lights and porters with skin dark as bittersweet chocolate (darker for the starched white jackets they wore) rustled discreetly down the aisles, attending to every need. There were paddlings administered to pink, yielding bottoms, sodomies of every variety known to man, petticoats cast off and petticoats kept on for effect, women whose pleasure was to sit blindfolded behind the compartment door, awaiting the soft knock that signaled the arrival of the first, then the second, then the third of her anonymous satyrs. There were captains of state and industry whose aching hunger for humiliation equaled their lust for conquest, and women who could dance between the two poles. But the most singularly erotic event I ever witnessed involved a famous actress, her equally famous consort, and a dead horse.

The *Sportsman II* made no stops between Mount Pisgah and Front Royal, but on one fragrant summer night, an exception was made. They came aboard in the deserted mining town of Parkland, accompanied by two plain-suited agents. We had, of course, been told to expect them. Now, they say that *she* was able—in her last years—to wander unnoticed in crowds, disguised only in head scarf and sunglasses, but I am quite sure I'd have spotted her in any surrounding. The walk, seductive but sweetly clumsy, gave her away. That, and the nervous giggle and earnest chorus-girl handshake as she was introduced to me and my crew. *He* was godlike in spite of his affliction (the outline of the back brace was visible above the vent of his powder blue suitcoat). Of all the notable and notorious people I met, I don't recall seeing anyone who looked so much like the picture in my mind's eye. He shook my hand and offered a broad, gleaming smile, then unbuttoned his jacket and stepped into the club car, working the room with his blond chorine in tow.

Once the train had pulled away from the empty depot, they settled back into a plush booth and were allowed the zone of privacy which all honored guests of the Proprietor received. The bartender brought them each an aperitif and trimmed a fat Cuban cigar for him. After the first puff, he smiled widely, raised the cigar in the air, and said, "Thank you, Fidel," which elicited hearty laughter from all aboard. After that, the party went on about them as if they were king and queen hosting a feast of flesh. In the booth next to theirs, a woman parted her legs to allow a man's head beneath her skirts. On the opposite side of the car, a well-known lady writer hiked up her skirt and unhooked her garter while her admirer flicked his tongue across her distended nipple. When she could stand no more, she pushed him away, stood up, folded herself over the table, and cried, "For God's sake, Harry, fuck me before I expire!" The subsequent display, in which the lady writer seized the edges of the table and thrust her buttocks fiercely into the man's groin in exuberant synchronization with the *k-chunk-k-chunk-k-chunk* of the train's wheels on the track, so aroused the guests of honor that the actress rolled up her own skirt and wriggled onto her lover's lap, crying out sharply three times as he slipped into her. At the moment of her third cry, there came the sound of a horrible impact and the airbrake screeched into service, drowning out all but the most ardent moans.

We had hit something big. I could gauge its weight as a matter of simple physics; it slowed the locomotive almost as much as the brakes did. The dullness of the impact told me that it was organic and not mechanical. I shuddered, pulled aside the club car's heavy door, and stepped out onto the landing, flashlight ready, waiting for the train to slow to a crawl. Then I leapt onto the spongy, pine needle-strewn red earth and began the long walk to the head of the hissing locomotive, followed shortly by my chief porter and an assemblage of guests which included the actress and her companion (their coitus rudely interrupted by whatever unfortunate thing had impeded our juggernaut). I had a feeling of dread as deep as the black ravines which surrounded us.

It was a silver gray mare, fully saddled and festooned as if for a parade. A military horse. I reasoned that she must have bolted from the grove of cottonwood on our right, spooked perhaps by a black bear or a wild Virginia boar. I swept my flashlight's beam across the track and the gravel shoulders ahead and into the brush beyond; there was no sign of a rider. The collision had left gruesome damage: her neck and both front legs had been broken and her skull split by the impact, and yet—amazingly—she still drew wheezing calliope breaths through her flared nostrils. I felt myself get a little weak in the knees and turned to wave the passengers back and direct the porter to make a search of the bramble for her mount, though I somehow felt certain that she had come with her saddle empty. I glanced at the actress, who seemed both shattered and spellbound. Her escort, a man who had seen violent death in the Pacific theater, comforted her, though his own face was creased in evident distress, no doubt from the pain in his chronically troubled back.

The engineer jumped down from the cab and joined me at

the side of the beast, where we whispered plans for its removal and disposal. The local sheriff would have to be notified. Some money would probably have to change hands. The mare whinnied pitifully and tried to lift her head.

"Should we put 'er to sleep?" the engineer asked me. There was a hunting rifle in the engine compartment, never used. I nodded, and was about to go fetch it when I heard a whisper of satin and smelled Chanel and musk. It was the actress.

"No," she said softly, dropping to her knees on the splintered ties, just beside the mare's head. "Don't. She's almost gone, almost gone . . ." I didn't question her. She lifted the massive head with its gaping wound and laid it on the soft folds of her skirt, stroking the mare's nose and humming faintly. Within seconds, the pink satin dress was saturated with blood, and within seconds more, the mare was dead. I leaned in and slipped the head from her lap, then called for two of the porters to fetch shovels and rope. I helped the actress to her feet, assisted by her stoical companion, who brushed the hair from his forehead in a characteristic gesture and told me, "Thank you. We'll leave you some room to work. You'll let me know if I can help." I nodded, though a salute might have been more fitting.

All during the removal of the corpse, he held her close in the bright beam of the locomotive's Cyclops eye, not minding that the blood and tissue on her dress were now on him, as well. From time to time, I stopped working to wipe my brow and glanced at the two of them: rocking, whispering, both kissed by pitiless fate. A wind rose out of the grove from which the mare had raced and lifted the thick hair on his scalp, and I was struck by an awful vision.

Later, after we had resumed our journey, I made my customary rounds of the sleeper cars with the head porter. Though initially our patrons had gamely tried to continue the festivities in the club car, most had now retired to their private compartments and were conspicuously silent. Only the cabin assigned to the actress and the statesman rocked with libido. The door was slightly ajar, whether by force of the train's movement or deliberately, I can't say. I could see the bloody dress and a pair of silk stockings hanging from the bunk. She was astride him, rising and falling in ever more rapid strokes. The porter halted and turned, and I put my finger to my lips. Then she came softly, and after that rose and shut the door.

That was the summer of 1963. In April of 1964, the Proprietor discontinued service on the Number 96, and her engineer and I hauled the club car and two sleepers to the great, sprawling train yard in southern Ohio, where they remain today, and where I have come to stir my memories and pay my last respects to those two souls who flaunted eros in the face of death.

A Red Dress Tale:
La Jodida Guarra

susannah indigo

Once there was a girl who wore only red dresses. Short, long, tight, loose, and free, it was all she owned in her closet. At first she thought she did this because she wanted men to *stop* looking at her, like a traffic signal, but then one day she realized that her secret fantasy was simply to be rolled out like a red carpet and be walked on.

She was too pretty for anyone to want to walk on her and men were always polite to her, which drove her crazy. Sometimes she would walk through the worst parts of some strange city just to hear men say dirty things to her. *Cunt* was her favorite word, but even strolling in her tight, strapless spandex red dress that barely covered her garters and stocking tops, the best she could get out of a man was *Hey, pretty cunt*, said with way too much affection.

So one day she decided to hire a man who would use her and be rough with her and fuck her hard and never be polite. She made up a contract, and it said that if he would do that, and not just pretend to be enjoying it and not just do it occasionally, she would give him anything he wanted.

"Anything?" the young man, Frank, who was known for his investigative skills, asked.

"Yes, anything," she answered, because she was both quite rich and quite creative and couldn't imagine a single thing that a man could want from her that she couldn't provide.

He wrapped his fist in her long strawberry blond hair, pushed her to the floor on her knees, and opened her mouth with his fingers, sliding them in and out like they were his cock.

"Wider, cunt," he told her, and she was in heaven. He began to massage her throat on the outside, just above the red dress, while the other hand reached into her mouth and opened it wider and wider. His fingers went deeper and deeper until she could barely breathe, and then he stopped.

"Take my belt off," he ordered.

She unhooked his belt and removed it from his pants.

"Lift your skirt."

She stayed on her knees and slid the red skirt up to her waist.

"Put the tip of the belt inside your cunt."

She spread her knees apart on the floor and slid the tip of the black leather into her wetness and it felt hard and tight and good.

"More."

She tried to slide more of the belt inside of her, but it was difficult so he reached down and began to shove it in, harder and higher, until she was gasping and he had the entire thin black leather belt inside of her right up to the buckle, which he left hanging from her cunt.

"It will hurt more that way if it's nice and wet when I use it on your ass," he said as he dropped his pants and stood in front of her with his hard cock close to her face. "Open."

She opened her mouth as wide as she could, but he opened it wider for her. He began to massage her throat again, and told her the secret of how sword-swallowers swallow swords. She understood, and then he rammed his cock into her throat all at once and she did not gag, but she felt herself getting dizzy, and this made her very happy. He stroked his cock in and out in long strokes, and when the tip was firmly lodged in the depths of her throat he pinched her nose closed with his fingers so that she could not breathe for a few seconds. The rhythm of *breath/no breath* built until it was like good music, and they were both lost in it. His cock stayed longer and longer in her throat until her eyes got wider and wider, and he knew that if he touched the side of her neck just right that he could make her pass out at exactly the same moment that he came hard and long down her throat. But he did not give her this yet, and instead stopped, and then pulled the wet belt from her cunt in one long stroke.

"This is the first thing I want," he told her when she was stripped down and securely tied face-down to her big king-sized bed with the red velvet scarves he found on her dresser. "The first thing I want is to hurt you."

The belt was so wet from her cunt that it stung like a towel in a locker room on first touch and she loved it. *Harder,* she thought to herself silently. *More,* she thought over and over again until there was more, and it was just like in her dreams, and then he stopped and raised her hips in the air and began to fuck her hard. "Like an animal," he said, "like the slut that you are, like the little rich filthy whore that you want to be, like the piece of ass that is all that you are, you're just a hole for my cock, you're like a dog in heat . . ." and he came inside her cunt with his finger high in her ass, collapsing on top of her and holding her there for a long time.

"Before I go," he finally whispered, "I will write you the contract the way it is." He rose from the bed, found a red felt-tipped permanent marker, and untied her and stood her in front of the mirror. "Watch," he said. He began to write down the front of her body, words in Spanish that she could not read. *Soy una jodida guarra.*

"Tomorrow you will come to me, in Five Points, in the alley behind Sabor Latino at Fourteenth and Federal. There is a woman I want you to meet. Dress like a streetwalker for me; do not wash the words off, be there at five o'clock sharp, and do not say a word when you arrive. Do you understand?"

She smiled in a way that she could not remember ever smiling before. "Yes," she said. "Yes."

After he left, she stood in front of the mirror for a long time, trying to decipher the words, admiring her red ass, feeling the rawness of her throat, feeling well-fucked and completely used. Finally she wrapped herself in a bright red blanket and fell asleep right there on the floor and began to dream about the next day.

She thought maybe she'd have to pay Frank a lot of money for making her feel so cheap, so she rolled up thousands of dollars in hundred-dollar bills and hid them in the bottom of her big black purse underneath the lining where nobody ever looked. She took everything else out of her purse except the money and her makeup and her car keys, and then she went to a Super-K store and followed his instructions exactly. She bought a little red velvet dress in the girl's department so that it was very tight and short and cheap looking, and she wore it off of her shoulders with no bra so that the words he had written would show at the top. Underneath she wore a red g-string, no stockings, and she put on a pair of red patent-leather spike heels. She looked in the mirror and remembered to tease her hair on top and layer the red lipstick and apply black eyeliner, and then she whispered to herself, "Anna, you look hot—nobody will ever know who you really are."

When she got to Sabor Latino at five, she couldn't see Frank anywhere around the alley in the back, so she stood

out front by the streetlight. A man drove by and proposi-
tioned her and this made her feel good, but somehow she
knew it would get too confusing when she would have to
offer him money to walk on her, and then anyway he might
know how to read Spanish and be shocked by the writing on
her body. *God, I hope it doesn't say I'm a nice girl, or a pretty cunt,
or something like that. I should have taken more Spanish in high
school.* She looked around but couldn't think of quite how to
ask anyone to read her body to her, so she just waited for
Frank to show up.

The fist in her hair jerked her head around and he was not
smiling at her. "I told you the alley, slut." He pulled her
roughly toward the back of the building and shoved her up
against the brick wall, kissing her hard with his tongue down
her throat and his knee shoved between her legs.

She did not, could not, speak. But she thought that *Slut*
was a lovely name, and that maybe she could change her
name to that and get less respect, and then she wondered if
her passport said *Slut* if she would even be allowed to leave
the country when she had to go to Switzerland in June.

Frank's kiss felt a little bit like love, so she was glad when
he stopped and pulled away from her. She looked him up and
down as he walked around her, looking *her* up and down.
Frank was tall and handsome in a serious way, but he never
wore the color red. He wore black from head to toe, as though
he was prepared to sneak off in the dark of night and hide not
far from her wildest dream.

"You look good, Anna," he said, and she frowned and
hiked up the hem of her skirt and posed a little like she
thought a good slut would. She knew that when her skirt rose
higher on her thighs the tail end of the words *jodida guarra*
were visible running down each thigh, and she hoped that
this would remind him of why she was there. She thought she
might be happy if he would just color her red with dirty

words from head to toe, and then she wouldn't have to buy any more dresses.

Frank brought out a red leather collar and lifted her hair and buckled the collar around her neck, fastening a long leash to it. "I promised her I'd bring you on a leash for her pleasure, slut. Open your mouth." She opened her mouth and he placed a small red apple there, instructing her to bite down on it and not say a word. He led her up the wooden stairs on the back of the building behind Sabor Latino and into a small room with black walls and a ceiling that looked liked it was lit by the stars.

Anna thought she should be scared, but when Frank tied her leash to a cement post near the wall and pushed her to her knees, she couldn't wait for more. A woman appeared from the shadows—tall, dark, big and busty, short black-cropped hair, lips painted with dark purple, wearing black like Frank, and smiling, always smiling no matter what she said or how mean her eyes looked. She circled around Anna, looking, touching, tapping, slapping lightly. "Excellent," she said to Frank, and they shook hands. "How much money?" she asked.

Frank turned to Anna kneeling on the floor. She nodded to her big black purse beside her, having no idea how much she had stuffed in there. The woman turned it upside down and dumped it out and counted the bills slowly right in front of Anna. "Eight thousand three hundred dollars. A good price." Anna couldn't tell if she was serious, because she kept smiling, and it might have been too much, or maybe not enough.

"Take her dress off," the woman instructed Frank, handing him a switchblade. He sliced down through the red velvet and tossed the dress in the corner, leaving Anna bare and shivering in her red g-string and her collar and high heels.

"Turn her over and fuck her while I watch."

Frank grabbed Anna and turned her over on the cement floor, pushing her head to the ground, lifting her hips in the air and spreading her knees apart. He stayed dressed but unzipped the fly on his pants and kneeled between her legs and brought his hard cock out and ran it up and down from the crack of her ass to her wet cunt and back. The woman circled and watched. "Her cunt first, and hard," she ordered.

He posed the tip of his cock at her pussy, grabbed her hips, and pushed all the way in on one stroke, hearing her cry out through the apple in her mouth, fucking her hard the way it was meant to be. Nothing extra, nothing kind, just a man's cock driving home, slowly and then faster, in and out, using her as nothing more than a hole to get off on. He closed his eyes and thought of all the words he would write on her before he was through.

"Stop," the woman said, and he did, pulling his pulsing cock from her cunt. "Stroke yourself and come on the floor next to her face." Anna's hips were still moving like a woman who can never be fucked enough, but he put one hand in her hair and stroked his cock until he groaned and his cum landed next to her face. The woman stood over Anna, pulled the apple from her mouth, put her hand next to Frank's in Anna's long hair, and said, "Lick it all up."

They both watched as Anna licked up every drop of Frank's flavor from the cold floor, and it was hard to tell whether they were guiding her head or she was guiding them. When she was done, Frank sat back against the post and watched as the woman turned Anna over, straddled her, and sat on her chest, running her fingers over Anna's wet lips. "My name is Zelda, sweet cunt," she said. "Tonight, I become the queen of your universe."

She put the apple back in Anna's mouth and tied a red scarf over it and behind her head. She nodded to Frank. "Truss her up, over the railing. And spread her legs wide." She turned back to look in Anna's eyes. "You may not be a *fucked pig* yet, darlin', but you will be."

* * *

Frank picked Anna up and stretched her out across the narrow wooden plank that was on top of the stair railing, belly down, her head turned and facing to the right so that she was looking down the stairway. This railing-top often held people's drinks during parties, but tonight it would hold only Anna. He arranged her small breasts so that they hung down on either side of the railing, and tied her hands securely to one of the dowels that held the railing up. Her bottom was posed right at the end of the railing, at the place where people would turn to enter the room after coming up the stairway. He took her g-string off, pausing to whisper to her that "Little pigs don't get to cover their holes, sweetheart," but left her heels on. Her legs were spread on either side of the railing and tied loosely below, with the rest of the red satin rope wrapping around her again and again, tying to her leash and her collar until she was as secure on top of the railing as if she was a permanent fixture. Then Frank began to write.

It was not quite like writing his great American novel. *Fóllame,* he wrote in big red letters across her ass. *Soy un coño bonito,* he wrote down the inside of her thighs. *Puta de la noche* he finally wrote across her back, the words facing the stairway where any stranger entering could read them. When he was finished, Zelda came over carrying her camera to admire his handiwork and took several pictures from each side. "We can use them as advertisements for *Zelda's Tuesday Night Special,*" she said. "I'll have to make many copies, *sí*? How long do you think pictures like these will last in the clubs after I put them up?" And she began to laugh, a laugh that delighted Anna, a laugh that said that everybody in the world was dirtier and sexier than Anna was, but if she was really good they would bring her into their world and teach her all the things that they could do.

Frank pulled up a barstool and sat next to Anna, stroking her back, talking softly to her while Zelda started the music—

some kind of West African high-life music, sophisticated, but still primal. "Only on special days will I bring you here, slut," Frank said. "The rest of the time you're mine. But I'm a generous man, and tonight I'll share everything you have with my friends here." He ran his hand down between her legs and slid one finger inside her cunt. "You're so wet all the time this is hard to imagine, Anna, but if it gets to be too much for you, all you have to do is turn your head to the left side to look at me and I'll make it all stop."

Anna shook her head vigorously, never turning left, appalled that he could think of stopping before it even began. Frank shrugged and laughed and called Zelda back over.

"It's time."

Zelda sent Frank down to unlock the door, and she began to lay condoms in every color and size, along with clothespins, on a table near the railing. "I was once a caterer," Zelda told her, "and you are a work of art. Pig roasts were my specialty." She brought out a bowl and began to brush barbecue sauce in two stripes down Anna's back. She leaned over to check the gag and gave her one hard biting kiss on her neck. "I think we'll take the gag off later, cunt, but only when I think you might be ready to squeal."

As each person came up the stairs Anna could look them directly in the eye. They only paused for a moment when they saw her trussed and gagged on the top of the stair railing; these were not people who came to Zelda's for anything but hard sex. Anna tried to smile at each man and woman but could not move her lips, so instead she tried to tell them with her eyes that she was not just a pretty cunt, and that she wanted to be used and fucked hard. Somehow they seemed to know this— each customer would enter, talk to Zelda, who stood behind Anna with her riding crop, and then come back toward Anna and begin to touch her. She could not see them once they had passed her on their way up their stairs, but she could feel the different touch of each one's hands, and she could feel each one pause as they decided what to do to her. She felt shapes, textures, and the unique sizes and curves of each cock when each one began to fuck her in one of her holes, but she could only try to tell from the voices whether it was a man or woman, and then she realized that it didn't matter. Some of the customers put clothespins on her first, decorating her, or pinched the clothespins that were already hanging from her nipples courtesy of the very first person who fucked her. Some of them licked the sauce from her back, some of them took the riding crop from Zelda and beat Anna's ass before they grabbed a condom and shoved their cocks hard and fast up inside of her cunt; some used their hands to hold her ass cheeks apart as they slid their cocks into her ass and fucked her hard.

More, Anna thought, *more . . . there is just never enough.* More, and then *more*, and then one man turned her head to the left and had Zelda take her gag off and fucked her mouth, but Anna made sure to turn her head quickly back to the right when he was done so that Frank wouldn't stop any of this.

Some of them asked Zelda to untie Anna so that they could use her in other ways, but Zelda explained that she was just a pig and that pigs hardly dance or kneel or do anything but lie there and get fucked, and they understood. "Lock the door, Frank. It's time to make her squeal," Zelda finally said.

The customers pulled up chairs, sixteen in all, in a semicircle around Anna. They drank and smoked cigars and watched as Zelda began to work over Anna's body from top to bottom, pinching all the clothespins, adding more, pausing to slap her breasts and then her thighs hard with the crop, then returning to the pins. Anna was crying out just a little, but never turning her head, and mostly her cries sounded like little gasps of joy. Zelda turned and said, "Frank, choose your hole."

Frank had watched for so long, with his cock hard at attention, that all he wanted was the deepest, tightest hole to bury it in. "Her ass is mine, Zelda. You take her cunt, and let Gianni here stand on the stairs and take her mouth." Gianni looked quite pleased, since he had already sampled her pretty cunt and run his fingers into her ass.

Zelda brought out a large dildo while the men watched, paying close attention. All three of them posed: Frank between Anna's spread legs with just the tip of his cock pressing against her asshole, Zelda standing next to him with the dildo teasing her swollen lips, Gianni on his tiptoes on the stairs running his cock around Anna's lips as she reached for him. "On the count of three, one hard long stroke all together," Zelda ordered and she counted, one, two, three, and then they all entered Anna long and hard and stopped there and Anna felt the fullest she had ever felt, and her head felt lighter and lighter and they all pulled out and did it again, beginning to stroke to the rhythm of the music in the background, three holes filled, Frank's cock almost touching the tip of Zelda's dildo inside of her, the force of three cocks at once driving her into herself in an ocean of sensation and she began to come like she had never come before and it *continued and continued* until she was crying out every time Gianni's cock came out of her mouth. From somewhere in the room there was the sound of animals and it could have been her or it could have been the men, but she didn't know and didn't care as long as they kept carrying her on this cloud of sex until she completely floated away.

They did not stop for a long time, Zelda challenging the men to last as long as she could, which was forever. When the sounds coming from Anna finally began to sound more like an animal in heat than a woman in control, Zelda removed her dildo and let the men begin to finish her off. Zelda picked up the small apple that had been in Anna's mouth most of the night and pressed it up against Anna's wide and wet cunt lips and pressed it half way in until it was held there by her cunt contractions. Zelda began to snap all of the clothespins off as the men drove Anna back and forth on the railing with their strength, rocking and fucking and grunting and finally coming, Frank deep inside of her ass and Gianni all over her face.

"Untie her and fix her up, Frank," Zelda said, almost softly, pulling the apple from Anna's cunt and replacing into her mouth. "Let everyone see what they've had before they leave."

Frank had to hold Anna up. He wrapped his arms around her waist and stood her in front of him naked, teetering on her heels, all of the bonds off, the collar and leash off, her heavy makeup washed away by the sweat and her hair matted down. He left the apple in her mouth, but her smile was visible around it. He tied her hair back with some red rope, and draped her torn red dress around her shoulders. Her eyes looked like she was not quite there, but rather up floating on the bright ceiling. Her body was marked all over, with words, with tiny bruises and red marks, with the stains of cum and with handprints and marks from the crop. Frank whispered to her that he would take her home and tuck her into bed soon, and that they would start again the next day, *over and over and over again* until she knew her place and he got what he wanted from her, which he suspected but did not tell her involved owning not just her body but also her heart and all of the dark secrets that had been hidden there so long.

The customers began to pass by her to pay their respects before they left. Each of them was given a hundred-dollar bill by Zelda, and as they walked by Anna they read the words on her front side that they had never seen: to a one, each could be heard murmuring as they left *Sí, es una jodida guarra.*

The Devil in Her Eye

maggie estep

She wasn't the kind of girl to make a bishop kick in a stained-glass window, but she got to me all the same. Her name was Sylvia. Dirty blonde. Five-foot-four, 122 pounds, thighs just shy of ample. She was quiet. Seldom looked at you straight on, but once she did, you never forgot it. Which is what happened. She looked at me. Right into me.

And I melted. I'm not the kind of guy to go around melting, mind you. I'm pushing thirty-five. I've been locked up a few times, and when I wasn't inside, I worked on the back side of racetracks. Mucking horse shit and what have you.

I'm not a melter. But Sylvia got me.

The night I met Sylvia, I was minding my own business sitting on the couch over at Sammy Diabelli's place, staring at Tina's ass as she served a plate of salami and cheese to the assorted denizens gathered there. I'd been getting cozy with Tina for three weeks by then and this was it, the first night she'd brought me to her Uncle Sammy's.

"I gotta have Uncle Sammy take a look at you," Tina had told me the night before. We were lying on the bed. Or I was lying; she was standing nearby, not a stitch of clothing on her and that immense chest of hers a little shiny with sweat.

"Who's Sammy?" I said.

"My Uncle Sammy. If I'm gonna keep seeing you, Sammy's gotta inspect you," Tina said.

I had feigned being a little nervous at the prospect of meeting the uncle, but in truth, it's what I was there for. To get inside Sammy Diabelli's house and see what was what.

The Feds had busted me six months earlier for sponging racehorses—which is when you stuff tiny sponges up their noses, which doesn't really hurt them, just impairs their breathing enough to make 'em run a tiny bit slower and lose the race. When I got busted, they offered me a deal. Either I did time again or I did them this one little favor. Get in with Sammy Diabelli and his clan in South Brooklyn. Not, mind you, that they were gonna have me wear a wire or do anything that might drastically impair my staying alive, no, they just wanted me to feel things out, let them know a few things, then, they'd take it from there. So they told me go to this bar where Diabelli's son, Little Sammy, hangs out shooting pool. I went and sure enough, I saw Little Sammy there. With him was Tina, who, I'd been informed, was Diabelli's niece. Now, mind you, the Feds didn't say: Go fuck Diabelli's niece. No. But I took one look at her and figured that's how I'd do it. All in a day's work.

She was a little dark-haired girl. She had on a skimpy tank top affording a healthy view of her disproportionately large breasts. I didn't even approach her. Just stood at the bar, sipping a glass of seltzer and watching. Watching her chest touch against the green felt of the pool table when she leaned over to set up her shot. Eventually, she felt my eyes on her. Looked over at me. In a few more minutes, sauntered over.

"Have we met?" she says to me.

"No, but we should," I say.

She giggles. She has tiny teeth. I want to touch them.

"I'm Tina," she says, flipping her hair.

"So you are," I say.

She does an encore on the giggle.

"You got a name?" she wants to know.

"I do."

"It's a secret?"

"I'm Benjamin," I finally say and stick my hand out to shake hers.

"Hi, Benjamin," she says.

About an hour later, I'm walking her home. She's got a little place she shares with two other girls on Forty-third Street in Sunset Park. She tells me she works at a beauty parlor a few blocks from home.

"I got a lot of family around here," she tells me as we're walking. "Mostly I end up just doing hair for people I'm related to."

This concept seems to amuse her. She laughs.

I laugh too.

Her bedroom looks like a twelve-year-old's. There's a lot of pastel-colored things and stuffed animals, and I feel particularly perverted as I push her back onto her bed and shove a bunch of stuffed animals aside.

"How old are you anyway?" I ask her as I pull her shirt off and find myself face-to-face with that huge chest, barely contained by a bright red bra.

"How old do you want me to be, Daddy?" she says, and I wince, I mean, I'm probably a good fifteen years older than her, but I'm not into playing any little-girl games and I let her know this, ripping her pants off her and grabbing hard at her little hipbones and saying: "You're a grown woman, Tina, don't go playing games with me."

She blushes a little, which gets me incredibly hard.

"I'm twenty-two," she says, adding an "Ouch, Benjamin!" as I pinch one of her nipples.

Her panties don't match her bra. They're powder blue like her bedsheets, and there's a tiny hole in the seam at the front of the crotch and I get the end of my finger in this little hole and rip, yanking the crotch of the panties completely out, making Tina gasp as I reveal her quaint little black bush, very well-manicured because I guess she applies her beautician skills to every hair on her body. And then, in no time flat, I've gotten a condom out of my wallet and she takes it from me and unrolls it on my cock and then climbs aboard and starts grinding away at me in this totally fierce way and I'm going to come immediately so I shove her off of me and she looks angry and puts her hand between her legs and starts touching herself, looking tortured, then says, "Gimme," and grabs my cock, rips the condom off, and starts sucking the living hell out of me. I pull out of her in time to let loose all over that chest of hers. I watch her jerk off. She makes a purring sound like an overgrown kitten as she comes.

Three weeks later, it's time to meet her uncle.

I'm on the couch there. Getting inspected by Sammy Diabelli and his clan.

"So, Benjamin," Sammy says to me, "Tina tells me you work at the track?"

"Sometimes. Not right now, but sometimes," I say. Truth is, right now I'm not working at all. Once in a while I act as a lookout for guys I know doing little heists and whatnot. But that's it. That and being the Feds' bitch.

"You worked there doing what? You look a little big to ride," Sammy says.

"Oh, no, I wouldn't get on top of those horses," I clarify, "those horses are nuts. I worked as a groom."

"Oh yeah? Well, that's nice. Good for you," he says, and then I guess he's done with me for the time being.

And now I start getting guilt pangs. I had no qualms about banging Tina for three weeks to get here, but now, Sammy's

just one of those instantly likable guys. I start to feel uncomfortable, having a dilemma, if you will. And then, whammo.
She walked in the front door. It's not like she made some
grand entrance or anything. But I noticed her. She walked in
and went to stand near Sammy's chair. She's wearing a navy
mid-calf skirt and tan pantyhose. Just to look at her I knew she
was wearing big white panties. She had dirty blond hair blunt
cut to her jaw. She had a good shape, some meat on her, but
she didn't make herself jiggle when she walked. She was very
contained. I guess that was part of the appeal. Part of why I
instantly envisioned hiking that navy skirt up over her ass.

Eventually, Sammy felt her standing there, looked up, and
beamed at her: "Hi, baby," he said to her.

She leaned over and kissed Sammy's cheek.

"Benjamin," Sammy said to me, "this is my daughter,
Sylvia."

And right away, I got a hard-on. You'd think it'd be the
opposite. You'd think finding out this chick was the daughter
of a guy I'm supposed to help take down for the Feds might
make any vestige of sexiness evaporate like a raindrop in hell,
but no. It added to my fire.

"Hi," I said like a stone moron.

She offered a smile, at first not even looking at me, too
busy listening to what Sammy was telling her about what
Little Sammy did to the family car. But then, all of a sudden,
for no reason I could really discern, she looked at me. Right
into me. Her eyes were medium blue with little gold flecks in
them.

Right at that moment, maybe sensing something, Tina
came over. She'd gotten rid of the plate of salami and cheese
but she was still wearing this ridiculous little serving apron.
Normally, my imagination would instantly swell with notions
of what to do with Tina in that apron, but I have to say I don't
get real far with it. I right away picture *her* in it. Sylvia.

Can you imagine falling for a girl named Sylvia? The only
other Sylvia I ever knew was my great aunt Sylvia. She'd had
a wooden leg because, as a young girl, she'd fallen victim to
one of those crazy rides they had at Dreamland, one of the big
amusement parks at Coney Island back then. The place went
up in flames in 1910, but not before the rides had taken a few
limbs, my Aunt Sylvia's left leg among these. They put a
wooden leg on her and she went through life just fine and
married my Uncle Aloisius and had a bunch of kids and lived
to be 103. By the time I met her of course she was an old lady.
An old lady with a wooden leg and actually a hair or two on
her chin.

So Aunt Sylvia with the wooden leg was the only Sylvia I
knew, and it's not like the name had any major erotic connota-
tions for me. And as I have now documented for you, Sylvia,
this Sylvia, wasn't your Come Hither type of girl. Not at all.
But she looked at me. Looked right into me.

I waited until I saw Tina go in the bathroom then I went
out in the yard for a smoke, praying Sylvia would follow, and,
to my astonishment, she did. I was sort of tongue-tied, but
then she asked me for a cigarette and the way she smoked it,
like a girl who's basically never smoked a thing in her life,
that got me harder than I was already. It got painful.

It transpired that Miss Sylvia Diabelli had a mind for num-
bers and was very interested in going to the racetrack and
learning to handicap horse races. This I could help her with.

Three days later, Sylvia and I are on the A train heading
out to Aqueduct. I've got the *Daily Racing Form* spread out in
my lap, and we're sitting with our shoulders touching as the
train rattles through the bowels of Queens and I explain how
to read each horse's past performance and how to factor in the
many things one has to factor in. I'm having trouble concen-
trating. The girl is like a virus. A weird, understated, tan
pantyhose-wearing virus.

Sylvia either has beginner's luck or she's instantly an ace handicapper because she has a place bet come in in the first race and hits an exacta on the second. Me, every horse I bet runs dead last. By the ninth race, we're both cold to the bone, because it's spring but early spring, and Aqueduct, situated as it is there at the very tip of Queens, is subject to gusting winds, and I insist on wrapping my sweatshirt jacket over her shoulders and she looks so completely disarming with my blue sweatshirt jacket over her tan sweater that's lightly distended from her very well-shaped breasts and we're standing on the platform, waiting for an A train to transport us back into Brooklyn, and I'm not sure what's what now, not sure where to take this, not sure of anything at all.

"I can come over?" Sylvia says to me now, just as the train groans up to the platform.

"Uh . . . well, I, uh . . ." I say, not because I don't want her to come over, not that I care if she sees I live in this little hole of a place, an attic I rent for $472 a month from an old Polish woman who's convinced I'm one day going to break down and go diving down at those cobwebs between her sizable ancient thighs. No, I have no qualms about Sylvia seeing anything that's mine, but the thing is, I actually don't want to just screw her. I mean, there are complications. There's the Feds. And Tina. And the fact that Sylvia is a tan pantyhose-wearing bank teller who works in Brooklyn Heights and probably wants to get married and start popping out kids and I can't say that's a route I'm interested in. But what the hell. I let her come over. No sooner are we inside my place than she pulls the tan sweater over her head revealing a very sturdy white bra. She stands there looking at me. I briefly get this image of her reaching up her skirt and jerking herself off for me, but right away I realize that's just not gonna happen. This is Sylvia at her most brazen, and she's already pushed it to the outer limits. And then I just go insane. I cup her ordinary yet beautiful face between my hands and I kiss her very lightly and I can feel those breasts pressing against my chest and she pushes her hips against me and her height is such that she's basically pushing her hips right into my crotch and I really don't know how I got into this. I mean WHY, right? Why me? I know I never should have done that sponging with the race-horses. I fucking love horses. I hate myself for the sponging but what the hell, I got busted anyway and I don't plan to revisit that particular occupation, no, the plan was: Tell the Feds what they want to know about Sammy Diabelli and then find some down-on-his-luck trainer who doesn't mind giving a second chance to someone like me and go back to working as a groom and find myself a nice exercise rider, one of those tough little muscular chicks with a sailor mouth and an ass of iron and we'll shack up in Queens near the track and do our thing. You know. That's what I thought. But now this. This *Sylvia* with her tan pantyhose. And her hips are pressing into me and I reach back and start pulling down the zipper on her skirt and my hand meets with the distinctly unsensual tan pantyhose fabric and she lets out this little whimper and then her skirt falls down to her ankles. There's a run at the top of her pantyhose and I insert my finger just like I inserted my finger in the rip in Tina's panties and I pull and rip the panty-hose and Sylvia covers her face with her hands, like she's sud-denly totally ashamed of everything as she stands there, so homely and lovely in her cotton white underwear with a pat-tern of fucking *butterflies* on them, and now I pull these big white panties down too, revealing a patch of brown and slightly unruly pubic hair and I just shove my hand between her legs and she moans but she's still got her hands over her face and then I turn away, like some troubled teenager, like no one I'd ever want to know, I pull back and turn away from Sylvia and there's this weird horrible silence and then I just say it: "I've been sent by the FBI. To find out about your dad. I think you should leave now." And it's not like I've got this great deep love for the girl, it's not like I think her and I could have a good run together, in fact, she's probably not even that great a lay, I mean have you ever known anyone to wear big butterfly panties and be a great lay? No. Not gonna happen. So I don't know what the fuck I'm doing. I'm basically begging for a death sentence is what I'm doing. All for the sake of a woman in butterfly panties. And that is basically all there is to this story. Sylvia stood there in her butterfly panties and her torn stockings and she looked at me and I felt guilty and crummy and she said she wasn't going to tell her father but I'd better make myself scarce. I made myself scarce all right. I told the Feds I couldn't help them. And presto. I'm locked up. In *New Jersey* no less. Eighteen months. Of which I've served two. As for Sylvia, well, she's doing just fine. I guess having me rip the tan pantyhose off her must have shaken something loose. She sends me letters now and then and even money. Which I guess she can spare. The fucking girl hit the Pick Six. *Twice.* That's when you pick the winning horse in six consecutive races. She even got written up in the *Daily Racing Form.* They took her picture for it. She sent me the picture. In it, she's wearing what looks like a slightly racy outfit, like with actual cleavage showing. In the picture, she looks like she's got devil in her eye. She probably does. And all I got is eighteen months in New Jersey.

Snow

jameson currier

Outside the window, the snow obliterated the view of the highway, but since Tyler was less than a mile from the airport, there wasn't much to see except ramps and lanes and traffic. The snow had started that morning when he had landed in the city for his meeting: small, enchanting, romantic flurries. By the time he had hailed a cab in the afternoon, four inches were already on the ground and flights were being delayed. He'd gotten one of the last rooms at the hotel, just as everyone—the receptionist, the cab driver, the airline reservations clerk—had started to mouth the word "blizzard" to him or, rather, started to mouth *two* words, *"big blizzard,"* as if the description *blizzard* was not an adequate enough weather forecast to instill a sense of urgency to get someplace and stay there for a while. Now, in Tyler's fourth-floor hotel room, the snow was so fierce it drained the color from everything, the dark green bedspread, the hunting print above the bed, the cherry wood of the desk and chair. Even the air in the room seemed as if it had been washed away, or, rather, had been sucked into a clear bottle and frozen, waiting to be thawed.

Tyler, stripped of all his clothes, pressed himself close to the window pane, the stale coolness seeping through the glass like an undetected leak of gas. His shoulder felt sore so he rotated his arm, then rubbed his dry hand across his drier skin. Winter, he thought. Aches. Arthritis.

Tyler stood at the window with his back to a young man named Brad or Chad or Tad or something like that. Tyler didn't care anymore what the guy called himself. He had cared the night before, when Tad had arrived, but for the last twelve hours he hadn't cared at all. Any sense of intimacy Tyler had felt for Brad or Chad had evaporated long ago. Tyler was bothered by his growing callousness—wasn't this what he had always wanted? Time alone with a young man? They had stayed up late drinking a bottle of wine, snuggling against each other, and watching television till Tad, or Brad, fell asleep. Tyler had absorbed the alcohol quickly, the wine fading into a headache and insomnia. Tyler had held whatever-his-name in his arms until he felt himself sweating, then pushed the young man away so that he slept on his side.

But by morning a weighty restlessness had seized Tyler, like a mouse trapped in a maze searching for the right way to a piece of cheese he could smell. At the window, Tyler rubbed his hand along the fine hair of his own chest and realized he might be attracted to Brad if he had become someone else. *Another* Brad. Maybe a *Chad,* he said to himself with a laugh. I've had Brad, he thought. Now give me Chad. Tyler then watched with bored interest as he looked down at his testicles and watched them shrink the closer he moved to the window. If anyone were in the parking lot looking up at his window, Tyler knew they would be unable to see him up there, striped by the blinds, with freezing nuts and a painful shoulder.

Todd—it was Todd, Tyler decided—lay on the floor wearing only his red flannel boxer shorts, an item of clothing he had sexily revealed with a flourish the evening before. Todd was young and lean. A brunet. Handsome with a nose too big for his face. Now he was busy touching his knee to his nose doing stomach exercises and shooting annoying breaths out of his mouth as if he were about to hurl a spitball. He'd been doing this senseless thing for almost an hour.

"Let's go down to the fitness room," Todd said. "Mr. Tyler?"

His voice, in this air, stayed even after the meaning was gone from his words. The room remained full of his voice— dropped into corners like packed snow on the roadside in spring. "I'm sure the fitness room is more like a fitness *closet*," Tyler said. The edge in his voice was easily detectable. "And it's not 'Mr. Tyler.' It's just 'Tyler.'" He didn't bother to look back at Todd. He had studied and studied the body till it no longer excited him. Todd had finely carved abs like the cuts of a diamond, and it was a magnificent display watching them flex and twist and breathe. But what was the purpose? Tyler wondered. He had seen them and now they were ancient history. He wanted something else. But even more, he wanted to be *somewhere* else.

"At least the electricity works," Todd said. "Last year we lost power."

"How long did it last?" Tyler asked.

"Three days," Todd said. He held his knee to his nose. "Can you see anything?" he asked.

Tyler didn't respond. He couldn't see anything beyond the white wall of snow. When he arrived at the airport yesterday he had been delighted to hear that the flight had been canceled, not from the snow—snow was always expected in this region—but because of the wind gusts. The airport closing gave him a legitimate reason to stay overnight, a bona fide expense-report item to submit, a chance to have some fun before returning back to the closeted grind of corporate meetings and lunches and lectures and conference calls. Tyler had seized the opportunity to order room service and a hustler.

Todd had arrived quicker than the food. By the time they had finished, though, there were already four more inches to the snow, frozen granules mixed in with the lighter stuff—and the television said bus service had been suspended until the roads could be cleared and sanded. And Tyler hadn't been so eager to see Todd disappear.

"Everybody's always in a hurry to get somewhere," Todd said.

Tyler didn't answer.

"Do you like my stomach?" Todd asked.

It was only the thousandth time he had asked Tyler that question. He heard the insecurity creeping into Todd's voice and if he could placate Todd without using too much energy, he decided he would. So he nodded. He could have easily turned Todd out into the snow last night. Wham, bang, here's your money, so long, don't hurry back even though you are gorgeous and it was incredible sex. But it was late and dangerous outside, and early on Todd had tapped into that warm fuzzy paternal spot Tyler always felt for the young and pretty boys who looked put upon. Now, Todd's company had worn thin. Tyler turned and took a long look at Todd's stomach and managed to work up a grin, trying not to be one of those sour old businessmen, who, well, float into town and hire hustlers. "What's not to like? You should do movies."

Todd stretched both legs out in front of him and pointed his toes, then sat up straight at the waist, a perfect right angle, sure of himself. "I guess," he said, then smiled at himself. "Best abs in Hollywood."

Tyler started to turn back to the window, wondering why he was the one now doing the pampering. Wasn't Todd supposed to be indulging *him*?

"I was in a commercial once," Todd said. "I did an internship at a television station my sophomore year. One of the camera guys was filming a diet commercial. I got to be the 'after' guy. Did you know that it's not the same person? I always believed that they could lose the weight."

Tyler did not react. Too much chatter, he thought, and he tried to tune Todd out.

"Wanna play around?" Todd said, dropping his voice into that low whispery octave that had so excited Tyler last night. "No charge since you're letting me stay."

"Too beat," Tyler said, and looked back at the window, weary and bored.

"I'm going to go downstairs," Todd said, making it sound like a threat, though Tyler couldn't imagine what kind of threat it could be.

"Better put something on first," Tyler replied.

Todd didn't move from the rigid shape he'd got himself into. With the lamp on inside the room, Tyler could see Todd's reflection in the window and he studied that—the reflection— squinting to see if he could detect the definition of Todd's abs in the snow.

Then he looked beyond the reflection. Back into the snow. It swirled and curled and danced in front of his eyes like an over-programmed computer screen saver. The warmth of the room was pulled up through the window and sucked off into the snow. He looked down at the parking lot and thought he could detect someone racing out into the snow, their hands pumping together like clapping, probably to keep the circulation going.

At the window he looked deeper into the snow, believing for a minute he saw thousands of men clapping their mittened hands together. They were sure they were going to freeze if they remained motionless, never to arrive someplace warm. Then they disappeared.

"Tyler?" Todd asked.

Tyler ran his hand down to his groin, running his hand across his cock. He was aware of Todd looking at him.

"Is it still hard?"

"Sure," Tyler answered, playing the suggestive innuendo game but unable to mask the cynical tone in his voice.

"How much longer?" Todd asked.

That raspy voice again. How much longer snowing? Tyler thought, or in this room? or in this room *with him*?

"What's your hurry? Am I that unpleasant company?"

"Of course not," Todd said. He pouted in a boyishly self-absorbed manner.

"It's just the snow's making me cranky," Tyler said.

"Let's play some more," Todd said. He stretched out his body and cupped his balls.

"Aren't you worn out?" Tyler asked.

"No," Todd said, his grin taking on a fake, impish quality. "Are you?"

"Yes," Tyler said. "You're too much for me."

"So let's just neck some more."

Tyler didn't really want to be unkind to him, though he knew he was being hustled now. "Neither of us has shaved."

"Want me to shave you?"

Years ago he would have been delighted with the offer. *Hours* ago he would have been delighted. "I'm not twenty anymore, though I wish I were, sometimes." Tyler turned and looked at Todd. "Or I wish I was twenty and knew what I know now."

Todd smirked. Tyler turned and faced the window again. As he did he caught sight of his own reflection this time, his white hair crossing against the currents of snow. Everything would be all right again soon. All he had to do was wait.

"Tyler?"

"Huh?"

"Wanna shower together?"

"Hmmm."

"Or soak in a bath?"

"My joints are damp enough." Tyler said.

Todd went into the bathroom. Tyler heard him take a leak and flush the toilet. Then he turned the water on. Then he heard the shower begin and the sound of the water change as Todd stepped into the flow. Tyler stayed at the window and ran a hand over his chest and pinched the slackness at his hips. He was still there when Todd came back into the room, dripping onto the carpet.

"Tyler?"

"Huh?"

"I'm going crazy in this room."

"Put something on. You're going to get a cold."

Todd put his boxers back on and a T-shirt and ran the towel through his hair. Tyler watched the process in the reflections of the window, momentarily imagining Todd was a soccer player, toweling off after a game. The image burst apart in another flurry of snow and Tyler again felt old and vulnerable in his sagging flesh.

"Wanna get something to eat?" Todd asked.

"If you want."

"Room service?" Todd asked.

"Sure."

Behind him, Tyler heard Todd pad across the carpeted floor and sit at the desk, thumbing through the hotel journal till he reached the room-service menu.

"What do you want?" Todd asked.

Tyler smirked at the loaded irony of the question. I want to be out of this room, in an airport, on my way home, away from *you*, on my way to someone else. For a moment he thought about running out like a lunatic—racing down the hall and into the lobby with nothing on. At least he might be arrested. At least it would take him to jail. *Somewhere else.*

"Nothing heavy," he answered.

"How about some ice cream?" Todd asked. "Or a milkshake?"

"Coffee," Tyler said. "I'd like something warmer."

The ice cream and the coffee came ten minutes later. Todd's spoon clinked against the glass at an annoying speed. Tyler sat in a chair facing the window, a cup in his hands.

"That killed a half-hour," Tyler said when he had finished his coffee. Tyler finally pulled himself away from the window and sat on the edge of the bed and turned on the television. Todd curled up on the bed into a fetal position, a pillow crammed between his legs, as if waiting to be petted.

"Wanna watch a movie?" Todd asked. "They have a movie selection here."

"Let's check the news first," Tyler replied. He flipped the channel, wondering if God would give him a respite with the snow. Even a little one. He shook his head to clear it.

"Something the matter?" Todd asked.

Tyler shook his head to indicate *No*. The moving images on the screen made his vision blur. He lay down, exhausted from the anxiety of trying to decide how long he might have to stay. He thought that maybe he couldn't last—that he'd have to cancel his appointments for tomorrow as well. The snow had become his business now. Something tugged at his inner ear. A rumble that seemed to shake the foundation of the building. He lay still and quiet and then felt it again. "What?" he asked.

"I didn't say anything."

"Are you sure?"

"Yes."

Maybe it was Todd's voice again, stirring in the room from some dead sentence. It tugged again, and Tyler realized it was a sound outside the room, far off. "Hear that?"

"I don't hear anything."

"It was the parking lot. Someone's leaving." Tyler felt his pulse quicken and, as he lifted himself off the bed, he struggled to overcome a dizziness. He padded across the carpet and looked out of the window again.

"Maybe they're salting the highway."

"No, listen," Tyler said. In another minute he heard it again, barely above the blood beating in his ears. Todd joined him at the window. Tyler smelled the soap Todd had used. He was aware of Todd's heat and the hairs on his leg stood up, warning him of Todd.

"It's lighter," Tyler said, looking out through the snow, the tone of his voice brighter, breezier.

"Sure is," Todd added.

While they were watching the snow, a man walked beneath them through the parking lot. Tyler's eyes followed him, watching the man's mittened hands clap together. The snow swirled in thinner gusts now, flaking against the window before melting.

Tyler walked to the phone and dialed. "Are they back on schedule?" Tyler asked. As the receptionist explained that flights were now leaving, Tyler thought that his giddiness would give him a heart attack, his blood now a roar in his ears. He hung up the phone, smiling.

Tyler packed with a hurry and a determination he had not possessed since he had arrived in the city. He kept looking outside as he packed, watching the flurries thin out. He could now see the sharp line on the horizon where the highway was.

Todd was dressed in his jeans and coat in a matter of seconds. Tyler waited for him to ask for more money, but as Tyler lifted his suitcase off the bed and moved toward the door there was nothing. Impulsively Tyler stopped and kissed Todd abruptly on the lips with a passion he hadn't shown the boy since he'd first arrived in the room. Todd slipped his arms under Tyler's jacket and returned the kiss. Suddenly they were all hot and bothered at the idea of losing each other. "I'm here often," Tyler said. "Could I see you again?"

Todd nodded and Tyler knew that if he wanted more he

would have to pay the price of it. In the elevator he felt relaxed. Peace, he thought, and studied Todd with his clothes on, finding himself mentally undressing him and growing hard at the thought of the young man.

By the time Tyler reached the airport he was as exuberant as the sun, the light bouncing off the snowdrifts so brightly he paused only to search for his sunglasses.

A Cool Dry Place

r. gay

Yves and I are walking because even if his Citröen were working, petrol is almost seven dollars a liter. He is wearing shorts, faded and thin, and I can see the muscles of his thighs trembling with exhaustion. He worries about my safety, so every evening at six, he picks me up at work and walks me home, all in all a journey of twenty kilometers amidst the heat, the dust, and the air redolent with exhaust fumes and the sweet stench of sugarcane. We try and avoid the crazy drivers with no real destination who try to run us off the road for sport. We walk slowly, my pulse quickening as he takes my hand. Yves's hands are what I love best about him; they are calloused and wrinkled, the hands of a man much older than he is. At times, when he is touching me, I am certain that there is wisdom in Yves's hands. We have the same conversation almost every day—what a disaster the country has become—but we cannot even muster the strength to say the word disaster because such a word does not aptly describe what it is like to live in Haiti. There is sadness in Yves's face that also cannot be aptly described. It is an expression of ultimate sorrow, the reality of witnessing the country, the home you love, disintegrating around you. I often wonder if he sees such sorrow in my face but I am afraid to look in a mirror and find out.

We stop at the market in downtown Port-au-Prince. Posters for Aristide and the Family Lavalas are all over the place even though the elections, an exercise in futility, have come and gone. A vendor with one leg and swollen arms offers me a box of Tampax for twelve dollars, thrusting the crumpled blue and white box toward me. I ignore him as a red-faced American tourist begins shouting at us. He wants directions to the Hotel Montana, he is lost, his map of the city is wrinkled and torn and splotched with cola. "We are Haitian, not deaf," I tell him calmly and he relaxes visibly as he realizes that we indeed speak English.

Yves rolls his eyes and pretends to be fascinated with an art vendor's wares. He has very little tolerance for *fat Americans*. Just looking at them makes him feel hungry, and feeling hungry reminds him of the many things he tries to ignore. Yves learned English in school, but I learned from television—*I Love Lucy*, *The Brady Bunch*, and my favorite show, *The Jeffersons*, with the little black man that walks like a chicken. When I was a child, I would sit and watch these shows and mimic the actors' words until I spoke them perfectly. Now, as I tell the red-faced man the wrong directions, because he has vexed me by his mere presence in my country, I mouth my words slowly, with what I hope is a flawless American accent. The man shakes my hand too hard, and thrusts five gourds into my sweaty hand. Yves sucks his teeth as the man walks away and tells me to throw the money away, but I stuff the faded bills inside my bra and we continue to walk around, pretending that we can afford to buy something sweet or something nice.

When we get home, the heat threatens to suffocate us. The

air-conditioning is not working because of the daily power outages, so the air inside is thick and refuses to move. I look at the rivulets of sweat streaming down Yves's dark face and I want to run away to some place cool and dry, but I am not sure that such a place exists anymore. My mother has prepared dinner, boiled plantains and *griot*, grilled cubes of pork. She is weary, sweating, slouched in a chair. She doesn't even speak to us as we enter, nor do we speak to her, because there is nothing any of us can say to each other that hasn't already been said. She stares and stares at the black-and-white photo of my father, a man I have little recollection of, because he was murdered by the Ton Ton Macoute, the secret military police force, when I was only five years old. Late at night, I am plagued by memories of my father being dragged from our home and beaten as he was thrown into the back of a large green military truck. And then I feel guilty because regardless of what he suffered, I think that he was the lucky one. Sometimes, my mother stares at the picture so hard, her eyes glaze over and she starts rocking back and forth and it is as if he is dancing her across the small space of our kitchen the way he used to. And in those moments, I look at Yves. I know that should anything happen to him, it will be me holding his picture, remembering what was and will never be, and I have a clear understanding of a woman's capacity to love.

We eat quickly, and afterwards Yves washes the dishes outside. My stomach still feels empty. I rest my hand over the slight swell of my belly. I want to cry out that I am still hungry, but I don't because I cannot add to their misery with my petty complaints. I catch Yves staring at me through the dirty window as he dries his hands. He always looks at me in such a way that lets me know that his capacity to love equals mine, eyes wide, lips parted slightly as if the words *I love you* are forever resting on the tip of his tongue. He smiles, but looks away quickly as if there is an unspoken rule forbidding such minor demonstrations of joy. Sighing, I rise and kiss my mother on the forehead, gently rubbing her shoulders. She pats my hand and I retire to the bedroom Yves and I share, waiting. It seems like he is taking forever and I close my eyes, imagining his thick lips against my collarbone and the weight of his body pressing me into our mattress. Sex is one of the few pleasures we have left, so I savor every moment we share together before, during, and after. It is dark when Yves finally comes to bed. As he crawls under the sheets, I can smell rum on his breath. I want to chastise him for sneaking away to drink, but I know that partaking of a watery rum and coke is one of the few pleasures he has for the savoring. I lie perfectly still until he nibbles my earlobe.

Yves chuckles softly. "I know you are awake, Gabi."

I smile in the darkness and turn toward him. "I always wait for you."

He gently rolls me onto my stomach and kneels behind me, removing my panties as he kisses the small of my back. His hands crawl along my spine, and again I can feel their wisdom as he takes an excruciating amount of time to explore my body. I arch toward him as I feel his lips against the backs of my thighs and one of his knees parting my legs. I try and look back at him but he nudges my head forward and enters me in one swift motion. I inhale sharply, shuddering, a moan trapped in my throat. Yves begins moving against me, moving deeper and deeper inside me and before I give myself over, I realize that the sheets are torn between my fingers and I am crying.

Later, Yves is wrapped around me, his sweaty chest clinging to my sweaty back. He holds my belly in his hands and I can feel the heat of his breath against the back of my neck.

"We should leave," he murmurs. "So that one day, I can hold you like this and feel our child living inside of you."

I sigh. We have promised each other that we will not bring

a child into this world, and it is but one more sorrow heaped onto a mountain of sorrows we share. "How many times will we have this conversation? We'll never have enough money for the plane tickets."

"We'll never have enough money to live here either."

"Perhaps we should just throw ourselves in the ocean." Yves stiffens and I squeeze his hand. "I wasn't being serious."

"Some friends of mine are taking a boat to Miami week after next."

I laugh, rudely, because this is another conversation we have had too often. Many of our friends have tried to leave on boats. Some have made it, some have not, and too many have turned back when they realized that the many miles between Haiti and Miami are not so small as the space on the map. "They are taking a boat to the middle of the ocean where they will surely die."

"This boat will make it," Yves says confidently. "A priest is traveling with them."

I close my eyes and try to breathe, yearning for just one breath of fresh air. "Because his kind has done so much to help us here on land?"

"Don't talk like that." He is silent for a moment. "I told them we would be going too."

I turn around and try to make out his features beneath the moon's shadows. "Have you taken complete leave of your senses?"

Yves grips my shoulders, to the point of pain. Only when I wince does he loosen his hold. "This is the only thing that does make sense. Agwe will see to it that we make it to Miami, and then we can go to South Beach and Little Havana and watch cable TV."

My upper lip curls in disgust. "You will put your faith in the same god that traps us on this godforsaken island? Surely you have better reasons."

"If we go we might know, once in our lives, what it is like to breathe."

My heart stops and the room suddenly feels like a big echo. I can hear Yves's heart beating where mine is not. I can imagine what Yves's face might look like beneath the Miami sun. And I know that I will follow him wherever he goes.

When I wake, I blink, covering my eyes as cruel shafts of sunlight cover our bodies. My mother is standing at the foot of the bed, clutching the black-and-white photo of my father.

"Mama?"

"The walls are thin," she whispers.

I stare at my hands. They appear to have aged overnight. "Is something wrong?"

"Gabrielle, you must go with Yves," she says, handing me the picture of my father.

I stare at the picture trying to recognize the curve of my eyebrow or the slant of my nose in his features. When I look up, my mother is gone. For the next two weeks I work, and Yves spends his days doing odd jobs and scouring the city for the supplies he anticipates us needing. I feel like there are two of me because I go through the motions, straightening my desk, taking correspondence for my boss, gossiping with my coworkers while at the same time I am daydreaming of Miami and places where Yves and I are never hungry or tired or scared or any of the other things we have become. I tell no one of our plans to leave, but the part of me going through the motions wants to tell everyone I see in the hopes that perhaps someone will try and stop me, remind me of all the unknowns between here and there.

At night, we exhaust ourselves making frantic love. We no longer bother to stifle our moans and cries and I find myself doing things I would never have considered doing before; things I have always wanted to do. There is a certain freedom in impending escape. Three nights before we are to leave, Yves and I are in bed, making love. We are neither loud nor quiet as, holding my breasts in my hands, I trace his muscled calves, his dark thighs with my nipples, shivering because it feels better than I could have ever imagined. Gently, Yves places one of his hands against the back of my head, urging me toward his cock. I resist at first, but he is insistent in his desire, his hand pressed harder, fingers tangling into my hair and taking firm hold. In the dim moonlight, I stare at his cock for a few moments, breathing softly. It looks different to me, in this moment, rigid and veined, curving ever so slightly to the right. I part my lips, licking them before I kiss the strangely smooth tip of his cock. His entire body tenses, Yves's knees cracking from the effort. I pretend that I am tasting an erotic new candy, slowly tracing every inch of him with my tongue. I drag my teeth along the thick vein that runs along the dark underside of his cock. My tongue slips into the small slit at the head of his cock. He tastes salty yet clean and my nervousness quickly subsides. I take Yves's throbbing length into my mouth. It becomes difficult to breathe but it also excites me, makes me wet as he carefully guides me, his hands gripping harder and harder, his breathing faster. Suddenly, he stops, roughly rolling me onto my chest, digging his fingers into my hips, pulling my ass into the air. I press my forehead against my arms, gritting my teeth and I allow Yves to enter my darkest passage, whispering nasty words into the night as he rocks in and out of my ass. At once I feel so much pleasure and so much pain and the only thing I know is that I want more—more of the dull ache and the sharp tingling just beneath my clit, more of feeling like I will shatter into pieces if he inches any further—more. At the height of passion, Yves says my name, his voice so tremulous that it makes my heart ache. It is nice to know that he craves me in the same way I crave him, that my body clinging to his is a balm.

Afterwards, we lie side by side, our limbs heavy and Yves

talks to me about South Beach with the confidence of a man who has spent his entire life in such a place; a place where rich people and beautiful people and famous people dance salsa at night and eat in fancy restaurants overlooking the water. He tells me of expensive cars that never break down and jobs for everyone; good jobs where he can use his engineering degree and I can do whatever I want. And he tells me about Little Haiti, a neighborhood just like our country, only better because the air-conditioning always works and we can watch cable TV. The cable TV always comes up in our conversations. We are fascinated by its excess. He tells me all of this and I can feel his body next to mine, tense, almost twitching with excitement. Yves smiles more in two weeks than the three years we have been married and the twenty-four years we have known each other, and I smile with him because I need to believe that this idyllic place exists. I listen even though I have doubts and I listen because I don't know quite what to say.

The boat will embark under the cover of night. On the evening of flight, I leave work as I always do, turning off all the lights and computers, smiling at the security guard, telling everyone I will see them tomorrow. It is always when I am leaving work that I realize what an odd country Haiti is, with the Internet, computers, fax machines, and photocopiers in offices and the people who use them living in shacks with the barest of amenities. We are truly a people living in two different times. Yves is waiting for me as he always is, but today, he is wearing a nice pair of slacks and a button-down shirt, the black shoes he wears to church. This is his best outfit, only sightly faded and frayed. The tie his father gave him is hanging from his left pocket. We don't talk on the way home. We only hold hands and he grips my fingers so tightly that my elbow starts tingling. I say nothing, however, because I know that right now, Yves needs something to hold onto.

I want to steal away into the sugarcane fields we pass,

ignoring the old men, dark, dirty, and sweaty as they wield their machetes. I want to find a hidden spot and beg Yves to take me, right there. I want to feel the soil beneath my back and the stalks of cane cutting my skin. I want to leave my blood on the land and my cries in the air before we continue our walk home, Yves's seed staining my thighs, my clothes and demeanor hiding an intimate knowledge. But such a thing is entirely inappropriate, or at least it was before all this madness began. My face burns as I realize what I am thinking and I start walking faster. I have changed so much in so short a time.

My mother has changed as well. I would not say that she is happy but the grief that normally clouds her features is missing, as if she slid out of her shadow and hid it someplace secret and dark. We have talked more in two weeks than in the past two years, and while this makes me happy, it also makes me sad, because we can never make up for the conversations we did not have and soon cannot have. We will write, and someday Yves and I will save enough money to bring my mother to us in Miami, but nothing will ever make up for the wide expanse between now and then.

By the time we reach our home, Yves and I are drenched in sweat. It is hot, yes, but this is a different kind of sweat. It reeks of fear and unspeakable tension. We stare at each other as we cross the threshold, each mindful of the fact that everything we are doing, we are doing for the last time. My mother is moving about the kitchen, muttering to herself. Our suitcases rest next to the kitchen table, and it all seems rather innocent, as if we are simply going to the country for a few days, and not across an entire ocean. I cannot rightly wrap my mind around the concept of crossing an ocean. All I know is this small island and the few feet of water I wade in when I am at the beach. Haiti is not a perfect home, but it is a home nonetheless, and I am surprised that I feel such overwhelming melancholy at a time when I should be feeling nothing but hope.

Last night, Yves told me that he never wants to return, that he will never look back, and lying in bed, my legs wrapped around his, my lips against the sharp of his collarbone, I burst into tears.

"Chère, what's wrong?" he asked, gently wiping my tears away with the soft pads of his thumbs.

"I don't like it when you talk like that."

Yves stiffened. "I love my country and I love my people, but I cannot bear the thought of returning to this place where I cannot work or feel like a man or even breathe. I mean you no insult when I say this, but you cannot possibly understand."

I wanted to protest, but as I lay there, my head pounding, I realized that I probably couldn't understand what it would be like for a man in this country where men have so many expectations placed upon them that they can never hope to meet. There are expectations of women here, but it is in some strange way easier for us, because it is in our nature, for better or worse, to do what is expected of us. And yet, there are times when it is not easier, times like that moment when I wanted to tell Yves that we should stay and fight to make things better, stay with our loved ones, just stay.

I have saved a little money for my mother. It started with the five gourds from the red-faced American, and then most of my paycheck and anything else I could come up with. This money will not make up for the loss of a daughter and a son-in-law, but it is all I have to offer. After we leave, she is going to stay with her sister in Petit Goave. I am glad for this, because I could not bear the thought of her alone in this stifling little house, day after day. I am afraid she would just shrivel up and die like that. I am also afraid she will shrivel up and die, regardless.

I walk around the house slowly, memorizing each detail, running my hands along the walls, tracing each crack in the floor with my toes. Yves is businesslike and distant as he remakes our bed, fetches a few groceries for my mother, hides our passports in the lining of his suitcase. My mother watches us but we are all silent. I don't think any of us can bear to hear the sound of each other's voices, and I don't think we know why. Finally, a few minutes past midnight, it is time. My mother clasps Yves's hands between hers, smaller, more brittle. She urges him to take care of me, take care of himself. His voice cracks as he assures her that he will, that the three of us won't be apart long. She embraces me tightly, so tightly that again my arms tingle but I say nothing. I hold her, kissing the top of her head, promising to write as soon as we arrive in Miami, promising to write every single day, promising to send for her as soon as possible. I make so many promises I cannot promise to keep.

And then, we are gone. My mother does not stand in the doorway, waving, as she might were this a movie. We do not look back and we do not cry. Yves carries our suitcases and quickly we make our way to a deserted beach where there are perhaps thirty others, looking as scared as Yves and I. There is a boat—large, and far sturdier than I had imagined, for which I am thankful. I have been plagued by nightmares of a boat made from weak and rotting wood, leaking and sinking into the sea, the only thing left behind, the hollow echo of screams. Yves greets a few of his friends, but stays by my side. "We're moving on up," I quip, and Yves laughs, loudly. I see the priest Yves promised would bless this journey. He is only a few years older than us, so to me, he appears painfully young. He has only a small knapsack and a Bible so worn it looks like the pages might fall apart at the lightest touch. His voice is quiet and calm as he ushers us onto the boat. Below deck there are several small cabins, and Yves seems to instinctively know which one is ours. At this moment, I realize that Yves has spent a great deal of money to arrange this passage for us. I know he has his secrets but I am momentarily irritated that he has kept something this important from me. He stands near the small bed, his arms shyly crossed over his chest, and I see an expression on his face I don't think I have ever seen before. He is proud, eyes watery, chin jutting forward. And I know that I will never regret this decision, no matter what happens to us, because I have waited my entire life to see my husband like this. In many ways, I am seeing him for the first time.

Little more than two hours after the boat sets sail, I am above deck, leaning over the railing, heaving what little food is in my stomach into the ocean. Even on the water, the air is hot and stifling. We are still close to Haiti but I had hoped that the moment we set upon the ocean, I would be granted one sweet breath of cool air. Yves is cradling me against him between my bouts of nausea, promising that this sickness will pass, promising that this is but a small price to pay. I am tired of promises, but they are all we have to offer each other. I tell him to leave me alone, and as his body slackens against me, I can tell that he is hurt, but I have too many things happening in my mind to comfort him when I need to comfort myself more. I brush my lips across his knuckles and tell him that I'll meet him in our cabin soon. He leaves, reluctantly, and when I am alone, I close my eyes, inhaling the salt of the sea deep into my lungs, hoping that smelling this thick salty air is another one of those things I am doing for the last time.

I think of my mother and father and I think that being here on this boat may well be the closest I will ever come to knowing my father, knowing what he wanted for his family. My head is splitting because my thoughts are thrown in so many directions. All I want is a little peace and I never feel more peaceful than when I am with Yves. Wiping my lips with the back of my hand, ignoring the strong taste of bile lingering in the back of my throat, I return below deck where I find Yves, sitting on the end of the bed, rubbing his forehead.

I place the palm of my hand against the back of his neck. It is warm and slick with sweat. "What's wrong?"

He looks up but not at me. "I'm worried about you."

I push him farther onto the bed and straddle his lap. He closes his eyes and I caress his eyelids with my fingers, enjoying the curl of his eyelashes and the way it tickles my skin. He is such a beautiful man, but I do not tell him this. He would most likely take it the wrong way. At the very least, it would make him uncomfortable. It is a strange thing in some men, this fear of their own beauty. I lift his chin with one finger and trace his lips with my tongue. They are cracked but soft. His hands tremble but he grips my shoulders firmly. I am amazed at how little is spoken between us yet how much is said. We quickly slip out of our clothes and his thighs flex between mine. The sensation of his muscle against my flesh is a powerful one that makes my entire body tremble.

I slip my tongue between his lips and the taste of him is so familiar and necessary that I am suddenly weak. I fall into Yves, kissing him so hard that I know my lips will be bruised in the morning. I want them to be. Yves pulls away first, drawing his lips roughly across my chin down to my neck, the hollow of my throat, practically gnawing at my skin with his teeth. I moan hoarsely, tossing my head backward; a gesture of acquiescence and desire. My neck throbs and I know that here too, there will be bruises. He sinks his teeth deeper into me and I can no longer see the fine line between pain and pleasure. But just as soon as I consider asking him to stop, he does, instead lathering the fresh wounds with the softness of his tongue, murmuring sweet and tender words. Such gentleness in the wake of such roughness leaves me shivering.

The weight of my breasts rests in Yves's hands and he lowers his lips to my nipples, suckling them. He looks up at me as he suckles and it is unclear whether this is a moment of passion or a moment of comfort for him . . . for me. And then I cannot look at him so I rest my chin against the top of his head, my arms wrapped around him, my hips slowly rocking back and forth. My cunt brushes along the length of his cock, hard beneath me. I am wet already, and I want him inside me, but I wait. This moment, whatever it is, demands patience. He turns our bodies so that I am lying on my back and slowly, almost too slowly, he draws his tongue along my torso, inside my navel, the round of my belly. He is reverent in his touch and I can feel the tension in my body easing away as I surrender my trust and fear and hope to this one man.

His hands massaging my thighs, Yves places a cheek against the soft, wiry patch of hair covering my mound. And then he is tracing the lips between my thighs with only one finger. His touch is tentative at first, and then it is possessive and insistent as he covers the most sensitive part of me with his mouth, tasting and teasing me with his tongue, that one finger sliding inside of me so subtly that I gasp, and clench around him and hear a distant voice begging him for more. It is agonizing that at a time like this, Yves is making love to me in such a manner when all I want is him fucking me so hard that I feel everything and nothing at all. His tongue is moving faster, so fast that it feels like a constant, and then I cannot take it any more.

"Fuck me," I say harshly, and he blinks, looking at me as if he too is seeing me for the first time.

"Oui, ma chère," he whispers, crawling up my body, kissing me as he slowly slides his cock, inch by inch, into the wet heat of my cunt.

Yves takes hold of my knees spreading my legs wide and pushing them upward until they are practically touching my face. I rest my ankles against his shoulders and shudder as he pulls his cock to the edge of my cunt and then buries himself to the hilt over and over again. I am intimately aware of his pulsing length, his sweat falling onto my body, into my eyes, mingling with mine, the tension in his body as I claw at the wide stretch of black skin across his back with my fingernails. Tomorrow, he too will have bruises. My cunt loosens around his cock and Yves groans, hiding his face in my armpit, trying to stay in control.

"Let go," I urge him.

Then, he is fucking me faster and harder, so much so that I cannot recognize him and my chest heaves because I am thankful. A cry that has been trapped deep inside my throat is finally released and the sound of it is peculiar. It is a sound that only a woman who has known what I have known can make. I can feel wetness trailing down the inside of my arm. It is Yves's tears. My thigh muscles are screaming at me, so I wrap my legs tightly around his waist. I am tender inside but I don't want Yves to ever stop because with each stroke of his cock he takes me farther away from the geography of our grief and closer to a cool dry place.

Man and Woman:
A Study in Black and White
rachel resnick

She was meeting a gorgeous black man she'd recently and violently fallen in love with, and the obsession was at full throttle. As she waited, she worried about not looking good enough for him. When she stood, this angular, show-stopping redhead with the frantic green orbs, she was painfully aware of the new garter belt slipping from her waist and the garters themselves poking into the excess fat of her thighs. He liked it when girls went without underwear, so she'd purchased this garter-hose ensemble, not expecting the discomfort of her nether lips chafing together as she walked or the chill that would rise from beneath her filmy skirt and strike her where the soreness began; after she came under the expert ministrations of his tongue, he liked to jam his fingers deep inside her to make her scream, only she never did. Instead, her vaginal walls were raw and bruised. She secretly delighted in the sensation, a forget-me-not etched into flesh, proof of his desire. She had worried about indulging her fetish for blacks, reminding herself that she was always falling in love and had proved herself incapable of having casual sex even with men she didn't fancy, but she was resolved that this time would be different. This time she would be in control. He would be her fantasy stud, her own Ray Victory, starring with her in a new make-believe segment of her favorite porn video, *Black Ass/White Gash*. She watched this video frequently. It had choreographed her masturbatory sessions for some years now, though none of her terminally PC friends knew. And it prepared her for the real weekend he and she had spent together, the one when she vowed she'd keep it about raw sex and not trip out on the man; in less than a week, though, her plans had disintegrated.

Even the way she stood on the Promenade, leaning against the glass of a light-fixture store, seemed awkward, and she couldn't manage to arrange her legs properly. What stupidly long legs! They were hopeless. Her skin was so pale it was almost see-through. She might as well be wrapped in rice paper. She saw a thick throbbing purple vein on the back of her hand she'd never seen before. Were her organs showing through? But no, her skin was more like coagulated glue— opaque and pasty. A canvas for freckles and sunspots, veins and scratches. She hated pal e with a passion. If only she could go out in the sun without turning into a tomato face. The zip- per on the skirt was puckering; why hadn't she noticed ear- lier? Thoughts were ping-ponging around her head, zigzag- ging the heart chakra. Her belly pooched under the tight black stretch top, and she was sure she hadn't covered up the spots on her face where she'd been picking and prodding at acne. At her age (she was twenty-nine—OK, thirty-three—to his twenty-four) she shouldn't be getting acne anymore and she should know better than to pick, but then, if he could mark her, why shouldn't she mark herself as well? It was a week since they'd first met and spent a whole torrid weekend together, and she hadn't heard one peep from him until a few hours ago when he'd called her at the office to ask her out, and she'd said sure, she'd meet him for a movie later—then she'd freaked, realizing it was Friday afternoon and she was a chump for saying she was available. Why would a stud like him want to fuck with a pale, neurotic girl like her anyway? Correction: an "older woman," as he'd said (without even knowing her correct age!). He was probably not going to show, or he was going to dump her in some humiliating fashion, and it would be nobody's fault but her own. She was close to despair about its being over, so she'd stopped at a bar beforehand and had a few espressos along with a couple shots of Jack, which only contributed to her sense of fragmentation.

He was late. Perhaps he wouldn't show. Miserable, she wandered into a trendy clothing store and was instantly mesmerized by the gaudy displays, the raucous derangement of cheap finery. Everything seemed to vibrate in the anticipation of his arrival. Absently she ran her fingers through a rack of silken blouses, and thought of his skin, its ebonic perfection, turning away when an anorexic salesgirl wearing a hoodie top and yellow-tinted aviators moved toward her with predatory speed. When was it she'd first understood her craving for black skin? For Negroid men? Was it when she read *To Kill a Mockingbird* as a child, and sensed that behind the chifforobe, it was really about fear of black men's virility, and if there was that much fear, there must be something fearsome to back it up? Was it her childhood in podunk Florida, where she'd fantasized about the ripped blacks who ran track so effortlessly, who seemed to go airborne on the basketball court, who danced with a feral grace and moved through the cinderblock halls with warrior strides and whose physiques put the crackers to shame, and who would either look through her like she was invisible when she made eyes at them, or would say nasty, vulgar things to her at the lockers—either way, they were so close she could taste their sweat, see their muscles shifting underneath their skin, but never touch them. They were completely out of reach. Tantalizing and taboo. Maybe it dated to the first time she'd heard Jimi Hendrix as a kid, and throughlined into her lifelong predilection for sappy black pop. In the music, as in their presence, she maintained that black men were more rooted in their sexuality than white men, more confident, more attuned. Maybe it had something to do with the scalding memory of certain rednecks who jokingly dared each other, "Nickel for every nigger you hit," in the school parking lot, flooring their Camaros and pickups past the blacks who, too poor to own cars, were walking home to the projects. But until she met him (he was a purebred, African blood to the core, while she was a typical Made-in-America Euro mutt; white trash, to her own mind) she'd never actually slept with one. Sleeping with him, and having it surpass the most explosive orgasms she'd had during sessions with her trusty *Black Ass/White Gash* tape and Dutch, the ten-inch cyberskin motorized dildo, had soldered her preconceptions. A silk shirt with a hula girl motif was in her hands, and she held it before her dreamily, seeing the shirt enshrining him. She was hopelessly snared now, and she thought of the African tale retold by Amos Tutuola, about a man who meets a woman in Africa at the market, and he invites her home to visit. He is the Perfect Gentleman, handsome and courteous and kind. She follows him. Along the way he begins taking off his clothes, dropping them behind. Then he starts removing his limbs. Arms. Legs. Torso. Until he is nothing but a skull bouncing along the dirt road. Because she wears the cowrie shell necklace he gave her, she is under his spell and must keep following him. Where would he lead her? What was he taking, and what would he give back? The stupid saying *Once you go black, you never go back* kept cycling through her fevered brain. No wonder most people clamped the sewer grate down on their own subterranean appetites. She saw a dark clotted river of Lethe in an underground subway, choked with shit

and crawling with blink-eyed albino alligators, and shuddered. She returned the shirt to the rack. After all, he was
Jamaican. African by way of the Caribbean. Hula girls made
no sense.

The pulse of fluorescence and the oiled sweetness of an old
Johnny Gill tune that came on the radio spurred a vision from
last weekend of them lying entangled there on her bed, his
buttery blackness draped over the white of her. Checkerboard
girl. "I love you more than I've ever loved anyone. I want to
do things to you I've never done to anyone else," she imagined him saying, though he had said nothing of the sort.
Instead, he had charmed her with his growling and purring as
he fucked her so deep down and rough she still ached. In the
picture she conjured up, she marveled at how his ebony body
contrasted the whiteness of her and gave it buoyancy, density,
almost beauty—as if she were an unfinished sketch of blank
space, and he shaded her in. As she sank into reverie, her
groin inflamed and her chest palpitated. She knew the vision
was a cheesy BET video, sentimental, maybe reverse racist,
but she couldn't help it. The heat was on. When she'd first
learned of her appetite for black men, she'd understood what
it was to look at sexuality like a stranger, the stranger within,
but one who must be greeted and welcomed. Move over, Ray
Victory. This Jamaican was her dream man. If she weren't in
Los Angeles, so far from family, she never would have had the
guts. Lucky she'd gone to that stupid VIP nightclub party.
She'd seen him and thought, no way can he be straight; he
was too breathtaking, stylish, in shape. Before they even
spoke, he'd taken her out on the dance floor and led her in a
sexy slow dance grind, ending with a dip! and she'd changed
her mind. Even more serendipitous that he'd been there at all,
since blacks and whites, as well as other ethnicities, were
more segregated in L.A. than back home. Now, the thought of
losing him struck her with a panic. The world seemed sud-

denly flushed with bright white, starchy with unhealth and imminent collapse, and lacking the grace of salvation. Even the mannequins looked startled at their loss of innocence. That same salesgirl, her aviators now accusingly yellow, clopped toward her, bearing down.

She exited the clothing store, kneading her hands to slow down the nerves. From somewhere came the smell of fresh caramel corn, so sweet it was sickening. She tugged nervously at her hose, thinking they had slid around her thighs, and clutched her jacket about her. The sky was gray and drained of all color, and she wondered if she could survive such a need. Which is when she saw him coming around the corner and immediately creamed.

He was dressed casually, but self-consciously. Studied cool. She'd noticed last weekend he seemed to be a bit of a control freak, given to extra hand-washing and a certain fastidiousness, especially with food—only tofu for him. In a way, his pickiness and concern about weight reminded her of a woman. Perhaps that was part of the allure, too. Tonight he wore an expensive white T-shirt that hugged his sculpted chest and shoulders, a pair of worn jeans (what were called "date rape" pants) with holes in the ass and knees, fashionably baggy, but cinched at the waist with a black bandana for a belt. Black clogs. A leather jacket. Hair in shoulder-length dreads. Striking face with that pure, flattish African nose and flared nostrils, lively dark brown eyes, lush mouth. No jewelry. Didn't matter. He could've worn anything and stopped traffic. When he walked, the slight bow in his ballet legs was exaggerated, another sexy trait. Only a dancer could get away with clogs. She wondered again briefly if he was gay somewhere under there. Weren't they all? Meaning, all men. Women were just shadows to them, things to catch and break, to penetrate and impregnate, whereas other men were meat and muscle, car talk and jock walk. Solid, simple. Familiar. He was terribly late, but walked nonchalantly toward her, and though she knew she should be insulted, she could not help smiling. She pictured him in his Calvins. He had been an underwear model in Japan. Once, he had told her, during a nude photo shoot for a fashion mag, a model who had been lying on top of him during a complicated shot left a wet mark. "Your abs," she whispered. "I've never seen anything like them." He got a huge boner and had to excuse himself to go to the bathroom. The Japanese stared, mouths open.

"Bonsoir, chérie," he said, but he seemed distracted and mouthed the words as if he relished the sound of his mush-mouthed French accent more than the meaning, or the impact. She herself, a highly successful entrepreneur and certifiable workaholic, had never yet been to Paris, whereas he had done photo shoots and gone on a tour with his dance troupe there. Now, after a mysterious injury, he was retired from dancing and worked as a bartender at a posh Beverly Hills watering hole. As for modeling, he said he didn't like being stared at that way, like an object. Not that she cared about any of that. She had money enough for both of them, though he always insisted on paying his half. Why was he so spacey? Had he just come from seeing someone else? Although she impulsively went to hug him and kiss him on the lips, he hesitated, as if he'd blanked out on the whole greeting ritual—or, worse, forgotten who she was. Maybe she was being overly pushy, even hokey, and he preferred a cooler public demeanor? Her right eyelid began to twitch, very slightly, and she hoped he wouldn't notice. Did he see her shoes?

"Hey," she said. Trying to be laid-back, not mentioning the time. Wondering if he was hard.

"Check the shoes. Cute." He paused, long enough for her to fall into compliment quicksand, where she was still pleasantly sinking when he followed with, "Why so dressed up, girl?"

She felt the blush. Instant tomato face. Why did she think of a one-two combination? Hook-jab-jab. She looked at his face and wondered if she was only imagining that he looked somehow pleased with himself, pleased with hurting her, but at that instant he grabbed her arm and she spun out, dizzy with the sensation. If he asked her, she would drop to her knees and suck him off right there. Let all Santa Monica watch. *Melting, I'm melting*, flashed in her brain, and the witchy striped socks hissed and curled away.

"I want to be your slave," she heard herself say from far away.

"Speak up, girlfriend."

"I will be your slave."

He looked at her then, more intently. The corners of his thick-lipped mouth turned up slightly, like pan-fry fish that is just beginning to burn.

At the doorway to her canyon house, she had forgotten to flip the outside light, and it was swamped in inky canyon night. His hand was electrifying her hip, but when she craned around she could hardly see him; his skin was the night air. A fat yellow moth stuttered drunkenly toward the light, and bumped smack against the bulb. She thought she heard a wing fry as the light singed it. *Tsss.* Then he smiled, and each gleaming tooth acted as a cowrie shell, binding her to his will. She faced the door now, bending slightly so her hips and ass would move into his groin. So she could press against his hardness. As she turned the key in the lock, he reached his hand up under her skirt, between her legs. She heard him draw in his breath, but kept on with the key. The lock clicked. The door opened. He smeared her juice slowly on the inner thigh and gently withdrew his hand.

"Good girl," he said.

Then he was guiding her through the doorway, surrounding her like a cape, kissing her ear. The way his tongue scoured the cochlea, setting the eardrum to pounding, each lapping released another cunt wave. If this ear were a fig, she would want all the fruit flesh tongued out until she was deaf to everything but the sound of him. As her cunt flared in anticipation, she tugged at his springing dreads. He pulled back slightly and she panicked.

"I'm taking my time," he said into her ear. His tongue puddled deeper as her nipples strained to pop through the crisp lace of her costly bra. Black. Yes, of course. Gothic against her pallor. Lingerie as contrast. Enticement's in the eye of . . . sweet Jesus . . .

But then he withdrew his tongue and pushed her so that she stumbled, and clattered to the floor. Déjà vu. Was she dreaming this or was someone videotaping? She looked at her hand splayed on the cold Italian tile to see if it was a grainy video hand, but no. Who was directing? He pulled his T-shirt over his head and it was gone. There he was. She couldn't breathe. Could not. It would've been enough to simply stare, pray to that body, the arc of pectoral triumph, baby-smooth sable skin, physique's articulation of the perfect mean, the golden triangle, the hypotenuse of her desire for African splendor.

"Fold my shirt," he said. "Bitch."

Actually, he didn't say "bitch," but she wished he had. His mother had raised him strict backwoods Christian, island-style, and he had trouble with swearing, though not with fucking, thank the gods. This mother of his was partial to the switch, or cook pot, or hand, whatever was easiest. Besides the beatings, she'd also enjoyed dressing him up, more than her daughters. He was the cute one. There was no question he had a dark well to draw from in the sexual arena. And she'd been encouraging from the start, telling him no limits. She wondered where it would take her, and him. How could he not fall for her? Wasn't she liberating him?

Swooning with longing, with lust, she crawled to the pile of shirt, kissed it first (what was she doing?), shook it out, and made it into a tight little square, like they do with shirts in plastic packages (how did she know how to do that?). Then her hair was in his hand, being twisted, and he was leading her to the bathroom. Better than she could've imagined.

"Clean my ass."

What? He was really coming into his own. She thought of the scene in the video where Ray Victory shaves this white chick's legs with a cheap Bic razor and shaving cream while they're sitting naked in a tub in an empty House for Sale. The slap and slosh of water, and soap, and skin, his black arm moving down her perky leg . . . but before she could fast-forward to the good stuff, his hand on her bony but shapely ass returned her to now time. In her charming three-quarter-million-dollar canyon house, not a rinky-dink porn set. Everything red under a weird heat light, giving his impossibly smooth skin a devil sheen, and him handing her a wad of toilet tissue. Then a washcloth he'd dampened under warm water, and offered, moist, soapy. Single, antichildren, and addicted to maid service, she'd never even cleaned a baby's bottom, nor changed a diaper, nor taken a shit with someone else in the bathroom, nor on their chest even when they asked her to—sometimes there were limits. But not now. Not in now time. In the red zone. With this vision before her, this Jamaican hunk, who needed, who wanted, his ass cleaned. So be it.

Swabbing the black ass bathed in red glow as he leaned against the marble scallop sink, she who never even cleaned her house, nor swiped a counter, was in heaven. Squeezing one rocky muscular buttock while she rubbed the cloth in circular motions over his anus, gingerly pressing and working a corner into the hole and wiggling her finger there. But he tensed and her finger was ejected. Drawing the damp cloth slowly down to cup his balls as she involuntarily went for the other virgin ass cheek and kissed, and bit. Insane with need. Then traced a finger over that cheek. Worshipfully. Until her finger reached the rectal starburst, and stopped in wonder at the extraordinary lips she found here. Forming a perfect O. This was not her thing. No way. But impulsively, she moved toward the circular puckered flesh and began kissing those still slightly acrid lips, and tonguing, and licking, taking the flaps of anal flesh into her mouth, being careful not to bare any teeth. With the other hand she flicked the halogen on and gasped at the succulence of black ass before her as the bright light defined it.

He growled. Swiveling his ass. No one's mouth had ever entranced her so much.

He purred. With her other hand she reached up between the taut dancer legs and grabbed only the root of his cock. And squeezed, in time with her mouth's lapping, and felt the blood rush there, swelling, and imagined it coursing thick and red-black through the ridged and lovely veins. Give her a century, folded into a parcel of time, and she would spend it like this. Pleasing him. Then, keeping her right hand on his cock's base, and her mouth paying attention to his asshole, she moved her left hand between her own legs and dipped in a finger to see how wet she was, and could not believe it.

"Don't forget your own, dirty girl. Wash up good."

Keeping her hand on his cock, working it to the middle, squeezing, then to the top, right under the flared mushrooming uncircumcised head, squeezing, feeling the cock grow bigger—she rinsed the washcloth under the running spigot, and dabbed at her own still-sore asshole, and at her cunt, though the pressure was almost too much, she was so aroused. If he had not then risen up, circled her throat with his chocolate-black fingers, and pressed, and raised her up, and moved her before him as they glided into the master bedroom, she would've come just from the intimate worship he was demanding, and allowing. Gone was the girl in him. Only the warrior prince of lovemaking remained.

He picked her up then, and tossed her onto the bed. She understood. Just the skirt came off. Spiky heels dug into the mattress, her garters scraped, and her swollen pussy lay open to the world. Which was him. There he was, standing there looking down on her, his fantastic ten-inch (ten-foot?) cock arching and jerking on its own, making little stuttering probes into the air. Somehow he was completely and stunningly naked. The whites of his eyes shone; his body was mythical. As he looked at her she knew to spread her legs and slowly part the sopping lips with her fingers, showing what color she had, offering him the pink, and he took it. He descended onto the bed, her body—this black Adonis—and buried his head between her legs. After some minutes of licking her gently around the pulsating mound, making her mad with lust and impatience, sending more juices spooling onto the sheets, he sat up and wound a plastic key coil from his wrist around his dreads so they were gathered into a topknot, giving him a deliciously androgynous touch. Too sexy. Too much. Those bee-stung lips on her cunt lips, pulling and sucking, teasing the clit, soon sent spirals and circles, sunbursts and ricochets of almost psychedelic sensation ribboning through her body.

"Fingers," she breathed.

"Don't rush me," he said sharply. Hovering on the edge of orgasm, she didn't register the harshness. The contrast with his skill. Was he not giving her mind-blowing pleasure? With her own fingers, she twisted both her nipples, amped up the thrill. Then she pinched until they stood up like rosy peaks of meringue. He saw her, briefly reached up and cupped one of her small but supple breasts. Finally he entered a finger in her cunt. Her strong muscles immediately closed around the digit. Then a second. He reached her G-spot right away, as if by radar. Or, was it love? Was it? Soul mates? Wouldn't that make everyone crazy? She closed her eyes. As he kept licking her lips and clit, he pounded his fingers against the G-spot, so she had to keep zoning toward that place where she was approaching orgasmo light, then backing off because there was now too much sensation.

Then she couldn't hold back. She saw herself, supine, red hair matted and spread like a banquet around her head, green eyes glazed, long milky-white limbs, cream-white skin, spinning around the smoky-black pivot of him, like paints are spun in metal bowls and splatter onto paper, creating fantastical random designs. Things telescoped, got larger, then smaller. She was an elephant. She was Thumbelina.

"You're raining on me," he said, in awe. At their bond? At his skill? Holding one hand under her to catch the wetness as he continued ramming his fingers against her G-spot. At first this extra sensation added texture to the orgasm; then it became painful. She wriggled to get away, scooching up the mattress, but she cracked her skull against the wall. He rammed harder. Furiously. His breath grew shallow. He seemed unaware of her, unstoppable. It was then she remembered she was on the tail end of her period. Probably it was all gone, but there was a chance deep inside there was still some blood. She worried it might bother him, anal as he was, but dared not interrupt him now. The pain mounted, but he kept going, and going, until he was done. She realized then, as she concentrated on the awful stabbing in her cunt, that as hard as he'd made her come, he only stopped when he'd had enough, not when she had. There was an important message there, but she was not quite able to grasp it, sex-drunk as she was.

An aromatherapy Passion candle flickered suddenly, then guttered. Others danced and flickered wild, shaggy shadows against the walls. A stick of Nag Champa incense burned in the corner, dropping ash as it kept trying to reach the ceiling.

Gypsy fabrics hung over expensive tabletops, and Tiffany lampshades. So Topanga. He had opened her up and she could do nothing but wait to be filled, when and if he chose. The candlelight was low; she hoped he hadn't noticed any red on his fingers. Hopefully it was all gone. In the shifting glow of flame, his topknot looked regal.

"God, I love your dreads," she said with a sigh and tried to reach toward him.

"You know," he said, sitting up abruptly, stroking his licorice-black cock, his eyes shiny and sharp, "where I come from, it is not Kingston. In the hills of Jamaica live the Wharricks, my family. We are descended from slaves, but we escaped. It was the 1700s and the Spanish were there, then the British. They call us Maroons. And they say my family is descended from Grandy Nanny, who led the escape. She wore branches in her hair and they believed nothing could touch her. People don't understand. They ask me about these dreads. They call me 'Bob Marley.' I have never smoked ganja. I do not listen to reggae. My family is all preachers. Do you know what I am saying?"

She didn't have time to wonder at his strange monologue, to substitute endearments for his words, or even to respond. Instead he pulled her toward him and slid his cock unceremoniously into her slippery cunt. Time stopped. Clocks broke. Skies fell. Rivers rose. Trees walked. Time was now split. There was time before his cock penetrated, and after. Before, when things were black and white, and after, when things were Technicolor.

"Nice and hot," he said about her twat—his words, again, not matching her thoughts or mood. Not that she noticed, really.

The thrusting was brutal. Banging against all manner of vaginal stalagmites and bumps and hidden chambers. She grabbed at his sculpted shoulders, urging him deeper.

Subsumed the pain. Pain on pain, producing pleasure. She raised her womanly hips, braced her hands against the walls, contorted herself to take him all the way. I'm not your girl, I'm your gash. That's all. Slit. Slash. Gash. White gash. Got it? Take me. Take all I have, then I will have you. She was a wound waiting to be opened. Red underlines white, clashes with black. No, she didn't think it mattered, the very slight chance of remaining menstrual blood. But might it? With such a man, so clean. So newly clean.

"I'm almost done with my period," she whispered. Hoarsely. In case there was a last trace left. And to her horror, with only one quick grunt, he stopped. For a moment, an instant, he was inside her, not moving. He would stay there, wouldn't he? He understood he was home? Together they made home? But then there was a sucking, slurping pop, and he was out, and her cunt collapsed along with her heart. Kerthump.

"Ras clot," he said. And she could barely understand. The Jamaican patois.

"Bumba clot. Ras clot," he said. Again. This time she got it. Blood clot. Right. Shit. He'd told her about this last weekend, this Jamaican paranoia for menstrual blood. Shit. Blood clot was the biggest insult you could use on a Jamaican. It meant something like you came out of your mother's womb as a blood clot, not an ovum? Or did it mean you were a blood-soiled period rag? Whatever. It was bad. No point in explaining now how she was just being extra careful.

Then, still leaning over her, facing her, he grabbed for her ass. Her ragged, sore ass. Clean, yes. Bloodless, true. She cringed. Last weekend, one brutish time, had been enough. She'd fantasized about it, yes, she'd egged him on, but the truth was it had hurt like hell. Now he nosed his massive cock at her hole like some kind of shit-skin flesh missile, then shoved. All the way. Involuntarily, she cried out, "No!" forgetting her promise to him, her need. Didn't he know about lubricant? Or was he unleashing some demon? He began pounding hard and deep; she could feel his cock swelling even larger. Impossible that she could even take him. She kept crying out, stuff she didn't even clock. "Please, oh, no, stop. It hurts. No . . ." but he paid no attention; thrust harder. She thought of a multitude rowing somewhere they didn't want to go, plowing through a jet-black sea, rowing bodies that were stretched to the limit, until their muscles began snapping like rubber bands, shooting all over the ship's murky bowels, and he came, shuddering over her. There he was, her merciless ebony god, arching his glorious back, his eyes rolled back in his head, his topknot shaking like spongy twigs as he threw his head back and stretched his arms out to the sides as if he were welcoming his own mysterious god. It struck her then, as she lay ravaged, sober now, blood leaking from her torn asshole, pinpricks of pain throbbing in her rectum, watching his unseeing eyes, the smug satisfaction in his beauty, in his prowess, that this was all about him. She was merely a sacrifice. A white girl gift. A boon to his path toward sadism. Toward ownership. Perhaps toward retribution. This was not love. She, the fetishizer, was being fetishized! He was tripping on the pliancy, the devotion, of someone who worshiped him, Black Stud. He was checked out. Unconnected. Dominant. By fetishizing the fetishizer, he'd turned the tables. While she herself had broken the cardinal rule of objectifying: She'd made her Jamaican fuck stud into a beloved man and so lost all power. So she thought. But her cunt was still sloppily, slaphappily swimming in that inky black sea. Blissful. Wasn't that what it was all about? The heart is not so easy to harness.

He was still hard. Would he return to her? She pulled him closer, with elegant, spidery, pearly-white fingers. Probing for a weak spot.

"What's a little teeny bit of blood, if there even is any?" she whispered, overcome by her own need. Balance the ugliness with the primal merging she loved best, his fudge-black cock melting in the ice-cream dream of her white gash. Cajoling. "I mean, I'm bleeding now from my butt . . ."

He shook his head. "Nuh the same." And shuddered by way of explanation. Christ on a stick, she thought.

"C'mon, you're a stud. Blood can be hot. One time this guy, he went down on me when I was bleeding buckets. His face was smeared with blood. It was beautiful."

Silence sank over their tangled black-and-white bodies, like an invisible mosquito net, sank into the sweat- and come- and juice-soaked mattress, knitting everything together.

"Please?" Blushing that her voice had so betrayed her, softly cracking.

She was shocked when he began moaning. Had she turned him on? Seduced him with her plea? A smile played across her full lips. But when she reached down, the magnificent cock had dwindled to a soft wrinkled thumb, and now, what was this? He was curling, hunching, into a fetal position, moving himself into the warping shape of her, and his toned flanks shook. Was he trembling? Shaking. Quaking. She thought of a party balloon, overinflated to that dangerous tautness, shiny in its thin state—then the flatulent hiss as the balloon was released and scudded around the room until it landed there, in the dust, wet and darker and deflated.

"What're you doing to me?" he said, burying his head between her tiny breasts. "Mi nuh wan de ras clot."

"OK. Roger. Ten-four," she said, giving up. Giving up on the syrupy love dream she'd poured over the original checker-board fantasy. Clearly they were each orbiting in their own horny worlds with their own gods and monsters. Owning didn't figure in. Neither did love. Did they? She needed to get grounded again, plant her snow-white feet back in the brown-black earth. Amazingly, he was already out. Lightly snoring.

With one ivory-white hand she clicked on the VCR, to the

part in the tape where Ray Victory shaves whitey chick's pussy clean, with short, even, raspy strokes, dipping that Bic in the tub water, sudsing her cunt, taking his time, being thorough, and then he's done; he sets down the razor, there's a splashing as he rises up from the bathtub edge, facing her, moving toward her, parting those tub waters toward this dimpled white trash gash, placing his dark hands so firmly on either pale hip, giving them meaning, giving them definition, and finally, finally—watch how that mud-black cock goes in so smooth, that elegant inky snake entering the shaved white lips, parting them and feeding them what they've been needing, and finally he's wet-slapping his big black cock into and against her wet white flanks. Look at her dimples, her mouth an ecstatic O. Even she is surprised by just how big it is once inside her, that shadow man unleashed; look at her straining to hold herself steady against the faux-rock wall as he pumps her, drills her, shows her who's the man, who's the master, who's holding all history's cards . . .

. . . And with her other bone-white hand, now completely translucent in the unearthly glow from the TV, our enlightened redhead first stroked the springy dreads of her trembling black stud, then reached her hand under the covers and stroked her honky-tonk pussy.

The Boy Who Read Bataille

simon sheppard

Because he was actually French, he stood out in the class. That, and because he was gorgeous.

The class was Transgressive French Literature, otherwise known as Kink Lit 101. It was a popular one at my grad school. We got to read all the really twisted stuff: de Sade, Genet, Bataille. And Philippe was always on top of the class, not having to struggle to translate things; after all, it's not so easy to find the translation of "cocksucking motherfucking fag" in your *Larousse Dictionnaire Bilingue*.

I was attracted to him—I'm guessing everybody in the class was, both male and female—but he never gave a clue as to where his interests lay. His sexual interests, anyway; it was quite clear that as a reader he loved the thoroughly filthy works of Georges Bataille.

"God," he said one night, when a few of us—me, him, Ben, and Mary Anne—were polishing off a pizza at Vito's, "I could just read *The Story of the Eye* over and over again."

"Really?" I said. I was more inclined toward Genet, who didn't seem to always be straining to shock.

"*Oui*. Ah, Bataille. The scene with the piss and the wardrobe? *Magnifique*. And especially the one where Simone breaks raw eggs with her ass."

Well, I was glad he wasn't fixated on the part about Sir Edmond at the bullfight, or the one with Marcelle's eyeball in Simone's vagina. Eeewww!

"I'd love," he continued, "to try that out."

"Yeah?" I was excited, but cagey. I looked at his pretty, smooth face, which nearly always wore a quizzical, almost distant expression, eyes lively but remote behind his glasses, his countenance crowned by a shock of dark brown hair.

"Oh God!" said Mary Anne. "Not me! That's gross."

"But you're taking a class on transgressive literature," said Ben. "Lighten up."

"Just because I read *Macbeth*," Mary Anne said, "doesn't mean I want to kill a king."

Good retort, but my mind was elsewhere, wondering how Philippe, body obviously well-knit even when he was fully clothed, would look naked, sitting in a bathtubful of raw eggs. I finished the last gulp of my pesto pizza and followed the procession to the cash register, a picture of his imagined slick-wet butt throbbing in my mind.

Once outside the restaurant, I managed to get rid of Ben and Mary Anne without arousing suspicion. Philippe and I were by ourselves, walking back from the restaurant toward his place. The four of us had polished off a couple of pitchers of beer, so I'll blame what I said next on that.

"You really meant that? About the eggs?"

Philippe didn't look at me, just somewhere off in the distance, and he seemed a bit nervous when he nodded. "Very much, yes," he said, though he sounded more uncertain than that. "Why?"

"Because . . ." And then I hesitated, drunkenly tongue-tied.

Philippe helped me out. "Would you like to try something like that? With me?"

Well, I couldn't say I'd ever considered it before. In fact, I wasn't sure how committed I was to it even then. Kink had never been my thing, not even in my masturbation fantasies, which generally centered on smooth-bodied guys bending over to show me their buttholes. But if this was my big chance to see Philippe with his clothes off, maybe even touch him . . .

I nodded.

And soon we were gathering groceries at an all-night supermarket, my hard-on visible, I guess, to anyone who'd taken the trouble to look. What the hell, transgressive is transgressive, right?

It wasn't a long walk back to Philippe's, but it seemed endless. He lived on the third floor, but I swear there were nine flights of stairs. Once we were inside his small grad-student-cluttered living room, we set our bags on the thrift-store coffee table. Awkward silence. Without a word, he stripped down to his undershirt and jeans. Then, never looking me straight in the eye, he slowly peeled down his Levi's.

I'd never seen anything so ostentatiously perfect as Philippe standing there in just his undershirt. Slightly stocky, broad-shouldered, he didn't look like the kind of guy who'd want to discuss Derrida. His soft dick had a long, luxurious foreskin. His thighs were creamy white, muscular, perfectly shaped, amazing.

And then he turned around.

I've seen plenty of asses in my young life, but Philippe's was the best, by far the best, a Greek god's ass, a Michaelangelo-statue ass, the ass of the Heavenly Host. Philippe sauntered over to the bags on the table and pulled out the plastic shower curtains he'd bought. He tore open the package and, with the nonchalant attitude of someone decorating the high school gym for a prom, he laid the curtains on the floor, keeping his back toward me. I figured that he *must* have been aware of the effect his astonishing, creamy ass had on those lucky enough to behold it. He bent over to spread out the plastic, his pure white buttcheeks parting just enough to let me glimpse a thin line of dark hair around the hole. I almost came in my pants.

When the floor was covered in clear vinyl, he strolled over to the table again, his buttcheeks shifting with every step, and unloaded the grocery bags: two cartons of 18 extra-large eggs, a bottle of chocolate syrup, tins of vanilla pudding, spray cans of whipped cream.

"Are you ready?" he asked, turning to face me, his eyes quizzical behind his owlish glasses.

Turn around so I can see your ass again, I wanted to reply. Instead, I said, "Yes."

"And you want to do this? Really?"

I unbuttoned my fly and pulled out my hard cock. "See?" I said. "Now get down on all fours, okay?"

"Sorry," he said, pulling his undershirt over his head, revealing a flurry of armpit hair, nearly knocking his glasses off, "I guess I'm a bit nervous."

"Well, it's my first time, too. On the floor, okay?" I really wanted to be a bad-ass, kinky motherfucker, but as I stood there, watching Philippe getting on his knees, then all fours, stood there with my big, stupid hard-on jutting from my pants, I just felt tentative. If Bataille or de Sade or Genet had been watching, they would have thought: Pathetic! Or *pathétique!*

"Well?" Philippe's voice was giving nothing away.

"Can I, um, touch you first?"

"Of course."

So I got down on my knees, just behind him, next to the pure European beauty of his ass, and extended a shy hand. The flesh of his butt flinched a bit at my touch, then relaxed as

I stroked the cheek, running my hand over its classical curves, then gently trailing two fingers down the crack, down from the tailbone till I felt the soft warmth of his hole. With my other hand I reached between his lean thighs, brushing his pendulous ball-sac, then aimed upward till I grabbed onto his dick. It was getting gratifyingly stiff, but the generous fore-skin still covered the head; I slid it back and forth over the moist headflesh as my other hand massaged his hole.

"Les oeufs . . ." Philippe said. The eggs. He was sounding impatient. All I wanted to do was fuck him, and he was think-ing about groceries. Damn this kink stuff.

I reluctantly got up, walked over to the table, and opened an egg carton. The egg was slightly cool in my hand. I cracked it on the edge of the table.

"Ready?" I asked, like something momentous was going to happen.

He looked up at me, straight at me through his glasses, and sort of smiled. "Oui."

I stood above him and pulled apart the shell, letting the raw egg drop onto the smooth, white flesh of his ass. I wanted it to drip right down the crack, but my aim was a bit off.

Philippe was muttering something. In French.

"Pardon?" I said.

"I was just reciting Bataille," Philippe said, and when he started in again, I realized he was doing just that, apparently having memorized the bit leading up to Marcelle's suicide. The guy was amazingly weird. But his ass was amazingly fan-tastic. I got another egg, cracked it, and, holding it close to his flesh, hit the target, the yolk oozing right down his asscrack. I spit in my hand and worked my throbbing dick for a minute while I watched raw egg slithering down his thighs, down to the plastic-covered floor.

"Oh, fuck," I said. And meant it.

Then I went back to the table and picked up the open egg

carton. Sixteen left. Standing above him, I dropped the eggs one by one onto Philippe, onto his shoulders, the small of his back, but especially onto his wonderful, wonderful ass.

By the time I'd gone through most of the carton, the place was a mess and Philippe was thoroughly covered with viscous whites and bright streaks of yolk. I was about to suggest that we'd made enough mess, when he reached back with both hands and pulled his asscheeks wide apart. His deep pink asshole gleamed beneath a raw egg glaze: boypussy tartare. Sometimes it's a matter of hygiene-be-damned. I dropped to my knees right between his kneeling legs, stuck my face into his sloppy-wet ass, and started lapping at his high-cholesterol hole. He paused in his recitation of Bataille long enough to say "Fuck, yeah" and back up against my tongue. I reared back again, reached for an egg, and smashed it into his open hole. I was, my oozing cock and I agreed, beginning to really enjoy this.

The chocolate syrup was next. I stood over Philippe for a moment, looking down at his egg-slick ass, all its beauty slippery and wet. Then I opened the nozzle of the syrup bottle, inverted it, and let just a drizzle of dark-brown syrup fall onto his wet, white skin. If this was the final exam for the Transgressive Lit class, I had a feeling I was passing with flying colors.

I squeezed the bottle and a stream of sweet syrup hit his hole, drenching eggwhites, yolks, bits of shell. It was beautiful, that hole, those food-covered buttcheeks. As gorgeous as his ass had been when it was clean and white, it was even sexier all sullied, filthy with food. I wanted to fuck it. And I *was* going to fuck his ass. I was glad I'd slipped a package of Trojans into the grocery basket.

The syrup bottle sputtered to emptiness. I dropped it onto the dirty floor, then picked up the whipped cream container and shook hard. With a flourish, I topped the egg-and-chocolate slop with swirls of whipped cream, shooting a big white rosette right on Philippe's asshole. He took his hands away and his cheeks came together, squeezing out a big glob of chocolate cream. I ran my fingers up the crack of his messy ass, getting a handful of brownish goop, bringing it to my lips. Sweet.

I went to get the rubbers. I was tearing the packet open with my teeth, slippery fingers straining to get a grip on the foil, when Philippe asked, "What are you doing?" I glanced his way. He was looking up at me through those glasses of his, expression vague as ever.

It was a stupid question.

"What does it look like? I'm putting on a rubber," I replied.

"No." Just that, sounding the same in French or English. No.

While I hesitated, wondering if all the work I'd done still wouldn't get me into his butt, Philippe rose to his knees. He grabbed his dick with his filthy hand, quickly jacking his foreskin back and forth over his swollen, shiny cockhead.

At last his face changed expression. Looking somewhere in the room, but not at me, never at me, he scrunched his face up in a stereotype of preorgasmic lust. "Oh yeah oh yeah oh yeah," he chanted. His glasses were sliding down his sweaty nose.

If I'd been smart, I guess I would have gotten behind him and at least stuck my fingers up his ass. Maybe even my dick. But I wasn't smart. I was polite. I just stood there gaping as Philippe shot a big load of sperm, gush after gush, onto the swamp of eggs, chocolate, and cream.

"That's it," Philippe said, recovering quickly. "You can wash up in the kitchen sink. I'm going to go shower."

I didn't know what to say. "Fuck you, asshole" came to mind, but when I thought about how gorgeous his asshole actually looked . . .

By the time I'd rinsed my hands and stuffed my poor hard-on back into my pants, the shower was already running. I went into the bathroom to say good-bye. There behind a clear plastic curtain, the French boy was washing his butt. His back turned toward me, he spread his cheeks, soaping up, lathering, drawing small wet circles on his hole. My dick stretched to full hardness again.

"Philippe?"

He turned. Amazingly, he still had his glasses on. He didn't say a word. I'd been dismissed, my part in his little literary experiment apparently at an end; he'd had his transgressive fun.

When I left Philippe's, the door locked itself behind me with a click.

Old Tingo's Penis
geoffrey a. landis

You have to understand that we Dhameo people were here first. The other people came here later—we don't know where they came from, they just showed up—but we Dhameo were first, so we know stories from the old days, like the story of how old Tingo lost his penis.

Back in those days, things weren't like they are now. There was some weird shit in those days. For example, back then men didn't have any penises yet. Nothing, just a flat spot between their legs. The women had to make their fun with each other, but since they didn't have anything to compare to, that was okay.

Old Tingo wasn't a god—nobody had heard about gods yet in those days, that's something the people who showed up later told us about. But old Tingo was sure some old; he could remember back before there were any other people, before there were any mountains or rivers or trees, back when there was nothing of the world but gray fog. Yes, there are a lot of stories about old Tingo. Anyway, one day old Tingo decided that he would make himself a penis. It was a little thing, about the size of a peanut, but old Tingo was pretty pleased with himself, and went around showing it off to all the women. "What's that?" the women would ask, and old Tingo would say, "It's a new thing, I made it myself." And then the women might ask, "What's it good for?" and old Tingo would offer to demonstrate.

After a while, that woman Aminea came to hear about old Tingo's new thing, and she went over to see Tingo and ask him about it. Now, Aminea was not old like Tingo, but she knew a thing or two, and right as soon as she saw it, she could figure out what it would be good for. But she pretended she didn't know, and she got old Tingo to demonstrate for her, and she thought, yes, this is a good thing. And afterwards, she said to Tingo, this is a good thing you have made up, you should let me borrow it for a while. And Tingo wasn't sure that this would be a smart idea, but he couldn't think of a good reason to say no, and besides, right then he was feeling all relaxed, so he gave it to her and said, please take care of it, and be sure you don't lose it.

So that clever woman Aminea used Tingo's penis for a while, and after a while she loaned it to one of the other women, and you know how it goes, they passed it around from one to another to another. Then after a few days Aminea had an idea, and she found who had the penis and borrowed it back, and then what did she do but go and hide it.

So when old Tingo came to see Aminea, and asked for his penis back, she told him, oh, it was around somewhere, but she didn't remember where it was. Old Tingo started to get a little mad, but Aminea knew how to deal with him, and she told him what a good thing that penis he had made was, and why doesn't he make another one? But this time, she added, he should make it a little bigger, so it wouldn't be so easy to lose.

So old Tingo made himself another penis, this one about as

big as your little finger, and he was mighty proud of it, too. He told himself, this one is even better than the first one I made, and the women he demonstrated it to all agreed. And after a while he had to go brag to that clever woman Aminea about how good it was, and she said to herself, yes, this is a very good thing. And afterwards, she said to Tingo, this is a good thing you have made up, if you could let me borrow it for a while, I promise I won't lose it this time. And she remembered not to laugh when she said this, because of course she had no intention of returning it.

So old Tingo gave her the penis, and she passed it around to her friends, and then after a while, when she thought old Tingo might be coming back for it, she went and hid it with the first one. And old Tingo came, and she told him, oh, it's around here somewhere, but I can't remember where I put it. Why don't you make another one for yourself, but make it just a little bigger, so it won't be so easy to misplace.

So old Tingo made another one, this one maybe as big as your thumb, and he said to himself, wow, this one is better than either of the other ones. And, of course, clever Aminea lost that one too, and so he made another one a little bigger, and another one, and another one.

After a while Aminea had a whole collection of old Tingo's penises, and it was more than enough to please her every night of the year, but she was curious how far old Tingo would go. He made a penis as big as your arm, and then made one as big as the trunk of a palm tree. Fortunately clever Aminea had been around for a while, and knew the trick of expanding herself up to make herself bigger (she could shrink herself down like a mouse, too, but that's for another story), so she still had a good time with old Tingo even when his penis was as big as the thickest, highest tree trunk, and he had to stagger just to carry it around.

"But these are just little things, old Tingo," she told him.

"Why don't you make one that's a decent size, big enough that it won't get lost?"

And old Tingo resolved, I'm going to make myself a penis that's big enough that not even absent-minded Aminea is going to lose it.

So he made himself a penis that was, oh, I don't know, maybe a mile high, and almost as thick. It was so big he couldn't carry it around, he had to dig a hole and lie on his back with the penis sticking up in the air, and he couldn't even move. Maybe this penis is a little too big, he thought, but wait until that absent-minded Aminea asks to borrow it, then she can have it, and just let her try to lose this one.

So after a while that clever Aminea came, and she saw old Tingo's penis—she could hardly miss it, you could see it a hundred miles away—and she thought, now this is a real penis, yes, but where is old Tingo?

But she liked the new penis, and she rubbed it, and after a while it did what a penis does. But what shot out of that penis was lava, and quite a lot of it, too. It really made quite a mess. So she thought, no, I don't like this penis quite as well, I really think Tingo went too far on this one. So she went away.

And old Tingo, he was in quite a bit of trouble, buried underneath that enormous penis, and under all that lava, which solidified into a mountain right there on top of him, and I don't know how long it took him to wiggle himself out again. I guess he was plenty mad, and it took him a long time before he could see what a funny joke that clever Aminea had played on him.

So when he got over getting mad he went to Aminea, and Aminea was so sorry for him that she let him have one of his penises back, and he picked one that wasn't too big, and wasn't too small, really the one that's just in the middle, the best one, and he took it and stuck it back on, and told her that he wasn't going to give away his penis any more. Women were plenty welcome to borrow it, he said, but they'd have to use it right there stuck to him where it wouldn't get lost. And Aminea decided, well, that wasn't such a bad idea.

She still had all those other penises that old Tingo had made, even if old Tingo had taken the one that was just the right size, so she took those others and gave them away. There were just enough that every man could get one, although some got ones that are just tiny little things, no bigger than a peanut, and some got ones that are just way too big.

So that's how come, if you look at men's penises, they are all different, some little and some big, and none of them ever think that their penis is just the right size.

And old Tingo? He has the one that's just the right size. And I know that there are a lot of women still looking for it.

Spawning

joy vannuys

The first thing I learned in cooking school was how to wash my hands. The twelve of us chef-hopefuls sat on our stools in our crisp new uniforms, hair tied back and covered by squat white hats that made all the guys look hot and professional, all the women dumpy. Before we could get our hands on any food, we sat through two agonizing weeks on sanitation procedures. How to wash dishes, aerobic and anaerobic bacteria, the various types of food poisoning and how not to get them. Horror stories of rats and roaches. "No polish, no manicures, girls," our teacher warned us. I looked down at my bitten nails, ragged cuticles. At last, an excuse for my unladylike paws. By regulation, we learned, there's a special sink in every kitchen with a sign over it that says FOR HAND WASHING ONLY. "As a cook, you'll wash your hands a hundred times a shift," we were told.

The first thing I learned in a professional kitchen was how to take care of my hands. My chef, during the interview, moved his hands so fast as he talked that they were a blur of cuts, burns, and scars. He caught me staring, and laid his hands open before me, two masses of broad, shining meat. They were beautiful, fascinating. I wanted a pair just like them.

"Fryer burns," he said, running a long finger over his red-speckled wrist. "You don't even feel those at first." One puckered welt deep in the meat below his thumb. "Shucking oysters." He is missing the tip of one finger. "You know how your food processor at home won't turn on unless the top is on? Don't try this at work," he told me.

"What happened here?" I asked, brushing the pads of his left-hand fingers.

"When I worked in France," he told me, his voice calm and steady, "my chef would hold my finger in the flame when I made a mistake."

"Jesus Christ," I said, pulling my hand away. "Is that legal?"

He laughed, gave me a pitying look.

"I sometimes have trouble with carpal tunnel," I told him, whether to level the playing field or caution him before he hired me, I don't know.

"For the first hour after I wake up, I can't feel my hands at all. They're cramped into claws, totally numb. If you care, you work through the pain," he told me, staring into my eyes.

"Okay," I said, wondering what the fuck I was doing there.

From behind me, Anne, the sous-chef, said quietly, "I know some good stretches you should do before prep every day. You're gonna cut yourself, probably a lot. Just keep them clean, keep them covered. You'll be okay."

I remembered this when, three days later, I found myself stripping off a latex glove filled with my blood every fifteen minutes, replacing it with a clean one before it could drip on the artichokes I was cleaning. A finger condom is more convenient, but this wound was clean across my palm, no way to bandage it without going through a box of Band-Aids each time I shucked an oyster or cored a tomato.

I fell in love with Anne over a tube of Silverdene. "I got this from my doctor. It's the best burn cream in the world," she told me, holding my jerking hand still as she rubbed it in. "It's poisonous, but it'll help it heal." My first day on the hot line, 115 degrees in the kitchen. Too many days of grabbing lettuce, vinegar, chopped parsley, and I forgot the second rule of the kitchen: All pans are hot. Even if they're on the clean rack, they might have just come from the furnace of the dishwasher. Even if you know it's been in the walk-in for a week, it is hot. Don't touch it without a towel. Her face was tomato-red, framed by ringlets that escaped from her blue bandana. Her hair glowed like sunlight strained through a honey bear stored on a windowsill; mine hung like a heap of limp, dirty carrot peels, ready for the compost heap. A drop of sweat fell from her chin onto my hand, and I sensed its coolness before she wiped it away with her side towel. Like a nurse, she bandaged and gloved me. I watched her hands, gentle and strong, in a daze, staring at a full blister on her knuckle. I wanted to kiss it and make it better.

"Are you okay?" she asked me. There was a tear in my eye, but it was from the sting of sweat.

"Yeah. Thanks," I told her.

"Then fire me five scallop apps," she said, turning back to the wall of tickets that had accumulated as she took care of me.

"Five scallop apps," I repeated back, reaching my gloved hand into a bowl full of raw, off-white flesh. I'll never wash this hand again, I thought.

She eased her way into my heart with her touch. When you like someone that way, it's a mix of wondering whether you want her, or you want to be her. Classic teacher-student fixation, I thought, watching her reach up into the blazing salamander and imagining her in a black leather corset, bent over me with a ruler as I pull up my Catholic schoolgirl's plaid skirt to bare my ass. "Mmm, that smells so good," she told me as I stripped rosemary needles from their branches and chopped them fine. That phrase followed me for days.

When I drag my aching body home at night, she is there. She asks about my day as she squeezes my twitching feet, hard, between her strong hands, then kisses my forehead and runs my bath. She moves so quickly that I hardly see her as she dashes around the apartment, whisking up dust bunnies as she goes, fulfilling my every need. While I soak, she cooks for me. Not restaurant food, but French toast, crisp at the edges, napped with butter and syrup. Spaghetti carbonara, studded with bacon chunks, slips down my throat, lubricated by cream. The skin of her roast chicken crackles between my teeth and her apple brown betty lies lightly in my stomach, the memory of the cinnamon still teasing my palate as she takes my hand and leads me to bed, where her disembodied fingers soothe me into sleep.

In the morning, I don't dare to open my eyes, afraid to disturb the illusion that she is there, waking me with soft kisses, stretching my sore limbs, loving me beyond morning breath and rumpled hair. She is there in the shower, soaping my limbs, looking over my shoulder in the mirror as I study my face, acne like a fourteen-year-old, sprung up by the layer of grease that coats me day after day. Her skin, of course, glows like a newborn's. She walks me to work, holds my hand, murmurs comforting things. You'll be okay today. You won't burn anything, I promise.

As I step into the kitchen, I trade the ghost Anne for the real one, less perfect, perhaps, but flesh and blood. This Anne can flip a fourteen-inch sauté pan full of onions with a flick of her wrist. She can whip a just-presented sole from a runner's hand, filet it with four swift motions, and send it back to the table still hot. She can nail medium-rare, the most elusive of all temperatures, on the grill every time. She can taste, down to the molecular level, how much wasabi I have put in the avocado mousse, and how much more it needs. She knows how many new potatoes are in the walk-in, how many lamb chops will be ordered tonight, how many days it will be until the new pastry chef quits. God, how I want her.

There are two places to change in the restaurant, one less appealing than the next. A tiny, smelly bathroom, toilet and sink so close that I smash my knee every time I stand up, bang my hand on the light fixture when I stretch my arm up to pull on my chef's jacket. When I come into work, though, this is the only choice, since the other alternative is the locker area, across from the prep table. This is the domain of our two Mexican prep cooks, and it is an unwritten rule that women don't change there. At the end of the shift, though, it's another story. We, the cooks, are so sweaty and food-reeking that we begin to strip as we walk down the stairs. No one is a sexual being at that point, but just another hunk of meat like the ones we've been grilling all night, and, after the first few peeks at his boxers or her running bra, the thrill is gone. Anne stays late to do inventory, and by the time we're all gathered by the bar, making our one on-the-house drink last as long as possible before bending our creaky knees to go out into the real world, she breezes out in hose and heels, a low-cut blouse, the works. How she can do this every night shocks me, until I meet her boyfriend, a slick, older banker, who kisses her neck and helps her into his Mercedes. I look down at my filthy jeans, ripped tank top, and think about the smell of that white neck, its workday scent of turmeric and lamb shank, now scrubbed and perfumed just for him.

"Hey, can you do me a favor?" she asks one Saturday. Ride a Greyhound bus to Albuquerque? Lick the Friolator clean? Give Raoul the dishwasher a pedicure? Yes. Yes, I will.

"Sure."

"Can you do prep for a party tomorrow? I'll be working

brunch, but you can set up downstairs and I'll come and help when I can."

"No problem."

The kitchen is a blur as I step in the next morning. "Oh, thank god, can you do twenty salmon plates for me right now?" Anne asks me.

"Of course," I tell her, grabbing a package of sliced smoked salmon and maneuvering a stack of twenty plates down the stairs. Still in my street clothes, cutoffs, and a T-shirt, I wash my hands and lay out the plates, tiling each one with thin slices of fish, then wrapping it tight with plastic wrap.

A few minutes later, she runs down the stairs. "False alarm. I had a table of ten order salmon, then change to granola. Psychos."

"No problem. I'll just get changed and start prepping."

"Cool." She unsnaps her shirt, then pulls a clean one from the pile of linens near the lockers. She is the only cook who wears dishwasher shirts, the kind with the wide notched collar and snaps up the front, like Mel on *Alice*, a diner-cook shirt. She's confident enough in her position to look like a dishwasher, while I am still new enough that I struggle into a long-sleeved chef coat even on the hottest days. Oh god. Under the shirt she is wearing only a white cotton tank top. Her breasts are bigger than I had imagined, pressing out against the whisper-thin fabric, pushing up from the *U* of the neck hole. I want to kiss the sweat marks on her belly.

"Have you ever done salmon roses?" she asks me. I blink, thinking she's talking about a drug, a sex position, then look down at the plates I've been making.

"I don't think so," I tell her.

"I'll show you. We need a hundred and fifty for tonight." Her quick fingers lift a strip of salmon from the waxed paper, roll and twist it until it is a perfect . . . something. A mass of curved petals, pink and fishy. I can't help it—I laugh out loud.

"What?" she asks, smiling.

"It looks like . . . you know."

"I don't get it. What?"

"Well, what's the opposite of phallic? Vulvar?" She looks down and gets it. I blush, she laughs and snaps on a clean shirt, and I follow her up the stairs with my eyes. I tackle the fish, trying not to think about how fast those fingers moved, what swift, competent things they could do between my legs. Five minutes later, with three little floral salmon pussies to show for myself, I realize that if I don't jerk off right now, I will explode.

The sweat on my forehead evaporates as soon as I step into the walk-in refrigerator, but the heat inside my brain keeps circulating as the cold air perks my nipples hard. I push a crate of avocados in front of the door. Three dead bass loll in a bin of ice on a low shelf, and I throw a towel over their heads to protect their innocent, staring eyes from what I'm about to do with one of their cousins. Knowing that she is upstairs coddling eggs, warming scones, watching lumps of butter melt in her smoking sauté pan is all the more exciting. When will she run out of goat cheese, and sprint downstairs into my arms?

I slip out of my hound's-tooth cook's pants, leaving my clogs on to protect my feet from the cold, and slide the wax-wrapped salmon out of my pocket. The bands of flesh form perfect parallel *V*s on each slice. *V* for vulva. I turn it over so that it's no longer a *V*, but an arch. I imagine a clit, tucked inside a pink hood, curve the fish so that it looks like one. I stick out my tongue, tasting dill and smoke and salt at the tip, tasting nothing at the back and sides, teasing myself with the flavor. I take a strip into my mouth, pulling it in and out. Needing animation, reciprocation, I curl the fish around my finger and move it in and out of my mouth like a pointed, muscular tongue, increasing the suction with each thrust. Letting the fish slide into my cheek, I keep it there, like a chipmunk storing food for winter. I open my jacket, unhook my bra. I pull off two small slices and gather them around my puckered nipples, feeling their stiffness through the yielding fibers. The oil from the fish glistens, contrasting the bold pink of the salmon with the pale pink of my nipple, as I twist and pull, letting the fish become her soft, insistent lips. Friction makes the flesh flake apart, and I give up, wrap a strip around my right nipple tight, like a fishy nipple clamp, pinching to make it stay.

The last slice slips into my panties like it was spawned at last, found its true home. I slide it between my lips, feel the shock of cold meat, the chafe and wonder of the feeling. I let it warm until I can barely tell the difference between it and me, and close my labia around it, let it become part of my anatomy. I fold and pinch a strip around my clit, making a perfect rose. I dream of her arms and legs wrapped around me, and work my clit with her tongue of fish, rubbing back and forth and in circles, pushing back hard against my fingers, as if I'm pressing her mouth down on my wet pussy, forcing her to eat me, to lick out every drop of juice.

Winding a strip of fish around two fingers, I find my hungry hole at last, tease it with my fingertips. How clever she would be, opening me slowly, her slim fingers joining together to spread and stretch my walls until, yes, there it is. My fingers are buried to the hilt, moving rhythmically, seeking the sweet spots inside my body. For a moment, my aching tendons resist, then I feel her hand clenched around my wrist, controlling the timing and pressure, bringing me to a slow, hard boil.

Another strip for my mouth. In between my teeth it's soft and yielding, and I bite down hard on the luxury of completely edible pussy. As my lips grow slicker, so does the fish, sauced by my juice, her cunt on my mouth, her mouth on my cunt. Her fishy tongue licks and slurps, her fishy fingers fuck me deep. Ghost Anne whispers in my ear, and I come, choking down the flesh in my mouth, feeling her slide down my throat and into my stomach.

Slick and glossy, spent and used, I toss the rest of the salmon in the trash. The warmth of the basement brings down my goose bumps, embraces me back into reality. The spell is broken. I'll never get to have her. But I can taste her whenever I want.

I wash my hands like a surgeon, scrubbing each knuckle joint, each cuticle clean. The hot water brings up the scars, sets them in relief to the whiteness of my skin. The fish smell remains, but what do you expect?

"I had no idea you were such a pervert," she whispers to me, later, as I top each hors d'oeuvre with a squeeze bottle full of scallion mayonnaise. I freeze for a second, then realize. She doesn't know. How could she know? I smile back at her, then squirt another dollop of mayo, missing the salmon completely.

A Guest!
from *The Portable Promised Land*

touré

A knock on the door. A surprise visit. A beautiful girl! A Friday night. A wee hour. A quiet hello. A long hug. A tight sweater. A black leather boot. A lace up the seam. A seat on the couch. A record by Miles. A joke. A laugh. A glass of red. A joint. A pass. A puff. A laugh. A listen. A sharing. A Scrabble game. A war on a word. A begging to differ. A laugh. A sweet nothing. A tight shoulder. A slow massage. A Marvin song. A spellbinding bassline. A spontaneous dance. A Polaroid camera. A posed smile. A silly frown. A tackle. A tickle. A laugh. A stolen kiss. A Prince song. A nasty bassline. A close dance. A slow dance. A lot of friction. A nasty flattery. A mischievous hand. A bare thigh. A slap of the hand. A recent memory. A Friday afternoon. A boyfriend. A raised tone. A thoughtless word. A diss on a Moms! A heavy tear. A No-I-didn't-mean-it. A big fight. A gargantuan fight. A storming out. A long walk.

A Prince song. A room dark. A slow dance. A lust affliction. A stolen kiss. A dangerous look. A slow kiss. A quarter of wet lips. A feathery touch. A deeper kiss. A chipping of teeth! A hasty retreat. A sorry of two. A real kiss. A kiss that could kill.

A rush of kisses. A torrent of kisses. A monsoon of kisses. A mouth going south. A stop on the neck. A stop on the chest. A graze of a breast. A bungee-ing heart. A tackle. A tickle. A made bed. A messy bed. A lost shirt. A tossed bra. A mingling of lips. A tumble of tongues. A collage of bodies. A mélange of limbs. A dominant gesture. A submissive reply. A boy on his knees. A bitch in her boots. A blindfolding. A boot licking. A long spanking. A nipple ringing. A bearable pain. A growing pain. A burning! A burning! A screaming of mercy! A catching of breath. A boy on all fours. A bitch in her boots. A brown eye. A lube job. A finger. A trio. A hand. A fist. A thrust. A fist! A thrust! A squeal like a bitch!

A pause. A talk. A laugh. A mingling of lips. A tumble of tongues. A collage of bodies. A mélange of limbs. A cyclone of passion. A mouth going south. A breast. A belly. A bush. A box. A dive. A curious tongue. A located clit. A vacuuming mouth. A pant. A pant. A louder pant. A tongue. A tongue. A faster tongue. A scream. A scream. A falsetto scream!

A catching of breath. A catching of breath. A shared cigarette. A slow drag. A happy two.

A sound on the steps. A sound on the steps! A sound at the door. A key in the lock. A whine of a hinge. A snatch of a robe. A rush to the door. A roommate's return. A slick Casanova. A smile that's wry. A strut in the room. A short hello. A loss of a shirt. A zipper undone. A giant schlong! A mountainous dong! A losing of breath. A girl on the floor. A soaking punany. A schlong in her crotch. A boy in a chair. A thunderclap thrust. A masculine groan. A falsetto scream! A crash of a crotch. A masculine groan. A falsetto scream! A double explosion! A catching of breath. A catching of breath. A boy in a chair. A walk cross the room. A hand on a chest. A kiss of the boys. A mingling of lips. A tumble of tongues. A head on a schlong. A tender embrace. A hug of a three. A thought of a thing. A throb of a three. A girl on her back: A schlong in her snatch: A dick in his ass. A movement of frames. A body aligned. A groove of three. A falsetto scream. A masculine groan. An unending ooohh! A groove of three. A falsetto scream. A masculine groan. An unending ooohh! A groove. A groove. A very hard groove. A chain of explosions. A fall on the bed. A catching of breath. A catching of breath. A shared cigarette.

A rest.

A piss.

A breeze.

A joint. A puff. A pass.

A ring. A ring. A very close friend. A very wee hour. A rare situation. A short discussion. A dash down the street. A spring up the stairs. A knock at the door. A striking couple. A coquettish Lolita. A sly Lothario. A quick introduction. A peeling of clothes. A dive in of five, a symphonic congress, a blizzard of thrusts, a tsunami of sex: a kiss, a lick, a jerk, a smack, a hickey, a grab, a grope, a schlong, a nipple, a foot, a cock, a cunt, a clit, a tit, a tush, a toe, a tongue, a twat, a rimming, a reaming, a frightening velocity: a Caligula scene: a falsetto scream!, a masculine grunt, an unending ooohh!, a chirp of a finch, a suck-in of breath, a falsetto scream!, a masculine grunt, an unending ooohh!, a chirp of a finch, a suck-in of breath. A Goddamn G'Lord! A fucking fantasia. A bliss. A bliss. A frenzied bliss. A jism. A jism. A fountain of jism. A climax. A climax. A climax that's final.

A catching of breath.

A shared cigarette.

A slow rising sun.

A pretzeling in bed.

A catching of breath.

A catching of breath.

The Audit

dominic santi

It's not easy being an auditor. Everyone hates the IRS. Even I hate the IRS, and I work here. But I especially hate my boss, Lyle L. Lipton. He's one of those idiot managers whose "subordinates" send his memos to the guy who writes *Dilbert*.

L-Cubed was still ticked at me for winning the Superbowl pool the week after I transferred in from Omaha. That, along with what he sarcastically referred to as my "impeccable performance record," put me on top of his shit list. So, when the decision was made to audit The Lady again, I suppose I shouldn't have been surprised when old Lyle made a beeline for my desk. I looked up to see him smiling down with payback in his eyes and a large expand-a-file manila folder in his hands: "Gerald Randolph St. Michaels III." He dropped his present on my desk, said, "Tuesday, ten," and sashayed back into his glass-walled domain.

I felt the blood drain from my face. Gerald Randolph St. Michaels III. I'd heard the stories. He, or rather, *she*, was officially self-employed as an escort service. I'd even seen her business cards:

MISTRESS SHEILA, DOMINATRIX
ACCEPTING BOTH EXPERIENCED AND NOVICE SUBMISSIVES.
WILL TRAIN TO SUIT.

St. Michaels was the most beautiful drag queen in all New Charleston. And her reputation, well, let's just say it preceded her. Even a newbie like me knew that our entire department quaked in their boots at the sound of Mistress Sheila's name. No one had ever audited her more than once. The veterans either came back to the office terrified, or they disqualified themselves from future audits because of what they called "conflict of interest." I wasn't sure what that meant around here. I didn't think I wanted to know. I opened the file and started to read, wondering in the back of my mind if I could go into business with my brother, grooming cats.

Tuesday morning came all too soon. I was nervous about meeting Mistress Sheila, but I'd been pretty surprised by her file. Everything seemed in order—straightforward, no previous penalties. There was nothing to indicate why they'd audited her every one of the past fifteen years. I had the feeling that fact alone wasn't going to predispose her to liking me.

I wore my usual gray flannel power suit, though, this time, I added my Looney Tunes silk tie. Maybe not in the best of taste from old Lyle's perspective, but I already had an inkling that the audit was going to go in Mistress Sheila's favor. I figured I'd at least try to take the edge off of what had probably become a major annoyance.

Her home was a large Tudor mansion, set well back from the road on a walled, wooded property. My Honda Accord looked totally out of place. This was a driveway meant for

Rolls-Royces and limousines, both of which would have been well within the means of her reported income if she'd decided to have them. I parked at the end of the white gravel drive at 9:55 and let the smell of roses waft in through the open window while I admired the intricate stonework on the main building.

At exactly 10:00 A.M., I squared my shoulders, walked up the path to the carved mahogany door, and rapped on the brass knocker. Then I stepped back and waited for a servant to answer.

Mistress Sheila opened the door herself. She caught me completely off guard. Not that I'm interested in chicks, but this man was the most beautiful *lady* I'd ever seen. Her wavy brown hair cascaded over her shoulders. Her full red lips looked naturally soft and wet. She was wearing a red leather miniskirt—smooth and flat and rounded in what I assumed were all the right places for a woman. Her black silk blouse showed real cleavage where the curves of her skin disappeared into the rise and fall of the tight red vest. The supple lambskin seemed to breathe with her. Even the bejeweled collar that covered her Adam's apple was made of the same flowing red leather. I squirmed, shocked to feel my dick jump when she swallowed.

It was a total mind fuck. Visually, my mind was recording her as female. But her scent was masculine, like when you kiss a lover's balls in the shower and he still smells and tastes like himself, even over the scents of the soap and shampoo.

Mistress Sheila's lips framed the ghost of a smile. I looked into her velvety brown eyes, and I completely forgot everything I'd been going to say. I just stared at her, completely smitten.

It took me a minute to realize I was being rude. I shook my head and stammered out, "Ah, Mr. G-Gerald Randolph S-St. Michaels? The Third?"

One sculpted eyebrow shot up, but she just stood there, resting her fingers on the ornate doorknob, watching me while I wiped my hand on my pant leg. She glanced down and I blushed as I realized she was looking at my tie. Her lipstick shimmered, like she was trying not to smile.

I licked my lips and tried again. "Excuse me, um, Mr. St. Michaels?"

This time the eyebrow flicked up a bit more sharply. Her fingernail tapped on the doorknob, but right about then I figured out what I was doing wrong. The sweat trickled down the back of my neck. I cleared my throat and said, as politely and courteously as I possibly could, "Excuse me. Mistress Sheila, Ma'am? I'm Albert Smith, from the IRS."

I was rewarded with a smile.

"Good morning, Mr. Smith."

Her low, husky voice reverberated against my ears. My whole body relaxed in relief. She held out her hand to me. Without thinking, I lifted the delicate offering to my lips and kissed her smooth white skin. "Pleased to meet you, Ma'am."

This time, the smile went all the way to her eyes. "I'm very pleased to meet you, young man. Come inside." With that, her grip tightened, and she pulled me gently but very firmly out of the warm sunshine and into the cool shadows of her house.

Mistress Sheila was considerably taller than I. She would have been, I realized, even without the three-inch heels on her black leather boots. I tried to convince myself that her height was the reason I kept looking at her legs. And why my cock was swelling. I liked tall men. I liked the way her silk stockings curved into her knee-length boots. I especially liked how her long brown curls reached almost to where the soft red lambskin clung to her lean, narrow hips.

I also liked my job, or at least my paycheck. I concentrated on being professional, getting myself pretty much back under control while we walked. My nose still twitched as we entered her study. The room smelled of warm leather and books. I appreciate good taste, and Mistress Sheila's private domain was exquisitely appointed. I had no doubt the Picasso over the desk was authentic.

"Would you like something to drink, Mr. Smith?"

Two crystal goblets rested on the conference table. Mistress Sheila took one and motioned me to take the other. Needless to say, that's not the way I'm accustomed to being treated during an audit. I lifted the glass to my lips. It was raspberry lemonade, my all-time favorite. I tried not to gulp as I drained my glass.

"Thank you, Ma'am," I said, setting my goblet back down. "That was delicious."

The sweet-sour taste lingered on my tongue. Trying not to think about sex always makes me thirsty. When I licked my lips, Mistress Sheila laughed and waved me toward a small serving cart near the window.

"Help yourself, Mr. Smith. We have a great deal of work to do, and I'd prefer that you be comfortable."

I poured myself another drink. As I set the pitcher back down, I looked at her glass and noticed it was only half full. My hand froze in midair.

"May I refill your glass for you, Ma'am?" I asked politely.

Mistress seemed immensely pleased with my request. Nodding slightly, she held out her glass to me. Her red nails curved sensuously around the crystal. I was surprised to see my hand shaking as I poured the pulpy pink liquid into the sparkling glass. Her warm strong fingers closed firmly around mine. Her touch was electric.

"Sit down, Mr. Smith, and take off your jacket. It's going to be a long day."

The audit was over at 1:00. It was apparent right from the start who was running the proceedings, and Mistress Sheila was very efficient. I said, "Yes, Ma'am," and "No, Ma'am," handing her the appropriate receipts and records when she demanded them. Not that some of the deductions weren't a bit out of the ordinary: whips, vibrators, leather restraints. But the supporting paperwork couldn't have been more perfect than if somebody from my office had prepared her statements for her.

I was careful to put everything back in the order I found it. In fact, I only made one mistake. Everything was going so smoothly that as the sun moved across the table around noontime, I started getting sleepy.

"Mr. Smith!" Mistress Sheila's voice cracked through the quiet of the study.

"Ma'am?" I jolted upright, confused and suddenly very awake. Mistress Sheila picked up her little wooden ruler and pointed to where I had accidentally put an envelope on the wrong pile. I realized my mistake.

"I'm sorry, Ma'am." I moved the offending item back into its proper place.

"As well you should be," she snapped. "Give me your hand."

Without thinking, I did. She took my wrist. The next thing I knew, I was yelping as she stung my palm a half dozen times with her ruler. Then Mistress lectured me sternly for a good five minutes about the importance of keeping accurate records. Usually I'm the one giving that speech during an audit. This time I sat there, opening and closing my burning hand and nodding profusely while I promised not to make the same mistake again. I was mortified—more at my unprofessional behavior than at what she'd done. After that, I paid close attention to what I was doing. And I kept her glass filled with raspberry lemonade.

I also found myself watching her a lot out of the corner of my eye. Mistress Sheila fascinated me. As the sting faded from my hand, I realized my fingers were itching to touch her hair. I could feel myself sliding into a fantasy as I thought about brushing those silken strands into a thick curl and running that curl slowly over her cleavage . . .

I shook myself awake. Yeah, right—me and cleavage. That was certainly enough to wake me up! I put my pen down and leaned way back into the comfortable leather of my chair.

"I don't understand, Ma'am." I stretched my arms high over my head. "With everything in order like this, why do they audit you every year?"

Her laughter was followed by a wry grin. I lowered my arms, watching the leather band move across her throat again.

"You seem a bright young man, Mr. Smith. Perhaps if you reconsider my profession, you'll be able to figure it out."

Of course by then, I had. "I'm sorry, Ma'am," I blushed. "I forgot."

"Oh, did you!"

This time the laughter was different, full-throated, but huskier—definitely a man's laugh. I felt my balls tingle at it. And of course I was blushing again.

But before I could stammer out any kind of a reply, an elderly man in a black suit walked through the open door and announced that luncheon would be served in forty-five minutes.

I sat up quickly and started gathering papers. "I should be going, Ma'am. Thank you so much for your time. I apologize on behalf of the IRS for any inconvenience this audit may have caused you."

"I'm inviting you to stay for lunch, Mr. Smith." Her statement was more along the line of a command. I stared at her in surprise. Nobody invites an auditor to lunch!

"I, ah, really shouldn't, Ma'am." I was trying to bring order to my now rather sizable mess, but through the open door I suddenly smelled Italian spices and some sort of garlic

sauce cooking. My stomach growled loudly. I flushed to my
hairline.

Mistress Sheila laughed again. My cock twitched against
my underwear, and this time, it kept swelling. I was getting so
hard I was going to have to resituate myself soon, and I didn't
want to do that in her presence. I was sure she'd notice—and
most assuredly take offense. It was a losing battle.

"But you *are* hungry." Her voice slid over my ear. My
stomach growled again, this time more loudly.

I opened my mouth, thinking I should insist on going.
Then I looked into her eyes. They were twinkling, the warm
brown sparkle sending a shiver crawling all the way up my
spine. All I could do was let my papers fall to the table as I
gave up on trying to control both my stomach and my errant
cock.

"Yes, Ma'am." I smiled helplessly back at her.

She nodded. I felt like I was basking in her warmth. I
jumped when she turned abruptly to the servant and said,
"Leave us, Charles. Close the door behind you."

As soon as I accepted Mistress Sheila's invitation, Charles
broke into a wide grin. As the door clicked shut, I found out
why. Mistress looked me up and down once, quickly. Then
she snapped, "Stand up, Mr. Smith. Now!"

Surprised, I stumbled to my feet, tripping on the table leg
in my hurry. Her hand moved to her lips, like she was trying
to hide a smile again, but I was so embarrassed I couldn't tell
for sure. When I'd righted myself, she walked over to stand in
back of me. She put her hand firmly on my shoulder, purring
right in my ear, "I like a man who responds quickly."

I hoped she couldn't see how quickly the rest of me was
responding. Her voice slid over my skin, pulling the blood
straight down from my brain. I moved my hands in front of
my crotch, so she wouldn't see how hard I was getting. I
gasped as she dragged one of her long, sharp fingernails

slowly over the curve of my butt. I knew right then I was going to have to untangle my cock or do real damage to myself—I just don't bend that way.

"Um, Ma'am." I tried to keep my voice steady. "I need to excuse myself for a minute . . ."

My breath caught when her hand gripped my butt cheek. "No, Mr. Smith, you don't. You will take your clothes off right here."

I jumped as she smacked me, hard, connecting full on my butt just before her palm started rubbing away the sting.

"Ma'am?" I tried to turn back toward her, shocked. My backside tingled more than hurt, although my cock certainly didn't have any complaints about the stimulation.

The next swat wasn't so gentle. "You heard me, Mr. Smith. Everything but your underwear. Off!" SMACK! "Now!"

The last one really stung. I didn't wait around to think any more. I said, "Yes, Ma'am!" as I yanked my tie loose and over my head. Then I stripped off my shoes and socks and shirt, and undid my belt and the front of trousers. As my pants dropped, I reached into my shorts and untangled my poor cock from where it was caught in my fly. The sudden freedom was such a relief that for a second, I closed my eyes, rubbing myself. Then my eyes flew open and I looked up, mortified, to realize I was standing in front of Mistress Sheila, wearing only my boxers, holding my cock in my hand.

"Excuse me, Ma'am . . ." I choked, trying to step out of my pants without tripping. I was so embarrassed I could feel the heat flushing across my face.

Before I could stammer out an apology, though, Mistress Sheila started to laugh. In fact, she was laughing so hard she put her hand to the corner of her eye to keep her mascara from running. And as I followed her gaze, I remembered what else I was wearing.

"Looney Tunes, Mr. Smith?" she gasped. "You are wearing

Looney Tunes boxers to an IRS audit?" She leaned against the table, laughing so hard I was afraid she was going to choke.

"Yes, Ma'am," I said sheepishly, trying not to blush or smile and failing miserably at both. Unfortunately, neither reaction was making my cock one iota less hard. "It sort of goes with my job, Ma'am. I didn't think anybody would see them, and I like the way they let me breathe and all."

"I see," she said, carefully wiping the tears from the edges of her eyes. She took a deep breath and reached over to cup the front of my crotch. "You do have quite a handful here to let breathe."

"Oh, Ma'am . . ." I moaned, leaning into her touch. I was already leaking so badly the silk felt cool on my hot skin. Odd little mewls escaped from my throat as her fingers squeezed and stroked my cock and balls. She looked like a lady, but the strength and the touch of her hands were all man. I shivered when she pressed another drop from the head of my dick into what I knew was the general vicinity of Bugs Bunny's fur.

"You understand, Mr. Smith, that before we do anything else, we must first take care of the little matter of my displeasure with your employer, whom you represent."

"Yes, Ma'am," I whispered. I wasn't paying much attention to what she said. Her hands were caressing me, her long nails snaking up the open leg of my boxers to scratch delicately over my balls, her fingers reaching through my tenting fly to tickle up the underside of my shaft. My cock jumped at her touch, leaking as she teased the precome from me.

She led me, unresisting, over to the straight-backed chair near the bookcase. With her free hand, she pulled the chair well away from the wall. Then she sat down and drew me to her side. Her hands were stroking me again, one hand rubbing over my tingly bottom, the other open palm moving in large sweeps up and down my crotch. The sounds coming from my throat got louder with each stroke.

"You understand that your employer has taken up a good deal of my valuable time."

"Yes, Ma'am." I arched forward into her hands. Without thinking, I reached out for balance and rested my hand on her luxurious hair. It was silky soft. She shivered as my fingers caressed her scalp.

"You're a very polite young man, Mr. Smith."

Her voice vibrated in my spine. It was difficult to think with her hands touching me.

"Thank you, Ma'am," I whispered.

"You understand that I shall be taking you to task for the actions of your not-so-nice employer."

"Yes, Ma'am. Whatever you say."

I had no idea what she was talking about. All I noticed were her hands and her hair, and the smell of her perfume and the mansweat in her leather clothes. My balls tingled so much I could almost feel the sperm wiggling their way toward my dick.

With no warning, she tipped me over her lap. One second I was standing at her side, the next I was hanging facedown over her knees, my cock pressed firmly into her thigh, my bottom up in the air, and Mistress Sheila's hand resting firmly on my cartoon-clad posterior. Her hand smacked sharply over my right cheek.

"Ouch!" I lurched up in surprise.

She rubbed her hand firmly over the tingle. "Pay attention, Mr. Smith."

"Yes, Ma'am!" I nodded vigorously. I was trying to concentrate on what she was saying. But in spite of my precarious position, I was totally distracted by the friction of my cock rubbing against her leg.

"For the past fifteen years, your employer has wasted my time with these ridiculous audits. A minimum of three hours every year for fifteen years! That's a total of at least forty-five hours of my valuable time!" She emphasized her displeasure with another sharp smack. "Do you understand that, Mr. Smith?"

"Ow! Yes, Ma'am!"

That firm hand was starting to worry me. I could still feel the sting from the last couple of swats, although my cock was telling me rather loudly not to pay attention. But Mistress definitely sounded annoyed. I wiggled my pelvis against her skirt, sighing as the dampness of my boxers warmed against my skin.

"Fifteen years, Mr. Smith," she said again, although this time I thought I detected a bit of humor in her voice. "And this year, they send me a polite young man with a Looney Tunes tie and boxers." She smacked me again, not terribly hard, but enough to emphasize her point.

Then her hand rubbed over my bottom. "Mr. Smith," her voice held the husky sex of her amusement, "because you are such a likable young man, I will give you a choice. You may either remain over my lap and let me exact my standard retribution from your department—in this instance, forty-five sound smacks from my hairbrush, during which time I will also attend most properly to that excited young cock of yours. Or you may leave—immediately—and never return. The decision is yours."

"Ma'am?" I asked, lifting my weight up onto my hands. I couldn't quite believe my ears. "You want to spank me?!" Nobody had ever really spanked me before, not even my parents.

"Yes, Mr. Smith," she laughed. "I intend to spank your round little bottom until it positively glows."

The idea made my cock twitch, but I was still a little concerned. Her earlier swats had stung and forty-five seemed like an awful lot. "Or I have to leave?" I asked.

"Yes, Mr. Smith, unfortunately with that beautiful young

cock of yours still unsatisfied and drooling into your now very wet boxers."

I blushed at that. I really leak when I'm turned on, though I wasn't sure I'd ever been this hot before in my life. Her hand was rubbing the sensitive crease where my butt met my thighs. I pressed my hips forward, wriggling my cock against her.

"But I don't want to leave, Ma'am." I whispered. Nervous or not, I knew I was horny.

"Then you are willing to take the correction for your department?" Her fingers gripped my butt cheeks firmly, emphasizing just exactly where that correction would be administered.

"Um, I guess so," I whispered, arching my butt back into her hand, feeling my cock slide back over her skirt.

Her hand stilled. "Yes or no, Mr. Smith." She swatted me again, this time sternly enough to get my attention. "A spanking from me is serious business. You either consent or you do not."

For a minute, I hesitated. Out of the corner of my eye, I could see the hairbrush resting on the edge of the bookcase. The brush was dark—cherrywood, maybe—and highly polished with a long handle. The oval-shaped business end looked thick and sturdy enough to be pretty intimidating. In spite of what my dick was telling me, for a moment, I seriously thought of leaving. After all, it was still working hours. I was a professional.

That's when I realized I wanted to please Mistress Sheila— and myself—not old L-Cubed. I didn't care if I got fired. Summoning all my courage, I squared my shoulders as much as I could upside-down and said, "I, um, consent, Ma'am."

I took a deep breath, letting myself sag forward across her lap. I was surprised to discover I was more than a little bit scared. I leaned my face against her leather-clad ankle. Her hand rubbed over my bottom, teasing me until my skin seemed to reach back for her hand. Then I felt the hard wooden surface of the hairbrush rubbing against the warm silk of my boxers. I shivered.

"Count them, Mr. Smith. In groups of fifteen." Her voice was deep and reassuring.

"Yes, Ma'am." At the first smack, I jerked up, startled. "Ouch!"

That stung! But after a minute, I realized the swat had made my skin tingle more than hurt. I figured that meant the spanking wasn't going to be all that bad.

"One," I said, relieved, and lay back down over her lap.

By fifteen, it was hard to stay cooperative. I tried, I really did. But I was glad that her other hand was planted firmly in the small of my back, holding me down. I fought to hold back the tears. My bottom hurt so badly, it burned! And for some embarrassing reason, my cock was harder than ever.

She stopped and started playing with my stinging cheeks, rubbing and touching. After the pain of the spanking, her hands felt good. When I'd caught my breath, she stood me back up. The front of my boxers tented out in front of me.

Then she did the most amazing thing. She pressed the brush into my hand and said, "My hair, Mr. Smith. It needs attention."

I'd been lusting after her hair since I walked in the door. I couldn't believe she was giving me permission to touch it now. Tentatively, I stepped in back of her and ran my hands over her silky waves. They were so very feminine—soft and warm from the afternoon sun. I could smell the lingering rosemary of her shampoo. Yet as the faint dampness of her perspiration touched my fingertips, I caught a hint of something else—something that reminded me of the heavy scent of men playing basketball on a hot day. I picked up the brush and started pulling it in long gliding strokes through the luxurious fall of her hair. With each stroke I started at her scalp and ended with the soft tips curled around my fingers, working the sweaty male scent out from the roots to blend with the fragrance of the rosemary.

We stayed like that for a long time, the grandfather clock ticking by the window. My bottom was sore and hot, the damp silk cool where the precome wetness pressed against my throbbing cock. Just touching Mistress Sheila made me so hard my balls ached, yet at the same time, I didn't ever want to stop. After a while, she reached up and gently yet firmly started rubbing her thumbs against the insides of my wrists.

"That was exquisite, Mr. Smith," she said huskily.

She held out her hand. Without saying a word, I placed the handle of the hairbrush in her palm. I shivered as I did it. My bottom was really sore, and I knew if I just held onto that brush, she wouldn't be able to spank me again. But I didn't have the will to resist her.

She motioned me to her side. I jumped when her fingernail slowly scratched over the back of my shorts.

"Take them off, Mr. Smith. They're only getting in the way."

In spite of my trembling, my hands seemed to move on their own. I pulled my cock back from where the head had slipped through the fly and slid the damp silk over my hips. Then I stood naked in front of her, the afternoon breeze cooling my naked, burning butt cheeks.

"I'm sorry, Ma'am." I blushed, looking down at my cock. It jutted out at full mast.

"For what?" she laughed. Another pearl of precome seeped out of my slit in response to her voice. "Young man, this," my cock jumped at her touch, "is behaving exactly as it should. As are you."

I felt the frisson all the way up my spine. She used just the tip of her finger to smear the viscous fluid over my glans and down the shaft. Then, at the gentle tug of her hand, I was again lying over her lap. I moaned out loud, beyond embarrassment as my cock slid over the soft leather of her skirt. I barely felt her arm wrap around my waist.

The hairbrush smacked down hard on my left cheek. I yelped, my eyes flying open as I arched into her. The sting was a lot more intense on my bare skin, and she was spanking me much harder.

"Count, Mr. Smith," she said firmly.

"Sixteen," I groaned, shuddering at the rush of sensation where the swat had pressed me harder against her thigh.

Then she really started tanning me. I mean Mistress Sheila set my whole ass on fire. Each time she cracked that damn brush over my butt, my cock surged forward over her leather-clad thigh, getting hotter and fuller and so engorged I thought I'd burst. By the time she reached thirty, I was yelling and crying from the pain, and the only other thing registering in my brain was that one more stroke and I was going to come all over her leg.

The next thing I knew, she'd pushed me off her lap. I lay on the floor at her feet, trying to keep my poor sore butt from touching anything. She set the brush on the bookcase. Looking directly at me, she put her boot in my hand and said, "My feet, Mr. Smith. Attend to them."

My vision blurred with tears, I pulled off her boots and rolled down her silk stockings. With her leg lifted that close to my face, I could really smell her crotch. Her leather skirt held in the heavy aroma of her cock and balls. I can't begin to describe the effect that her male pheromones were having on my poor leaking cock. I massaged her feet, letting all my energies flow into each deep caress as I pressed the tension from her straining arches. I soothed my way up her smooth ankles and over the strong ligaments and tendons of her calves, then back down, milking each individual toe. Every so often she touched a polished toenail to my shaft and stroked. I closed my eyes at her touch, shivering as the precome oozed from my slit. It was exquisite.

The next thing I knew, she was drawing me back up to kneel beside her. She picked up the brush. Ignoring my incoherent cries, she carefully and deliberately scrubbed the bristles all over my blazing tender skin. I was still sniffling when she lifted the brush away.

"My lap, Mr. Smith." Her voice was quiet and firm.

It took me a minute to comply. I knew Mistress had said she'd take care of my cock, but my backside was burning so badly I really didn't know if I'd be able to hold myself still for the final fifteen. When she saw my hesitation, Mistress held out her hand to me. It seemed like I was watching myself in slow motion as I let her pull me back over that soft smooth leather and her hard, muscular thighs. She grabbed me firmly by my cock and balls.

"You needn't count the final fifteen, Mr. Smith. I very much doubt that you would be able to anyway."

"Yes, Ma'am," I whispered. "OW!"

The first smack was pure fire. Then Mistress Sheila rained molten flame on my butt. I cried and hollered, twisting and kicking my legs, straining to get away from the incredible pain. My ass hurt more than I could ever have believed possible. I tried to concentrate on just breathing, but even the air coming into my lungs felt hot. Every exhale came out as a yell. With each swat, Mistress spanked me so hard I felt the heat all the way through to my balls.

And with each searing crack of that hairbrush, she stroked my cock. I love the feel of a man's hand bringing me to orgasm. Mistress seemed to know just how to time her movements. I almost choked on my tears as her strong hand drew the boiling juices up into my shaft. I was beyond being able to control myself. As her husky voice purred "Forty-five," the final flame seared across my ass. I shot all over her leg. Even after she stopped spanking me, I kept rocking back and forth into her hand and the leather, sliding on my sweat and my come, my cock jerking like it would never stop.

At Mistress's direction, I didn't put my underwear back on when I dressed for lunch. I gingerly settled my poor blistered behind onto the hard wooden chair and fidgeted my way through three helpings of angel hair pasta and marinara sauce. I even had dessert—homemade spumoni ice cream so sweet and creamy that I only thought for a second about how nice it would feel on my scalded backside.

Over coffee, Mistress explained about L-Cubed and his campaign of audits. They'd had a run-in a while back, fifteen years ago, to be exact, when she'd refused to take on ol' Lyle as a client. So he'd set out to get his revenge. Even I had to smirk at that. He'd sure shown her who was boss!

Mistress Sheila said she knows she'll be audited again next year. My inability to sit still at work tomorrow will be duly noted. The wrath of Lyle L. Lipton will carry over into year sixteen, and I'll still be at the top of his shit list. However, I won't be doing the next audit. Since Mistress Sheila and I will be seeing each other rather frequently from now on, it would be a conflict of interest.

Girdle Boy

jerry stahl

So I'm like, six years old, home on a school day, faking a sore throat so that I can sit under the table during my mother's weekly bridge game. I'm under the table because I like looking up the ladies' dresses. Sometimes you can see hair. Mrs. Thuringer, the whitest, fattest, most enormous-breasted of my mother's foursome, shows more hair than anybody. Mrs. T, a dead ringer for Shelley Winters in her jumbo, blowzy phase, is open for business. Her big thighs pucker at the top, but shift every minute or so, as if their owner were sitting in something damp. When she shifts, she crosses and uncrosses her legs. That's when I glimpse the dark forest.

For entire minutes Mrs. Thuringer opens and closes those hefty thighs. It's almost like she knows I'm looking. Her hidden parts just fascinate me. Blond on top, her nether-thatch is a dirty brown, and reminds me of the stuffing in car seats. There are junked cars at the bottom of the hill behind my house, and when there's nothing else to do, I slash the interiors; the stuffing that pours out looks exactly like Mrs.

Thuringer's pubic hair. But more than the actual pubes, I love the shiny metal snaps that hang down from her girdle. I love the milky-white sheen of the girdle itself. I love the thick lip of flesh that forms where the girdle stops and the thighs start, the strangely musty-ripe smell that wafts like steam from under her dress. I want to warm my face in it. I want to crawl up and lick, and I don't even know why.

On TV, the Playtex girdle ads all talk about "midriff bulge." And I wonder, gazing at Mrs. Thuringer's ring of squeezed-out fat, if there's such a thing as "subriff" bulge, and if this is what I'm looking at. The problem is, I don't know where a woman's "riff" is, and don't know whom to ask.

I'm still mulling on this when, suddenly, the plump, skittish Mrs. Thuringer leaps out of her chair, startling the three identically beehived matrons around the card table. I poke my face between my mother's knees and peer up. Mrs. Thuringer is actually sweating. A sheen of perspiration coats her face, as if she'd dipped herself in sugar water and hadn't quite dried.

"If I don't relieve myself," she shrieks, "I am going to ruin Hilda's carpet!" She accompanies this announcement with a large spank on her own buttock. "I'm so packed in I may have to be buried this way!"

With this, she goes to work, groaning and tugging at the taut material. The sight of her curly hairs jutting from under her girdle as she claws away has my face burning. I feel like I'm watching a secret world, until my mother swings into action. "I could use a new shag," she snaps, "besides which, you said you had to pee twenty minutes ago, Dolly. And twenty minutes before that!"

"Well, it's not my fault, it's this damn girdle. It takes me an hour to squeeze my fat 'n' sassy into it, and two hours to squeeze it back out!"

Gasping with frustration, Mrs. Thuringer does a kind of hopping butt-dance away from the table. She raises her plum-colored Lane Bryant housedress and, unleashing a series of boar-like grunts, digs her thumbs in the girdle's elastic top and struggles mightily to hoist the snug appliance an inch or two south over her dimpled hips.

"Oh God, just kill me!" she cries after a few seconds, letting her eyes roll back in her head. "I give up!"

This performance brings all the ladies trundling over from the card table. "Here, let me help," says Sylvie, my mother's best friend, a tiny woman whose thyroid condition left her with bug eyes and the ability to inhale an entire box of chocolate turtles every day and not gain an ounce.

"Sylvie, you can't open a ketchup bottle," barks my thick-wristed mother. Mom worked in a canning factory as a girl and could still squeeze the juice out of a beet barehanded. "I'll do it!" she hollers.

Even my aunt Magda, who'd gone arthritic at thirty and could barely peel a banana, gets in on the act. "For God's sake, Dolly, let me!"

In that moment, though barely old enough to walk to school on my own, I find myself entranced, enraptured, engorged at the sight of a hefty lady's fur peeking out beneath the dirty white sausage-casing of her girdle. I can't see her actual labia, just that tangle, hanging down from her lips like Louisiana moss. On either side of that peeping bush, a bracelet of puffed-out white diamonds—flesh-divots formed by those metal snaps—circles the tops of her legs.

Before Sylvie spots me, wide-eyed and wiggling my pee-pee through my short pants, I get an eyeful of womanhood that scathes me to this day. My mother, Aunt Magda, and Sylvie, all on their knees, dig their fingernails under the top of Dolly Thuringer's Playtex girdle. At the same time, my aunt Magda, slightly emphysemic as well as arthritic, actually leans her forehead against Mrs. T's unnaturally flattened tummy, as though nuzzling it. It's all too much, and before I know what I'm doing, I ease over and press my face against that stretchy material. I take a deep breath of under-the-girdle lady-fumes and, feeling the room spin, keel over into the ropy arms of Thyroid Sylvie.

"Look at this one," she cackles, fondling my throbbing tickle-stick through my pants. "He's got a *pischer* the size of a niblet, and he's hard as a rock!"

Fast forward three decades and I'm in the bedroom of my Viennese girlfriend, herself something of a lingerie fetishist, by way of a career in fashion, staring at the most foul-looking, stained, wretchedly retro breast-high girdle apparatus I've ever seen. As if the color alone weren't enough: a yellow-tinged, dirty white that looks like it's been laundered in piss for fifty years, there's a flesh-tone tube extending out of the bottom, where she's literally scissored a pussy-hole in the crotch of what must surely be the world's oldest panty girdle. Below the tube, strapped to her thigh, is a plastic bag, half full of piss. I would of course be nauseated if I weren't so turned on.

Weird but true. The rubber tube and pussy-hole aren't exactly fetish items. Or not, at least, conceived as such. And that dangling piss bag—don't even ask. As it happens, Miss Vienna has had stomach surgery, repairing damage from a five-year-old cesarean. And this evil corset, along with its attendant accessories, is something the hospital gave her: her boudoir-wear for a week or two. But whatever the cause, here she is, bagged-and-tubed, poured into her foul *über*-girdle, an item so heinous, so perversely utilitarian, that it looks like something designed in the Soviet Bloc, circa 1955, for stalwart Communist party girls. Which is, of course, beyond hot.

Surprising myself—not to mention the slightly horrified, grudgingly wet belle of Vienna—I reach for that wanton tuft of cunt-hair, slip in a finger, and find myself hard and monstrous for a woman who's only just had her insides rearranged, and still has the bandage to prove it.

And yet . . . fucking her is such a delicate operation. I feel like I'm performing a hysterectomy, probing her somehow inappropriately sopping vagina with my prick like a dull scalpel. It's as if, on some level, she shouldn't even be aroused. She should be anesthetized. In fact, she is—more or less. The doctors gave her heavy painkillers. And her opiated, Demerol-soaked state is one more reason to feel like I'm violating some lubricious trauma victim.

One hand on that Stalinist girdle, one hand easing the rubber pee-hose to the side, I slide myself in and out as gingerly as a man walking barefoot on broken lightbulbs. Normally I might slap her, squeeze my hands around her throat, twist her nipples until she screams. But now, now the hottest thing in the world is the near-stillness of our coupling—those sacred, weirdly dainty thrusts. I fuck her the way you touch the soft spot on a baby's skull. If I push too hard—if I let myself go—something awful will happen: Stitches will break loose, hemorrhaging commence, my fresh-scarred lover collapse like a gutted doe on the prong of my hard-on.

This is (there's no other way to put it) end-of-the-world sex. I-know-I'm-going-to-die-but-do-me-anyway sex. Miss Vienna is in pain, but she's pumping, too. In spite of herself, she begs me not to stop. Now I'm the one who wants to pull out. My mind races with awful consequences. I think, *I don't want to kill her.* I mean, what will I say to the police? "I know it's crazy, Officer, but that girdle was so fucking nasty, I couldn't help myself . . ."?

Then again, it occurs to me, if they let me keep the thing when they ship me to Quentin, it might be worth it . . .

Wax

i. k. velasco

Mark is open.

He is spread-eagled on the landing, his wrists bound by silk ropes to the curling balusters of the staircase. Two dozen candles of every shape, size, length, and breadth flicker in the dark. Sweat begins to dot his skin. Diagonal shadow lines crisscross his torso like the bars of a jail cell. He is naked, cock lying small and innocent against his thigh. He looks foreign to her.

Sydney stands over him, hovering like a transient specter of the night. He doesn't look at her. She imagines herself a goddess, glowing. He'll burn up if he looks, spontaneously combust into a cinder of sooty ashes, breaking apart and floating away. She wants it this way. She wants him to feel like he's about to shatter.

"I can't believe you're trusting me this much," Sydney thinks out loud. Mark has always told her that she should think out loud, and she does, even when it's not appropriate.

"Me neither."

She laughs, and then stops abruptly. She's always laughing. She laughs when something's funny, of course. But she also laughs when she's scared, when she's so angry she can't cry, when she's lonely and when something is so weird and wild and out of control she doesn't know how to react—a common occurrence when she's with Mark. Defense mechanism. She's not sure which kind of laugh that was.

"You know you can back out at any point."

"I know, but I want to do this."

She could have tied him to the four-poster bed. In her fantasies, he's lying in that bed, sinking into the softness of her feather duvet and percale sheets. But that was too nice, too neat, too comfortable for what she really wants. She wants him at attention, hyperaware of everything around him. She wants him sliding across the hardwood floor on his back, the cutting pull of silk on his wrists.

The candles have been burning for a couple of hours now. Pools of melted wax surround the half-black wicks and the cylindrical sides have collapsed in on themselves. She'd lit them in preparation. The match head had danced around each wick because her hands shook.

She takes a long look at Mark and can't quite believe the vision is real and not part of a waking dream. She's held off long enough. She takes a deep breath and fills her lungs with a little courage. Teetering on the edge between wish and fulfillment, she realizes the danger of one over the other.

"Are you sure this is okay?" she asks one last time.

Mark nods with finality.

She arranges herself over him, her thighs tangled in his, her rump resting on her heels. She takes pleasure in watching Mark's cock respond, awakening when she hasn't even touched it yet.

With the candle poised over his chest, Sydney stops. He is watching her. His gaze is too palpable to ignore and she can't will her hand to tilt that extra inch. She rises, retreats to her bedroom, and returns with a blindfold. Mark frowns as she secures it behind his head, but he doesn't say a word.

She doesn't hesitate this time. When she tilts the candle, the wax flows. He squirms with this first contact, jolting with first pain. She continues, spacing the pain at capricious intervals. As Mark writhes beneath her, Sydney realizes that he is not making a sound, not a whimper, a squeal. Even his breath is quiet.

She stares at the rivulets, the balling beads of wax congealing against his ribs. The wax pools, then cools quickly and forms a thin layer over the wide plane of his chest, a rainbow swirl of red, green, violet, white, hypnotizing her, consuming her with the desire to make him hurt.

The liquid drips down from the candle, dances on the mushroom-rubbery skin of his dick. Instead of shrinking away from the pain, his dick gets harder, twitching and rising up proudly. And then she is aching from the sudden deluge of sex and smell and wet, rapid desire.

She presses her palm on his chest. The wax cracks and peels, falls away from his skin, leaving faint red burn marks, a road map of past pain. She sinks down over him, and circles her hips, pulling and contracting on his dick, the remnants of wax on him coating her all up inside.

She rips the blindfold from his eyes and his head whips back with the force of it. "Look at me. I want you to look at me when you come."

He opens his eyes, and she can see the effort it takes, like he's prying them with a crowbar. His lids flutter, the thick brown lashes brushing against the translucent skin beneath the rims of his eyes. He struggles to look at her. He's looking but not really seeing, his vision blinded by the pain, pleasure, and sensation he feels.

He is there. Sydney can feel it. He jerks on his bonds, clenches his fists. Sydney blinks hard, afraid that he'll hurt himself. The staircase is shuddering vigorously and his hips shudder up and into her with equal force. A delicious grunt finally escapes his lips, and then he is still.

The edges of Sydney's ruby lips curl and she wants to laugh again. She didn't come, but she doesn't care. She knows she can't wipe the smile threatening to bust out, so she doesn't, and indulges herself in one loud giggle.

"What?"

"What?"

She smiles even bigger. "Nothing."

She dismounts, unties his bonds, and then sits next to him, cross-legged like a little schoolgirl. After rubbing his wrists, Mark turns on his side, rests his head on one hand. Sydney can tell from his expression that he is coming back into himself, coming back from whatever heaven or hell her pussy and her hand and her mouth had taken him, and she doesn't like that.

His hand is on one of her knees, tracing the bone underneath, around and around in descending concentric circles. He pushes her legs apart, his palms pressed against the inside of each thigh.

Mark reaches around her body and pulls a tapered pillar candle from its wrought iron holder. He holds it delicately between two fingers and brings the flame up close to both their faces. Sydney feels the heat from the candle and from him, all mingled into one pulsing source. Licking his fingers, his eyes turn to hers, expressionless save for the haunted glare always present there. She can see the flame dancing against his pupils, twin licking tongues against two lake-slick surfaces. He presses on the wick with his thumb and forefinger, extinguishing the flame with an audible hiss.

He traces the length of the candle on her—cherry red wax, matching the cherry blush of her sex. All at once, the candle is up inside her, the wick tickling her soft pink walls, the shaft coming away slick and wet and shining.

He's fucking her, fucking her hard with the thin candle. He adds two fingers, three, then presses the thumb of his other hand to her pulsing clit, building, building, until she's smoldering, flaming inside, rising up and arching. Sydney imagines the smoke snaking out between her fevered, red pussy lips, flames licking them up like a hot little tongue.

She comes, reaching for him. She's always reaching for him, and she dies a little, every single time.

Vegan Lesbian Boarding School Hookers in Bondage

lisa montanarelli

I got kicked out of high school for slipping secret-admirer notes in girls' gym lockers. The principal told my teary-eyed parents that I was displaying stalking tendencies.

"There's a boarding school near Boston that has extracurricular clubs for kids like her," he said, offering no explanation of "kids like her."

On the Amtrak train to Boston, I imagine what extracurricular clubs for teenage stalkers look like: beady-eyed, pimply-faced teens armed with binoculars, butterfly nets, and those metal tags we used to clip on birds' legs in my seventh-grade ornithology club. Perhaps they'd wear combat boots and install hidden surveillance cameras in bathroom stalls.

At the train station, I catch a cab to my new school. The dorm proctor carries my bags to my small, white room and opens the blinds above my new bed. Fifty feet from my window, an immense column of Saran wrap reaches into the sky. Under the plastic wrap, the hands of a clock keep watch over the students arriving at school.

"What is that?"

"The campus clocktower," he says.

"Is it under construction?"

"No. There's a lesbian secret society called Ozvuh that does that every year on the day before school. They call it 'Phallus Draping Day.' It's a protest against dicks or something like that."

Across the hall a girl with spiked black hair and army fatigues watches us from behind a slightly open door. She slinks across the hall and extends her hand to me.

"My name's Waverly. I can tell you everything you want to know about Ozvuh."

The dorm proctor winks at me. "Be careful," he says and leaves.

Waverly sits on my bed.

"Ozvuh," she explains, "is the Order of Student Vegans (OSV). We're the only lesbian group on campus, and we've all foresworn meat, milk, and men."

"Then what do you eat?" I ask.

"You should come to one of our meetings and find out."

The meeting turns out to be an orientation for new initiates. Halfway through, the head of the Ozvuh steering committee stands up in front of the room.

"You have been 'chosen' from the ranks of the new students to undergo a hazing process that will prove your fitness for the Order."

The lights blink off. A movie flashes on a screen at the front of the room. It's a scene from a slaughterhouse. Baby cows are taken from their cages and butchered; a tiny rabbit has its throat cut; farmers scrape shit off the bottom of chicken coops and feed it to their milk cows. Halfway through the film, I run out of the room and vomit in the restroom across the hall.

The lights are on when I return. Some girls in the front row are holding each other, sobbing. The head of Ozvuh paces in front of the blank screen, hands clasped behind her back.

"Who will be the first to swear never to eat or wear animal products again?" she asks.

Holding my stomach, I tentatively raise my hand.

After my oath, the steering committee gathers in a huddle of spiked hair and army fatigues. When they disband, they appoint me a vegan big sister named Brickley, who is about 5'8" with cropped brown hair, a high forehead, and a long boneless face. She tells me that one of the dorms—Brickley Hall—is named after her ancestor, who founded the boarding school in 1795. I wonder whether Ozvuh is a lesbian debutante society, a radical militaristic cult, or a bit of both.

Brickley is essentially my supervisor. She accompanies me to all meals and provides consultation on my food options. She will also help me choose my course schedule for the fall semester, guide me through my first Ozvuh demo, and generally support me throughout the hazing process.

We schedule our first protest of the year for "Calf Awareness Night"—the night when the student dining hall serves veal for dinner. The dining hall workers have tipped us off, so we know the date of Calf Awareness Night well in advance. A half-hour after the dinner bell rings, an Ozvuh member named Whitney sneaks into the back room of the dining hall and turns off all the overhead lights. The entire room falls silent. We enter the dark dining hall in full-body vegetable suits.

I am dressed as a green cherry tomato (the customary garb of the new initiate). Brickley is dressed as a yam. She stops me so we can hang back and watch the solemn, shadowy procession of vegetables march between dining hall tables in the dark. Their flashlight beams fall on the plates containing the infamous veal dinner.

"You all right?" Brickley asks in a whisper, squeezing my hand.

Earlier that evening, I confided to Brickley that veal is one of my favorite foods.

"*Was* one of your favorite foods," she corrects.

Courtney, a very tall dyke dressed as a stalk of broccoli, turns her flashlight on an open book. Slowly and methodically, she reads from Plutarch, "Was it courage that possessed the first man who used his teeth to break the bones of an expiring animal, who had dead bodies—cadavers—served to him, and swallowed up in his stomach parts which a moment before bleated, lowed, walked, and saw?"

Brickley pulls on my hand. We venture forward. The room is no longer silent, but filled with laughter and loud chatter. Brickley sweeps her flashlight across a table full of jeering faces in matching boatneck sweaters.

"Genocidal imperialists!" she hisses.

"Hey! Watch it, Yamhead!" My eyes adjust to the dark just in time to see the entire table raise their forks like slingshots and pelt us with wet clumps of mashed potatoes and half-chewed veal. We duck and run.

"That was the Mayflower Table," Brickley explains once we're out of range. "They all have ancestors who came over on the *Mayflower*. They get into food fights with the European Royalty Table. Sometimes they even throw animal products."

By the end of the meal, six of our full-body vegetable suits are ruined. The dean calls the members of Ozvuh to his office. I stand shuddering in front of his desk. (After all, I've just been booted from my last school for stalking.) He announces that we're all suspended for five days. The members of the Mayflower Table only have to mop the dining hall after dinner. As Brickley observes, the comparative lightness of their sentence proves we are living in a carnivorous patriarchy.

When we come back after suspension, Brickley tells me I have to have my class schedule approved by the Ozvuh steering committee. This semester all members of Ozvuh are taking a Comparative Religions course on cannibalism and Greek tragedy. The teacher is a sexy young French woman named Françoise Husset.

In the first class, Françoise explains how the Christian practice of Holy Communion emerged from Greek tragedy and the cult of Dionysus, whose followers—the sprightly wood nymphs called Maenads—tore the god's body to shreds and devoured his bleeding flesh.

"So you see," Françoise concludes her first lecture, "every Sunday in church, the veil is lifted on the mysteries, and the supplicants consume the dying god."

The entire class quakes as Françoise sounds the final notes of her lecture. A vegan dyke couple in front of me holds hands, sobbing.

"This is very basic stuff, but you have to know it," Brickley whispers in my ear as we leave the classroom.

Cannibalism is like no class I've ever taken. After three weeks, I'm on the brink of understanding something new— how the sacred is profane and the profane sacred. Clearly I am seeing deep into the nature of things. Walking around campus, I breathe the words "cannibalism" and "Ozvuh" like a mantra.

But each night I jolt up in bed in a panting sweat—running my hands over the surface of my skin to make sure it's all still there. In my recurring dream, the members of Ozvuh chase me through the woods waving thimbuses—the little wands the Maenads waved when they chased Dionysus. I run faster and faster, trees ripping past me like vertical stripes. Claws rip into my back. My eyes fly open as I plunge headlong into Brickley's angry vegan mouth, which looks like the jaws of a cartoon shark, a bottomless black pit with fangs like dinosaur ribs and a pink uvula dangling from the ceiling. I wake up panting, staring at the tiny glow-in-the-dark stars the last tenant pasted on the walls and ceiling of my dorm room. Something is wrong, very wrong. I don't tell anyone about my dreams—especially not Brickley.

I spend hours in the library, reading anything I can find that might explain my nightly visitations. In the *American Journal of Anthropological Psychoanalysis,* I stumble upon an article explaining how "oral sadism" (the desire to inflict pain by biting) is a compromise formation that allows modern man to sublimate archaic cannibalistic urges into the higher forms of art and culture. *Or-al say-diz-um.* Each syllable lurches in me like an involuntary muscle spasm. Then it hits me—the memories of strange scars and bruises I've seen on the Ozvuh members' arms. Teeth marks. So that's what they do in the inner circle—I am being inducted into a secret order of orally sadistic lesbian vegans, who sublimate their cannibalistic urges by hating carnivores!

The next Friday, after a particularly intense cannibalism class, Brickley takes me aside.

"It's time for you to appear before the steering committee and be judged on your sexual practices."

"My what?"

"Your sexual practices."

"But I don't have any."

"What do you mean you don't have any?"

"I'm a virgin," I say, looking at the floor.

"But you told the steering committee you got kicked out of high school for being a dyke and for stalking people!"

"No, I got kicked out for leaving notes in other girls' gym lockers. I've never had sex with anyone at all."

"You're making this really hard on me!" Brickley throws up her hands in frustration.

"But I'd do anything to be in Ozvuh." My eyes well with tears.

"Well, at least you haven't slept with a man. The problem is that the hazing process can be difficult—especially the sexual part. So it's probably a good idea to get some experience beforehand. That way, at least, you'll have some idea of what you're doing."

"How do I do that?"

"I'm not really supposed to help you. That would be what's called a 'dual relationship.' But I'll think of something. Meanwhile you'd better get an anatomy book and start answering some personal ads."

Brickley leaves, slamming the door to my room. Oh fuck, I think, now I'll never be a member of Ozvuh. I hardly know what a personal ad is.

In the newspaper recycling bin, I find a *Boston Free Weekly* and turn to the personals—"Women Seeking Women."

"44 yr old Taurus seeks soulmate for LTR, long walks on beach."

"SWF, 57, loving, compassionate. Let's go to couple's counseling before we need to."

"Temporarily incarcerated SWF seeks amorous bon vivant for monogamous LTR. We like classical music, cooking, epistolary romance."

"Acclaimed chef seeks gorgeous gourmand for sumptuous venison . . ." I flip the page quickly.

Then my eyes fall upon the ad of my salvation: "18-year-old sex tutor seeks generous gentlewoman for mutually beneficial arrangement."

That's what I need—a sex tutor! I dial the voice mailbox and leave a message.

The phone rings in less than half an hour.

"Hi, I'm Stacy the sex tutor. You answered my ad."

"Hi. How are you?"

"I don't have a lot of time to talk. I just want to see if we're on the same page here. Have you had an arrangement before?"

"No, I've never even answered a personal ad before."

"You sound young. How old are you?"

"18 . . . just like you!"

"So can you afford this sort of thing?"

"What sort of thing?"

"You know, like how much can you spend? I don't do charity, honey." She pauses. "You really don't have a clue what I'm talking about, do you?"

"I guess not."

"Well look, hon. I'm a tutor, right? And tutors charge money, you got that?"

"Uh-huh."

"So where are you located?"

I give her the name of my boarding school and dormitory.

"Do you have a trust fund?"

"A what?"

She cuts to the chase. "For $50, I'll come out to your place. The first session is strictly consultation, but you have to pay me the $50."

"Why is it so expensive?"

"Have you ever seen an ad for a sex tutor before?"

"No."

"Well, do you think you can find a better tutor?"

I don't know that I can. I've never found one before, so my prospects seem slim.

"Look, hon, I'm sure you could get this for less, but the question is, what kind of quality you want?"

"Good quality," I say, feeling—for once—quite sure of my answer.

"That's right. The very best. So what room are you in?"

"Number six, but it's locked after nine P.M."

"No problem. If you're in six, you're on the first floor. What window's yours?"

"How do you know so much about my school?"

She doesn't answer.

Once we get off the phone, I flail about the room—scooping dirty clothes off the floor and hurling them into the closet. In less than ten minutes, she raps on my window. She's gotten here very fast—but it's evident why.

"I've seen you before," I say, lifting the heavy window with both hands. "You're in my cannibalism class."

It's the girl with frizzy red hair who always sits in the front row—chewing bubble gum that makes the whole room smell like artificial strawberry. She drags herself over the window ledge on her stomach, tumbles headfirst onto the floor of my room, and picks herself up, dusting off her skimpy pink dress. She's wearing black fishnets and pink high-tops. I stare slack-jawed.

"Why didn't you tell me you go to this school?"

"Because I didn't know you took Cannibalism," she says. "You didn't seem that sophisticated on the phone."

"But . . ."

"No questions. First let's get the business out of the way. I'd like the $50 up front. This is just for the consultation."

I hand her a wad of crumpled bills. She sits down on the side of the bed and straightens them one by one. Finally placated, she looks up at me.

"So, what can I do for you today?"

I start talking. It's like she's pricked a bubble. I tell her how I got kicked out of my previous high school for leaving notes in girls' gym lockers, how I was sent here so I could be in extracurricular activities with dykes, and how it looks as if I'll never get into Ozvuh because I'm a virgin. I tell her the nightmares I've been having about running from the members of Ozvuh as if I'm Dionysus, how they finally catch me and rip me to shreds (she seems especially interested in this), and how I've decrypted the cannibalistic desires of the orally sadistic vegans. Why else would they have those teeth marks on their arms? About two-thirds of the way through this monologue, I realize that I'm telling her way too much. It might be unwise. Nonetheless, I've paid her $50, so I might as well treat her like a high school guidance counselor.

Finally I run out of steam. Stacy is grinning.

"Let me tell you about Ozvuh, sweetie. I'm so over them. They're a cult. You're either for them or against them. And if they don't like you, they entrap you. I was in Ozvuh my freshman year. Two of the members—who I thought were my friends—invited me to spend Thanksgiving with them. They served turkey and added milk to the mashed potato mix. All three of us ate it, but after Thanksgiving break they tattled on me. I was kicked out. I got so pissed I sabotaged the Ozvuh demos for the next year. I tore the cover off the clocktower and organized groups to spit veal at them on Calf Awareness Night. My advice, hon, is to ditch Ozvuh now. Your fantasies about them are much more interesting than they are."

I stare at her, stunned.

"Anyway," she continues, "you still want to be devirginated, and I can do a lot more than just devirginate you. I think I know just the thing that'll *really* get you off. You just have to come to my room tomorrow night around eight and bring $200."

"I don't have $200."

"Well, honey, you'll just have to work for me to pay the rest of it. That'll be easy, since you're a girl. You can make $200 an hour easy if you want to."

"No way! How?"

"Just trust me. We'll talk about that afterwards. It's important that you have your first sexual experience first."

I nod. She glances at her watch.

"Well, looks like your consultation time is up. Are we on for eight?"

"I guess so."

"If you chicken out, just give me a few hours' notice. Gotta go." She strolls over to the window, throws one fishnet-covered leg over the ledge, and glances back at me over her shoulder.

"You know, the thing I hated most about Ozvuh was not being able to eat meat. Don't you miss meat?"

"Not after those movies." I say, trembling a bit.

"Oh right, the movies. They got to me for a couple weeks too. See ya." She hoists her other leg over the window ledge and jumps.

The next day I can't stop thinking about Stacy—and the chance of losing my virginity and making $200 an hour. That evening I tell Brickley I have too much Cannibalism homework to meet her for dinner. I go to the dining hall early to grab a tofu sandwich.

It's the first time I've been to the dining hall without Brickley's supervision. The moment I walk in I smell it. The dining hall workers are setting the tables with napkins and silverware. In the middle of the center table sits a stuffed, roasted pig with an apple in its mouth—like a dead thing still eating, or killed in the act. I shiver, recalling the cows in the movie being fed and slaughtered. Saliva leaks out the corners of my mouth. I'm sweating, and my crotch stirs the way it does when I daydream in class. I turn and run.

I buy a bag of pretzels from the vending machine in my dorm. But by 7:30, my hunger feels like a dog scratching at the inside of my belly. I walk over to Brickley Hall—the dorm where Stacy lives, named after Brickley's ancestor. I wait until three minutes after eight, then take a deep breath and knock on Stacy's door.

I jump a little when she opens it. Instead of the skimpy dress and Converse high-tops, she's wearing knee-high black leather boots, black satin gloves, and a tight leather bodice that shows lots of cleavage. I notice how the freckles are dense on her shoulders and sparse on her neck and breasts. She motions me into her room.

Lingerie and piles of twenty, fifty, even hundred dollar bills lie scattered on the floor.

"You're loaded! Do you sell pot or something?"

"No, silly."

She hands me an IOU for $200, which she produces from

her laser printer. My hand is shaking so much that I can't read a word of it. I'm sure I'm entering a diabolic pact, but I can't turn back. I don't want to lose face. We sign it, and the deal is done.

Or almost done.

"Let me put this on you for just a second," she says, blindfolding me. I can't see a thing.

"Hey! Take those off me!" I yelp as the cold metal clamps around my wrists. "I'm not paying you for this. That's not fair."

She leans close to me so I can feel her warmth. "This is all a part of losing your virginity. I'm trusting you to pay me the $200, so you trust me with this. OK? Just go with it. I know you'll like it—I just know."

She takes my wrists in her hands, pulling me somewhere. I follow. I don't have much of a choice. The situation seems incredibly unbalanced to me. She's trusting me to pay her all this money, so I have to trust her with—something I didn't even agree to in the first place.

She walks me over to the wall and fastens some fur-lined leather cuffs around my wrists below the handcuffs. If Ozvuh ever finds out about these leather cuffs, that's the end of my career as a vegan lesbian—virgin or not. She removes the handcuffs. Chains rattle. She fastens my wrists to the wall, high above my head, and has me pull on the chains—to show me I can't get away.

"Before we go any further," I breathe, "just tell me one thing."

"What's that, hon?" she asks.

"What the fuck does this have to do with losing my virginity?"

"I just don't want you to run away. All right?"

"I won't run away, so let me go."

She takes her hands off me.

"Hey! Where are you going?"

"I'll be back in a second." Her stiletto heels click on the

floor. A door squeaks open. She's letting someone else in the room—several people, whispering inaudibly among themselves. Suddenly, sharp teeth pierce my arm, then my thigh.

"Hey! What are you doing to me? Ow!"

Like rats—scavengers—they scurry around me, ripping off my clothes, pawing me with their mealy hands. Snarling and hissing, they dig their teeth and fingernails into me. I squirm and tug on my wrist straps, until my body goes limp, and I hang there, resting just enough weight on my feet to keep from pulling my arms out of their sockets. I imagine my body covered with bite marks, an interminable future of long-sleeved turtlenecks. What will the people in my Cannibalism class think?

Finally the biters scuffle out of the room, giggling.

"I think you've been up here long enough," says Stacy. She fumbles with my wrist cuffs and unfastens me. I let my arms down. I've been hanging from them for so long, they feel funny dangling at my sides. The cuffs are heavy. I'm surprised how much my body weighs.

Stacy grabs me by the arm and leads me several steps, until my knees bump into a piece of furniture. I feel it with my hands. A bed.

She helps me lie down. I suddenly realize how sore my feet are. She picks up one of my arms. It's flaccid in her hands, like rubber. She lifts it over my head and fastens the wrist cuffs to the bedposts. Then she walks away.

"Where are you going?"

The door squeaks open again. Someone's cooking wafts in from next door. Dining hall smells. The hungry dog inside me wakes up and rolls over. Something heavy rolls toward me, its wheels churning on the hardwood floor. It stops alongside the bed. Stacy rips off my blindfold.

She is standing beside a metal cart, wearing a black strap-on dildo—so big it hurts to look at it. On the metal cart, the roast pig from the dining hall stares at me blindly, its body half-eaten, the apple still in its mouth.

"How in the world did *that* get in here?"

"Let's just say I have a special relationship with the dining-hall workers." Stacy smiles.

She picks up a ladle, scoops some hot grease out of the pig's tray, and drips it on my chest. It burns like hell.

Smiling, she picks up a knife and saws a thick slice of ham off the side of the pig. My stomach gurgles. Vegan or not, I've had nothing but pretzels since noon. The hungry dog claws at the insides of my belly.

"Here, little vegan girl." Stacy lowers the slice of ham to my mouth. "Eat this meat." A drop of blood-red juice drips off the meat and hits me under the eye.

I crane my neck, open my mouth and bite—the air.

"No you don't! Those fur-lined cuffs are quite enough for one day." She drops the ham on the bed. It lands with a wet thump. I watch the brownish red juice soak into the white sheet, just like I've watched it spread out on other people's plates for the past month.

"Here. Eat this meat. It's vegan." She pokes me in the cheek with the dildo.

"Open up." She slides the tip of the dildo into my mouth. It tastes like plastic, but in my hunger, anything is better than nothing.

"That's enough. You're enjoying it too much." She yanks it out and kneels on the bed.

"Open your legs."

I squeeze my thighs together. I've had cucumbers, carrots . . . all manner of vegetables inside me, but that thing is too big for words.

"Come on. This is what you're paying me for. Do you want to stay a virgin for the rest of your life?"

That's right. I did promise her $200. A minor fortune for

me, but I'd almost forgotten. I carefully open my legs—squeezing my eyes shut, as if I'm getting a shot at the doctor's office.

She spreads something cold and wet between my legs.

"Wha—?"

"It's just lube."

Something round and wet slips inside me. It's just the tip. It feels like the cucumbers, but it's strange having someone else put something in there. I'm about to reach for it with my hands, but the wrist cuffs stop me.

I open my eyes. Stacy is staring. She looks like my dentist when he reaches into my mouth. Her eyes ask, "Is it OK?"

I nod, as if she'd really asked.

She moves inside me, fills me all the way up, until something sharp pierces me deep inside.

"How far are you in?"

"All the way."

I clamp down on the dildo.

"It's happening." My eyes fly open. I hardly know what I'm saying. My back arches like a bow pulled taut. My whole body is trembling, balanced on my neck and heels. Then the warm sensation floods me. Digging my heels into the bed, I grip the dildo like a fist, making sounds and faces I'm not sure I want anyone to see. I sink into the bed, panting and laughing out loud.

Stacy blushes bright pink under her freckles.

"God, you came fast! You're not a virgin anymore."

She leans over and kisses me on the lips.

"Now let me at that pig!" I say, grinning ear to ear.

Joanie
james strouse

Mitchell Rogers kept staring at my mother's parts all through dinner. My father pretended not to notice, but I could tell it bothered him. Mitchell's gaze was blatant. Whenever he spoke, he addressed my mother's breasts.

"More roast, Mitchell?" my mother asked.

"Yes," he told her boobs. "It's lovely."

"Oh, good," she said. "I hope you're saving room for dessert."

Mitchell drummed his gut and smiled. "I think I'll have room," he said to Mom's freckled cleavage. Mitchell's lust was more obvious than that of the teenage boys in my class, and their hormones could have powered a whole town.

My mother stood up from the table to get dessert, and Mitchell fixed his eyes to her ass as if it were the last bite of meat. When she disappeared into the kitchen, he greedily forked the remains of his dinner.

My father and I kept our eyes on him. We didn't look at each other, just at Mitchell and then back to our plates.

"I'm sure glad you could make it to dinner tonight,

Mitchell," said my father. "I think it's important to get to know people outside of the office."

"Yes," grunted Mitchell, no hint of comprehension in his voice.

"After a while you start to think of people as extensions of their desks, don't you think? You forget the people you work with even have legs." My father laughed, as if he hadn't told my mom the same thing in despair a thousand times before.

Mitchell didn't laugh. "I don't forget your secretary's legs," he said. "How could you ever forget legs like that?"

"Ho, ho," my father laughed, a little helpless. He had told my mother that he'd gotten a new secretary, but he hadn't mentioned her legs.

This dinner was going all wrong for my dad. He had invited Mitchell over for supper, hoping to make an alliance at the office. Dad was afraid that he wasn't liked at the company and blamed this for his failure to advance. Month after month, he watched as promotions were offered to less capable men, simply because, my father thought, they knew how to talk bullshit with the boss.

Mitchell Rogers was the boss's third cousin, or some such distant and meaningless relation. My father wasn't even sure what Mitchell did at the company, only that he almost never came in on time, took two-hour lunches, always left at five, and had a larger office and a more impressive title than my father: Senior Director of Management. There were no Junior Directors of Management at the company as far as my father could tell, but Senior lent more distinction to the title than his own: Assistant Production Manager.

My mother returned from the kitchen wearing oven mitts and holding a warm butterscotch pie with freshly whipped meringue. My father watched her nervously. Before dinner, he told her that butterscotch pie was a strange dessert to serve, but my mother had insisted. Butterscotch was my favorite and the pie would be my reward for sitting through dinner.

Mitchell watched my mother's crotch as she crossed the room with the warm pie. He was obese and his weight hid his age. His small black eyes were vacant, and his open, huffing mouth exposed little more than a thick horse tongue.

"Butterscotch," said my mother with a smile. "It's Joanie's favorite."

"Your daughter has good taste," said Mitchell. I couldn't stand his filthy wet pig eyes on me. "I bet she gets that from her mother." He turned to my mom's tits and smiled.

Mom and Dad laughed like sitcom parents at a scripted joke. My mother cut the pie and dished heavy slices onto our plates. Mitchell asked for another sliver after he finished, and my mom gave him another whole piece.

"It's great pie, isn't it?" asked my father.

"I'll say," said Mitchell.

"Maybe I'll have another small piece, too," I said. My parents looked at each other and frowned. They were "concerned" about my weight.

"Of course, dear," my mother said, her voice a bit too eager. She cut me a thin slice.

Mitchell and I finished our second helpings. My parents watched intently.

"Well," said Mitchell, the last bite of pie still in his mouth, "I'm stuffed."

"I just hope you liked it," said my mother. "I think I might have cooked the roast a little too long."

"Nonsense," wheezed Mitchell.

"I'm still not quite the cook Roger would like me to be. Am I, honey?"

"Well, you're perfect in every other way, Toots," said my dad.

"Yes," said Mitchell, "I'd say she is."

My mother blushed.

"And your daughter seems to be blossoming into just as lovely a creature as her mother," he said, smiling blankly into my face.

"Luckily, she didn't inherit much of her father's ugly looks," said my dad.

"Lucky," said Mitchell.

"She does have her father's eyes," my mother chimed in.

"Yes, I've been meaning to talk to you about that, Joanie," said my father in a tone of mock sternness. "I'm going to need those back. I can't see a damn thing without them."

The table erupted in laughter. I faked dry heaves over my empty plate. No one noticed.

After dinner, my parents invited Mitchell to watch television with us. I think the offer caught him off guard. It was a corny thing to ask a near-stranger.

"No," said Mitchell, short and distracted. "I don't watch television."

"Who doesn't watch television?" joked my father.

"I don't," repeated Mitchell. "Anyhow, it's late."

It wasn't even nine o'clock. Mitchell was ditching us.

"Well, thanks again for coming," said my father. He handed Mitchell his coat, which looked like heavy gray drapes.

"Nonsense," said Mitchell, "the pleasure was mine."

"You'll have to come again soon," said my mom.

Mitchell stared into her bosom and smiled. "You'll have to invite me again soon."

"Don't hesitate to call, either," added my father. "For any reason, business or otherwise. I want you to know that you can depend on me for anything, Mitchell."

I couldn't look at my father as he groveled.

Mitchell stood with his head down in a concentrated gaze. "Well, there just happens to be something," he said. "But I wouldn't want to put you out."

"Just ask," said my father.

Mitchell looked up. "As you probably know, I have a vacation next week, and I've been having the damnedest time trying to find someone to feed my fish."

Silence.

My parents and I stared at Mitchell. Mitchell stared at the floor.

"Fish?" said my father, like he'd never heard of them before.

"Tropical fish," said Mitchell. "I never even wanted the stupid things. This girl I was seeing convinced me to get them."

I don't think any of us believed Mitchell had ever "seen" a girl.

"What do they eat?" asked my mother.

"Fish food," said Mitchell.

"Sounds easy," said my father.

"It's real easy. And I'd ask the girl, but we're not seeing each other anymore," said Mitchell.

"Oh, that's a shame," said my mother.

"You know what they say," said Mitchell.

None of us knew. We looked at him expectantly.

"There are many fish in the sea."

"Ha, ha, ha," they all laughed.

"So maybe your daughter could do it," Mitchell suggested.

"Maybe," said my father. And I knew it was decided that I would.

Mitchell and my father shook hands. Mitchell kissed my mother's hand, patted me on the side of the head, took one final look at my mother's chest, then left.

The smiles on my parents' faces faded as Mitchell's taillights trailed into the dark. We stared at the window in silence.

"Where is he going on vacation?" asked my mother.

"I don't know. Some island," said my father. "He's been going to a tanning bed every night this week to get ready."

"He can fit into one of those things?" asked my mother, mildly astonished.

"No," said my father drolly. "They have to tan the overhang separately."

"Oh, Roger," said my mom.

"Oh, Dawn," said my dad.

They looked at each other slyly. I wanted to butt their heads together.

My parents were fitness freaks. If they succeeded at nothing else, they'd at least look good failing. My mother had a tight hourglass figure with firm breasts that popped out of her chest to meet you. She was short and lean, perfectly curved like a sculpture of a fertility goddess. My father was tall and well-toned. His arms weren't thick, but solid and defined. I was a formless blob, forty or fifty pounds overweight depending on what scale I used. I was exploding into a trollish version of my mother, not blossoming into "just as lovely a creature."

To my parents, this was a source of endless chagrin. The fact that their own offspring was a fat, feckless groaner made them unsure of themselves. I was a constant reminder of their flaws: a heavy-bottomed, sharp-eyed suggestion of their negative potential. I was a fat girl. *Their* fat girl. They constantly did little things to help. My mother bought me outfits that were a size too small. "I thought you'd look great in this, Joanie," she'd say, holding a blouse or dress up to her own perfect frame, "if you just lost a couple pounds." But I did not lose a couple pounds. I got bigger, and the clothes fit tighter.

My father offered to buy me a gym membership or take me on his after-work runs. "We'll go at whatever pace makes you comfortable," he'd say. I'd tell him I didn't see any reason to run unless you were being chased. He would smile, then look at my mom gravely. "She'll grow out of it," they would agree, "once she discovers boys."

I was already sixteen and had long since discovered boys. Boys were mindless little animals full of smirks and grins. Boys were dumb, frightened little men who didn't know how to feign interest or hold polite conversation. Boys were undergrown Mitchells waiting to happen. Unfortunately, some boys also looked very good in jeans and these boys terrified me to no end. They not only disliked fat girls, they were downright cruel to us.

"Where does Mitchell live?" asked my mother.

"I don't know," said my father. "I'll find out tomorrow."

"Don't you think it's strange?" asked my mom.

"What?" asked my father.

"I mean, we barely know the man."

"He must be hard up. For friends."

"I bet his house stinks," I said.

"Joanie," said my parents.

"Did you smell him?" I asked. "He smelled like a bowel movement doused in Old Spice."

"That's not polite, young lady," said my mother.

"What about the way he looked at you all night? Was that polite?"

"What do you mean?" asked my mother indignantly.

"That's enough, Joanie," said my father. "Mitchell Rogers is a coworker and a friend. What if I remarked on the hygiene of one of your classmates? How would that make you feel?"

"Everyone at my school stinks too," I said.

My parents frowned.

"Mitchell Rogers does not stink," said my father angrily.

"Okay," I said. "Okay, I'm sorry." There was no point in fighting my parents' delusions. It might just undo them. But Mitchell Rogers did stink. I could smell a trace of his reek in the foyer as my parents looked at me with their sad, simple eyes. My mother's were narrow and dark. My father's were sky blue and wide, just like mine.

Mitchell Rogers lived a good fifteen-minute drive outside of town. I feigned annoyance when my parents asked me to feed his fish but I secretly reveled in the chance to use my mother's car. (Dad's '76 Ford Mustang was out of the question.)

Monday after school, I took my mother's Cutlass Ciera for a drive before going to Mitchell's house. I drove down Main Street, past the dueling antique shops and the travel agency. I drove past the movie theater that had been converted into a Methodist church. Its marquee read "Christ Saves," as if it were a Hollywood blockbuster. I drove past the men's tailor shop and the local Moose Lodge. Past the main strip of town, I drove straight out onto the flat land my parents wistfully referred to as "the country" and floored the Ciera to seventy.

I drove for miles. My parents never let me use their cars, and I wanted to make the most of the opportunity. I rolled down the window and sank into my seat.

Mitchell's house was set against a young forest of pine trees. A narrow limestone path led to his single-car garage. Mitchell's house was small. It looked more like a shed than a home. It had white aluminum siding, a black tar-shingled roof, and matching black shutters closed over all the windows. His doormat read "Wipe Your Paws" above embroidered dog prints. I lifted the mat and found the key. I held my breath as I unlocked the door.

The rooms were strangely scentless, like a show house, old but unlived-in. The odor of new carpet and paint had faded but hadn't been replaced with human scent. His walls were bare white, like blank sheets of paper. I could see why his "ex-girlfriend" had suggested he buy fish. This house needed some proof of life.

Mitchell's aquarium was in the living room, centered

inside his unused fireplace. I shook a can of dry fish flakes over the water and watched the little creatures go at it with their tiny dumb mouths. None of them were brightly colored or particularly exotic. Leave it to Mitchell to get the dullest tropical fish possible. I fed them some more. I looked around for the television, but he didn't have one in his living room. Just the aquarium in the fireplace and a tan loveseat.

I got up and went to the kitchen. My guess was that Mitchell and I had one thing in common, a deep and abiding lust for food. This would explain his surroundings. We had a singular focus that took up most of our time and energy: overeating.

But Mitchell had almost nothing in his cupboards; just health-food junk: fat-free soup, vegetable-curry mixes, granola, unsalted baked tortilla chips. He had unflavored rice cakes, for God's sake. How was he so fat? On his refrigerator there was a weight-loss poster with "before" and "after" pictures of a woman. It was typical self-improvement propaganda. The "before" picture was small and showed the woman's backside in a bathing suit as she looked over her shoulder without expression. The woman was an ugly fat Hun. The "after" picture was large. It was obviously taken in a studio. The now-skinny woman stood with her arms akimbo, an obscene smile on her face. She was still ugly. Superimposed over the bottom of the poster were the words "You Can Do It!" in boldface yellow script. Obviously, Mitchell could not do it. He was just about the fattest person I had ever seen.

I opened his fridge and, on a shelf, a light-sensitive plastic pig started oinking and blinking red from its eyes. Mitchell had skim milk and Egg Beaters. His freezer held Healthy Choice dinners and one small container of nonfat vanilla frozen yogurt. His diet was as bland as his home. The man had a nonaesthetic. I knew there had to be food hidden somewhere. I made it my mission to find it.

I searched his house. I looked in his utility closet behind his linens. I looked in his bathroom cabinet behind his bath towels and plumbing chemicals. I looked under his couch and up his fireplace. I even looked on his screened-in patio in back of the house. I looked in the desk drawers in his den and the file cabinets between his tax-return folders and life insurance policy. Then, I searched his bedroom.

Mitchell's bedroom smelled different than the rest of his home: wet, almost musty, an old scent like stale glue. I looked under his king-size bed. Nothing. I looked behind the TV/VCR combo by his bed. Lying bastard. Probably all he did was watch television. I rifled through his drawers, which only held clothes. I opened his closet, a walk-in full of suits and coats, all neatly pressed and hung. Then I noticed a red trunk in the corner, with a pile of shoeboxes stacked on top. It was the size and shape of one of those old chests you see in movies, the type kept in attics with war medals and treasure maps hidden inside. Except this trunk was new and red and padlocked.

I lifted the trunk a little and looked for a key. It was hidden underneath, just like the one to his house. People were so obvious. It was depressing. I undid the lock and opened the chest, careful to keep Mitchell's shoeboxes in order. There was no food in the chest. Only videotapes. Black, unmarked videotapes. I started pulling them out of the chest. One layer of tapes revealed another. At the bottom, I found Polaroids. Dozens of them. And they all contained just one image: Mitchell's gigantic penis.

My heart raced, and I screamed. Then I blushed, both from the sight of Mitchell's penis—I could tell it was Mitchell's because it was framed between a pair of hulking thighs—and the fact that it made me scream, alone, in his empty house.

I hadn't seen many penises in my life. Once, when I was a little girl, I glimpsed my father's as he was coming out of the shower. All I remembered was a blur of bald pink flesh that looked like a limp thumb. Later, in sex-ed classes, I got a better look at the things in drawings and diagrams. I learned that the urethra served not only as a urinary canal but also as a genital duct. I knew what dicks looked like and what they could do, but I didn't know they could get so big. I was horrified. I couldn't touch the pictures; I studied them as they were, scattered across the bottom of the chest.

Mitchell's dick looked almost a foot long erect and maybe seven or eight inches flaccid. He had plenty of pictures of it both ways. Some were taken head on, reflected in a mirror. Some were taken at arm's length from his crotch. Sometimes he held his cock with his free hand. Sometimes it dangled freely. Engorged, the tip of his cock was blue like a bruise. Limp, it took on a yellowish hue, like the skin of a sickly child.

The pictures made me nauseous and wild. I backed out of Mitchell's closet and went to the kitchen to get a drink of water. I watched his fish for a moment, ate some of his granola, and drank another glass of water. I walked back to his closet. I looked in the full-length mirror on the door and pictured Mitchell's fat naked body reflected back at him. Was he able to see his own penis without a mirror or a Polaroid? Seeing my own reflection there unnerved me. I felt goosebumps on my arms.

I got in my mother's car and drove straight home. I couldn't stop looking over my shoulder. After I parked the car in our driveway, I fidgeted to get the key out of the ignition for nearly a minute before I realized the car was still running.

"Where've you been, Joanie?" asked my father when I went inside. It was eight o'clock.

"I'm sorry. I didn't know I was being timed."

"Your mother needed her car tonight. She had to use mine. You know how she hates to drive stick."

"I'm sorry," I said.

"Dinner's in the fridge. It's probably still warm. Did you have any trouble finding Mitchell's place?"

"No," I said. I didn't want to talk to my dad. I was having trouble just looking at his face.

"Well, thanks for doing it."

I started for my room.

"Joanie," said my father ominously. I froze. "Bring the car straight home tomorrow in case your mother needs it. She's no good with the stick shift."

This was not true. My mother was fine with a stick shift. My father just didn't like my mother driving his car. "Okay," I said, but nothing was.

The next day, all through school, Mitchell's dick kept popping into my head. I saw it everywhere. Boys' fingers. Teachers' bald heads. Pencils. Flagstaffs. There was dick in my ham sandwich at lunch. The hallways of my high school were big genital ducts. The rank scent of sweat in the gym reminded me of the smell in Mitchell's bedroom. I couldn't get it out of my head. Dick. Dick. Dick. Even in short moments of distraction, I was aware of dick and the fact that I wasn't thinking about it.

After school, I took my mother's car directly to Mitchell's house. I ran into his bedroom and stacked the videotapes back into the chest, over the Polaroids, careful not to look at any of the pictures. Once this was done, I felt a little better. But I couldn't help wondering what was on the videos. Visions of Mitchell's dick in motion made me shudder.

I couldn't force myself to watch one, but I couldn't close the chest either. I bent over, and I could see my ass crack in the mirror. I was wearing pants my mother had bought me. I took a video out of the chest and walked into the kitchen. I ate some frozen yogurt. It had freezer burn. "You Can Do It!" read the weight-loss poster.

I went back to Mitchell's room and put the video in the VCR. I stood in the space between his bureau and his bed, inches from the television. A porno came on screen, right in front of my face. I felt mildly relieved. I knew what these were: the movies in the back room of the video store, rented only by pathetic men like Mitchell. They were what the old feminists deemed exploitative and the new deemed an "empowering business endeavor." I'd read things. I'd even heard a radio forum on pornography with Gloria Steinem and a surprisingly well-spoken adult-film actress. But I'd never *seen* one before.

Mitchell's porn was titled *The Fireman's Daughter*. It starred a blond girl named Sable. She looked like one of the girls who worked at my mother's beauty salon: ridiculous perm, over-done makeup. She was pretty, despite the stupid faces she made when she tried to act. She wore a lace slip and sat on a bed covered with stuffed animals. Suddenly, a fireman burst through her door. His hair was also permed, but he was not handsome. He had a big forehead and a snub nose.

"I thought there was a fire in here," said the fireman. He wore a fireman's coat and hat and held a hatchet. That's how you could tell he was a fireman.

"There is," said the girl. She pulled open her slip, revealing double-D plastic boobs.

"You know how to handle a hose like this?" asked the fire-man. He was naked underneath his coat and had a hard-on the size of Mitchell's.

"Oh," said Sable. "I think I do." Then some bad music with horns started and Sable started sucking the man's dick.

I stood transfixed, watching it like a nature program. I imagined narration: *Once the wild man's penis is engorged and the woman's vagina is properly lubricated, he inserts it thusly, rocking to and fro, not unlike the species of human known as the music-video dancer.*

I watched the entire video, then another. This one was about a team of cheerleaders called The Cum Squad. The actors had changed, but the corny dialogue remained. It was as pointless as my parents' dinner conversations. Why did they bother? I liked the movies better when they were just sex. The sex was fascinating. It made me forget about Mitchell's cock.

That night, I got home at ten. My parents were waiting for me in the living room.

"Where have you been, Joanie?" my mother asked, more angry than worried.

"Nowhere," I said. Suddenly I remembered Mitchell's fish. I had forgotten to feed them.

"Now look here." My dad always said that when he was mad, but he never indicated a specific place to look. "We gave you this responsibility because we thought you were adult enough to handle it. But if you can't, we'll just have to do it ourselves."

Do it ourselves. It sounded like the opening line to a porno sequence. I imagined my father turning my mother over and pulling down her pants, while bad horn music piped in. Then I envisioned Mitchell Rogers walking into the scene, his twelve-inch love wand putting my father to shame.

"You gave me this responsibility because you didn't want it," I said.

"Don't take that tone with me, little girl," said my dad, his temper rising. My mom nodded.

They repulsed me. "I'm not a little girl."

"Well, you're certainly acting like one," said my father.

"Fuck off, Dad." I couldn't stop myself.

My father stood up but didn't move toward me. "Fuck off?" He sounded stunned.

"Apologize to your father right now, young lady," commanded my mother.

But I wasn't sorry, so I said nothing.

"That's fine, that's fine," said my dad in a quiet voice on

the edge of hysteria. "Let her say whatever the fuck she wants. What's the fucking difference." This was his lame idea of making a point, by throwing the offense right back in my face. "I'm sorry, Joanie," he said. "You're obviously not a little girl. You're a big fucking woman to be able to talk to your father that way."

"Oh, shut up, Dad. You're just mad because you've got a little dick."

My mother went white.

"You're fat," my father snapped. He froze, his index finger in my face. He didn't yell at me again. He didn't say much at all. What could he say? We'd just insulted each other in the worst possible way, with the unspoken truth. I was fat. That wasn't a revelation, but it was painful to hear my father say it. My dad did have a small cock. I was sure now. Why else would he return the insult? He even acted like a man with a little dick, defeated and angry, never one hundred percent sure of himself, just like his overweight daughter. He compensated with working out and driving a Mustang. My mother was part of the compensation. I couldn't figure out what her inadequacy was, though, other than being a dumb bitch. She put her arm around my father and looked at me. My father was blushing.

I heard my mother whispering something into my father's ear. He shook his head. Then I ran out of the house. No one followed me outside.

I got in my mother's Ciera and drove straight to Mitchell's house. I locked his doors. I left the lights off and wandered through the dark. I fed the fish, shaking the flakes over the water again and again until there was nothing left. Their little fish mouths gulped at the surface maniacally. Nothing in their dumb fish brains told them they were full, so they kept eating and eating.

I went to Mitchell's room and put on a porno. I lay down

on his bed and watched the television sideways, my head propped against my arm.

My parents had brought this upon themselves by having sex like the dumb actors on Mitchell's TV. That's how I happened. That's what was behind all the boys' smirks at school, the notes girls passed in class, the after-dance parties at rich kids' houses, the ones with alcohol and swimming pools. My classmates were learning to be porn stars in darkened movie theaters and the backseats of their parents' cars. They were learning what my parents had already learned and what their parents had learned before them. They were learning to ram each other like dumb animals and breed more dumb animals who would grow up and learn to ram each other like dumb animals. But not me. Not Mitchell Rogers. Not the chubby girl or the fat man with the King Kong dick. For us there was something else. We had butterscotch pie and pornography.

On Mitchell's television, a short man in glasses gave it to a wild-haired blonde from behind. The man was skinny. The skin around his cheekbones was so tight that his head looked like a skull. He made short grunts between his teeth and determined, evil faces as he pumped the blonde. The blonde made awful sounds. The man's brow was sweaty. His jaw was clenched as he pulled the girl's hair. I wondered if my father grunted, if my mom faked it that loudly when I wasn't home. I wondered if Mitchell Rogers moaned as he lay on his bed watching other men. I thought about the boys at school. I imagined their weak little adolescent voices breaking in short squeals as they pumped and thrusted.

I squirmed in the indentation of Mitchell's bed and touched my hand to the bare skin of my belly. The grunting excited me. It sounded raw and dirty. It sounded naked and pure and awful and beautiful. I slid my hand between my fat thighs. I thought about Mitchell's Polaroids. I wondered how it would feel to look at my own crotch on film.

I touched myself like the women in Mitchell's videos. I started to feel things. Heat in my fingers and toes. The warm air of his room like breath on my skin. A thousand tiny thrills running over my body in warm, slow trickles. I felt like I would turn into light, like something was going to consume me from the inside out. I felt like I'd burst through the ceiling in a blinding ray and hurl straight up into the sky like an ascending star. Then the feelings started to ebb, and I stared into Mitchell's TV, blank-eyed and nauseated.

Later, my parents drove to Mitchell's house looking for me. They pounded on the front door and shouted for me to open up. They walked around the outside of the house knocking on windows and yelling my name. At least that's what they told me the next day. If they did, their voices just echoed through the pine trees, unheard, because I'd already fallen asleep, lulled to dreams by the grunts and screams of people fucking.

Contributors

Steve Almond's debut collection of stories, *My Life in Heavy Metal,* was published in 2001. He has won the Pushcart Prize and been named a finalist for the National Magazine Award. Visit him at http://www.stevenalmond.com.

Rachel Kramer Bussel is the reviser of *The Lesbian Sex Book,* coauthor of *The Erotic Writer's Market Guide,* and coeditor of the erotica anthology *Up All Night.* Her writing has been published in *Bust, Curve, Diva, Girlfriends, Playgirl, On Our Backs, San Francisco Chronicle,* and numerous anthologies. Visit her at http://www.rachelkramerbussel.com.

Alan Cumming's Tony Award–winning portrayal of the emcee in the Broadway musical *Cabaret* was one of the most celebrated performances in recent years. More recently, he coproduced, cowrote, codirected, and starred in the film *The Anniversary Party* with Jennifer Jason Leigh. Other films in which he's appeared include *Spy Kids, Titus, Emma, Eyes Wide Shut, GoldenEye, Circle of Friends,* and *X-Men 2.* He lives in New York, and on the Web at http://www.alancum-ming.com.

Jameson Currier is the author of a novel, *Where the Rainbow Ends*, and a collection of short stories, *Dancing on the Moon*. His short fiction has appeared in many magazines and anthologies, including *Men on Men*, *Rebel Yell*, *Best Gay Erotica*, and *Making Literature Matter*.

David R. Enoch is a government attorney. In addition to writing occasional stories for alternative press publications, he is currently working on a legal writing textbook. This is his first attempt at erotic fiction. Because of his job, Mr. Enoch submitted this story under a pen name.

Maggie Estep is the author of *Diary of an Emotional Idiot*, *Soft Maniacs*, *Hex*, a crime novel, and *Love Dance of the Mechanical Animals*. She has written for *Black Book*, *Harper's Bazaar*, *Spin*, *New York Press*, and the *Village Voice*. She lives in Brooklyn and likes to hang out at racetracks, cheering on long shots.

R. Gay is a writer who works with engineers, oddly enough. Her writing can be found in *Best Lesbian Erotica 2002* and *2003*, *Best Transgender Erotica*, *Best Bisexual Women's Erotica*, *The Mammoth Book of Tales from the Road*, *Shameless: Women's Intimate Erotica*, *Sweet Life*, and others. She is also the fiction editor of www.ScarletLetters.com.

A. W. Hill has been a musician, a motion picture exec, and a Grammy recipient. Erotica did not begin to flow from his word processor until he'd been through divorce, remarriage, and several near-death experiences. His first novel, *Enoch's Portal*, was published in 2002 and is currently in motion picture development at Paramount.

Susannah Indigo is the editor-in-chief of *Clean Sheets* magazine at http://www.cleansheets.com, and also the editor and founder of *Slow Trains* literary journal at http://www.slowtrains.com. Her books include *Oysters Among Us, Many Kisses: Stories of Dominant Love, From Porn to Poetry,* and *From Porn to Poetry 2.* Visit her at http://www.susannahindigo.com.

By day, **Geoffrey A. Landis** is a mild-mannered rocket scientist. In his spare time, he's the author of seventy short stories and two books. He has lived in Michigan, Maryland, Illinois, New Jersey, Pennsylvania, Massachusetts, and Rhode Island, and is currently in Ohio. His recent book, *Impact Parameter: And Other Quantum Realities,* collects his short stories.

Lisa Montanarelli is author of *The First Year— Hepatitis C,* with Cara Bruce. With a Ph.D. from U.C. Berkeley, she can imagine almost anything happening in a classroom. Her fiction appears in *Best Fetish Erotica, Best Women's Erotica, The Mammoth Book of Best New Erotica,* and other anthologies.

J. D. Munro, here writing as **Dawn O'Hara,** is an up-and-coming women's writer who's been in all the best women's erotic anthologies and journals this past year. She is racking up various writing awards in her home state of

Washington and is currently shopping a nonfiction book about female fertility issues: *Not Suitable for Children.*

Bill Noble is a great-granddad still two-finger typing in northern California. He edits fiction for *Clean Sheets* magazine, walked the 165-mile Tahoe Rim Trail in eight and one half days last year, and appears splendidly on the cover of David Steinberg's new book of erotic photography, *Photo Sex: Fine Art Sexual Photography Comes of Age.*

Rachel Resnick is the bestselling author of *Go West Young F*cked-Up Chick.* Her fiction has appeared in various literature journals and anthologies including *The Dictionary of Failed Relationships, L.A. Shorts,* and *Absolute Disaster.* She is contributing editor at *Tin House,* and her nonfiction appears in *Black Book,* the *Hartford Courant,* and the *Los Angeles Times,* among others. She lives in Topanga, California, and on the web at http://www.rachelresnick.com.

Dominic Santi has had dozens of erotic stories published in anthologies and magazines, and coedited the anthology *Strange Bedfellows* with Debra Hyde. For the record, Santi keeps all receipts, has an impeccably honest accountant, and has never (knowingly) spanked a government employee.

Simon Sheppard is the author of *Kinkorama: Dispatches from the Frontlines of Perversion* and the award-winning *Hotter Than Hell: And Other Stories.* He's also the coeditor, with M. Christian, of *Rough Stuff* and *Roughed Up.* His next short story collection, *In Deep*, debuts this year. His work has been published in more than eighty anthologies, and this is his fourth appearance in *Best American Erotica*. Visit him at http://www.simonsheppard.com.

Jerry Stahl is the author of the narcotic memoir *Permanent Midnight* and the novels *Perv—A Love Story* and *Plainclothes Naked*.

James Strouse is a writer and cartoonist currently at work on his first collection of short stories. When not writing or drawing, he sells used books at a not-for-profit bookstore in Manhattan's SoHo district. He was raised in Goshen, Indiana, and lives in New York City. "Joanie" is his first published story.

Touré is the author of *The Portable Promised Land*, a collection of short stories. He is also a contributing editor at *Rolling Stone*. His work has appeared in *The New Yorker, New York Times Magazine, The Best American Essays 1999, The Best American Sportswriting 2001*, and *Zoetrope: All Story*, where he won the Sam Adams Short Story Contest. He is a contributor to NPR's "All Things Considered." He studied at Columbia University's graduate school of creative writing and lives in Fort Greene, Brooklyn. His new novel *Soul City* debuts this spring.

Claire Tristram's stories appeared in *Best American Erotica 2000* and *2001*. Her fiction has been published in *Massachusetts Review, Hayden's Ferry Review, Alaska Quarterly Review, Fiction International*, and *North American Review*, and her essays have appeared recently in the *New York Times,* *Wired,* and *Salon.* She is currently working on her first novel.

Joy VanNuys is a chef and writer living in Brooklyn, New York. Her fiction has recently appeared in the anthologies *Grunt and Groan* and *Best Bisexual Women's Erotica.* She'd like to assure readers that nothing like the events described in "Spawning" ever happens in restaurant kitchens. Really. Visit her on the Web at http://www.JoyVanNuys.com.

I. K. Velasco is the pseudonym for a fledgling writer living in Dixieland. By day, she is one of many slaves to the corporate machine. By night, she is the master of her imaginative musings. Her work has appeared in several online magazines, including http://www.cleansheets.com and http://www.thermoerotic.com.

Sharon Wachsler is a poet, disability activist, teacher, and dog trainer. Her erotica has appeared in *On Our Backs, Moxie Magazine, Worcester Magazine, HLFQ,* and *Best Lesbian Erotica 2003.* She has a monthly humor column at http://www.abilitymaine.org and cartoons at http://www.sickhumorpostcards.com. Check out Sharon and her big dogs at http://www.sharonwachsler.com.

John Yohe has a BA in English from Michigan State University, and an MFA in Poetry from New School University. His erotic fiction appears periodically in *Leg Show* and *Tight* magazines. His fiction and poetry have appeared in literary magazines like *Fence, Rattapallax,* and *Left Field.*

Credits

Reader Survey

Please return this survey or any other *BAE* correspondence to: Susie Bright, BAE-Feedback, P.O. Box 8377, Santa Cruz, CA 95061. Or, e-mail your reply to: BAE @susiebright.com.

1. What are your favorite stories in this year's collection?

2. Have you read previous years' editions of *The Best American Erotica*?

3. If yes, do you have any favorite stories or authors from those previous collections?

4. Do you have any recommendations for next year's *The Best American Erotica 2005*? (Nominated stories must have been published in North America, in any form—book, periodical, Internet—between March 1, 2004, and March 1, 2005.)

5. How old are you?

6. Male or female?

7. Where do you live?
    ❏ West Coast   ❏ South
    ❏ Midwest   ❏ Other
    ❏ East Coast

8. What made you interested in *The Best American Erotica 2004*? (check as many as apply)
    ❏ enjoyed other *Best American Erotica* collections
    ❏ editor's reputation
    ❏ authors' reputations
    ❏ enjoy "Best of" type anthologies
    ❏ enjoy short stories in general
    ❏ word-of-mouth recommendation
    ❏ read book review
    ❏ erotica fan

10. Any other suggestions for the series?

Thanks so much; your comments are truly appreciated. If you send me your e-mail address, I will reply to you when I receive your feedback.